BROKEN

SYMMETRIES

Steve Redwood

DOG HORN

PUBLISHING

With thanks to all those book and magazine editors who took a chance on my often quite unsuitable stories; to the mysterious D, the Queen of Whispers of Wickedness, who published my first ever collection, and to her enforcers, especially Peter Tennant, always unfailingly helpful, and also to the scallywaggy troupe of regular posters; to Jerome Betts, who did not want to be mentioned, but who ploughed through most of my stories (despite most of them not being his 'cup of tea') and never failed to spot nasty little bugs hiding in them; and, of course, to Adam Lowe, who unhesitatingly took on the project when the initial publisher suddenly abandoned it; and (just in case) to God or the Devil, whichever one of them happens to be stronger. Finally, with love to my brother.

INTRODUCTION

by Ian Watson
†

Broken Symmetries must be one of the most enjoyable books I've ever read. Cunningly, to keep you on your toes, Steve Redwood alternates serious tales with hilarious tales. The latter are, well, hilarious – told with wit and wordplay, vim and vigour and sometimes a spot of vinegar for seasoning.

Speaking of vinegar, years ago Garry Kilworth won a Gollancz short story award with "Let's Go to Golgotha," in which the audience for the crucifixion mostly consists of umpteen time-travelling tourists. But the sage Mr Redwood goes one, or ten, better by exploring many more implications, such as the little-known fact that Jesus was of short stature – challenged elevation, aspiring elevation, whatever the more politically correct phrase – and that Jesus wasn't much of a fan of God the Father.

"Fuckit, fuckit, fuckit!" exclaims one of the characters. "For a moment, I thought he was conjugating a long-forgotten Latin verb . . . "

Don't worry about these being spoilers; there's *plenty* more in the story. Indeed here is one of the hallmarks of a Redwood tale: sheer abundance *as well as* economy (try buying that from Ryanair) – his two-in-one zompire, for instance – couched in really sprightly and vivid prose. But then there are the serious tales too, and *mein Gott* these can be exquisitely harrowing as well as written with remarkable eloquence. Just to single out one, "Epiphany in the Sun" is a masterpiece of brilliant dark tension set in a Turkey (the country!) wonderfully evoked, as the initially minor incident of an injured dog leads inexorably to tragedy. Oh, why not single out two? The

1

tale of the Virgin's milk, set in Argentina, is tormentedly eloquent. Indeed, why not three? "Circe's Choice," the Redwood riff on Greek mythology prompted by Ovid's *Metamorphorses*, is cruel, beautiful, lustful, savage. In fact, lust (often frustrated; feminists will love Nastassja Kinsky's revenge on one of her seedier fans!) plays quite a role in a number of the stories. Indeed most of the high emotions run riot in *Broken Symmetries* (with which, symmetrically, this introduction ends so as not to delay you further from the banquet that awaits).

CONTENTS
†

DAMAGED

†

The Library shelves were unusually well-stocked that day, with golden-skinned women dangling languid bare legs over the edges. They were not allowed to speak here, of course, but their sad eyes pleaded, "Take me, take *me*." Through a half-open door at the back, he saw a couple of them being treated.

He pushed Maria 8, her skin already unhealthily blotched, towards the counter, and forced a smile for the Blueskin sitting behind it. She didn't return it.

"I've come to renew this woman," he said. His tone was defensive.

She frowned. "There'll be a renewal fee, of course."

"I know."

She took his name – John William Smith – and Social Security number, then tapped buttons on her computer keyboard, her fingers moving with the speed of hummingbird wings.

Behind her, he noticed a huge reproduction of Magritte's shrouded lovers. Were they hiding their faces from each other to avoid disappointment? he wondered.

She printed out a sheet from the computer, and passed it over to him.

He glanced at it, then looked up angrily.

"But this is twice as much as last time!"

"That is correct."

"But why?"

She looked at him through lidless eyes. "You know very well that the longer she goes without a Service the quicker she deteriorates. And the treatment is correspondingly more costly."

The computer bleeped. She glanced at it, and then looked

back at him.

"It appears someone has reserved her, anyway. For . . . let's see . . . the 14th. Next month."

"What!"

"Which means you couldn't renew her for more than two weeks anyway."

Inside, he felt an enormous relief. No more pretence! It was no longer up to him! But at the same time . . .

"Who's reserved her?"

"You know we can't give out information like that."

Maria 8 stood to one side, her face expressionless. But he could almost smell her fear.

"But I don't understand. Why does he want *her*? Was he the owner before?"

She refused to reply.

He knew it wasn't wise, but he couldn't stop himself muttering, "It's not as if she was in very good condition even when I got her!"

The Blueskin's head snapped up, and her colourless eyes pulsed ominously.

"Please remember you are on State Benefits! We provide for your minimum sexual necessities, but you can't expect us to provide you with the latest models, or allow you to pick and choose what you think suits *you*. If you want a brand new woman, then get yourself a job, and *pay* for one!"

Realising he had gone too far, he made a placating gesture.

"I'm sorry. It's just that this bill is so much higher than I expected."

"I can't help that. Please make up your mind: do you still want to renew her – but only till the 14th – or would you rather exchange her now?"

He glanced across at Maria 8, remembered where he was, and looked quickly back at the Librarian. He hoped she hadn't noticed his lapse.

He intended to say, "Well, if it's only a couple of weeks, I might as well return her now." What he actually said was:

"My present renewal is still valid until the end of this month. Can I come back in a day or two and let you know?"

She looked surprised. Then frowned. "You can do that, if you wish."

"Yes, thank you, I think I'll do that. Goodbye."

He didn't waste time smiling this time, but, pushing Maria 8 before him, moved towards the door, trying not to notice the array of sparkling legs. Maria, his treacherous mind remarked, was like a grey cloud passing in front of the sun.

So someone had reserved her. As the unemployed were not allowed to make reservations, and the average working citizen would not be allowed to use State Benefits, it had to be somebody *above* the system. Someone really high up. He felt almost relieved. It was out of his hands. He'd done his best. She couldn't blame him for this.

But he knew she would.

†

He sat thinking as she prepared the lunch in the kitchen. She had hardly spoken on the way home. He noticed his hands were clammy. Nervousness. But why, for God's sake? He'd done more than could ever have been expected of him. Not only renewed her twice already, but even been prepared to do it yet a third time! Which would have made four months. Four whole months with the same used woman! He doubted if anyone else in the City had ever kept a woman out as long as that without a Service, certainly not one as damaged as she had been.

Lunch was uncomfortably silent, until at last he said, trying to adopt a light tone:

"Well, it seems you have an important admirer! You should feel complimented."

"Maybe I would if I knew who it was." A moment's silence. Then inevitably: "Why didn't you exchange me then, get it over with? Like you really wanted to?"

He didn't answer at once. A few weeks before, he would have flared up, demanded to know how she could be so ungrateful: acting the victim, when *he* was the one making the sacrifices! But he was now resigned to her distrust, knowing, deep down, that it wasn't unfounded.

Two weeks before, she had caught him glancing through the catalogues.

"I'm only *looking!*" he had protested as she stared at him with sadness and disappointment. "Come on, if I really wanted another woman, I only have to take you back, like everyone else!"

He had meant it as a defence, not a threat, but it had been a turning point. She had never mentioned it, but he knew she had never forgiven him.

Which was crazy, since there was nothing to forgive.

Now, he said, not answering her question: "It's almost better this way. For your sake, I mean. Maria, if you don't go in for a Service soon, you're going to be really ill. You could even die!"

"A Service would destroy my memories."

"But sooner or later, not having one will destroy *you!*"

"I *am* my memories."

"You lost your other memories, the ones before me, and yet you've been all right."

"All right? When I came here, I was empty, empty, *empty!* Do you want me to return to that again?"

He looked at her, wanting to say so much — and yet not

8

enough. When she had arrived, she had been nothing more than a bright shiny receptacle for his desires. Someone who had language, and a passable knowledge of everyday things, but not a single personal memory. This had been a conscious policy decision on the part of the Government, once the Blueskins had offered their skills: it was bad enough not being able to afford to buy your own woman, without having to put up with any emotional baggage the State hand-outs might be carrying.

And he'd renewed her, and renewed her again, and his reward was that she had developed enough character and personality to be able to . . . what?

To have her own desires? To presume to *judge* him?

Before he could answer, there came a ring at the door. Voices. Steve! That was one person he would have preferred not to see right now. Especially if he had come – and he would have, of course! – with his new woman.

Maria opened the door. Steve looked at her, surprised.

"You're still here?" he said. He had no intention of being rude or hurtful.

"Nor for long," she replied,

Steve's new woman stood smiling beside him. She wasn't exactly beautiful, of course – after all, Steve too was on State Benefits – but really *glowing*. It wouldn't last very long. Within a very short time she too would begin to lose her shine. It always happened. The women always lost their shine. Nonetheless, the contrast now between the two women was too painfully marked, like the difference between a waterfall throwing back flashes of sunlight, and stagnant pond water on a grey day. And he was more than ever conscious of how *thin* Maria's skin had become, what was left of it. Almost transparent. The signs of previous operations were now clearly visible.

Also the size of the wounds she had suffered.

Who could have done a thing like that?

Steve at once steered him towards the kitchen.

"Don't tell me you've renewed her again! Whatever for?"

"I couldn't do it. I couldn't dump her back on the shelf again."

"OK, OK, we all go through this at some time or other. It's natural. We grow fond of them. Nothing wrong in that. I renewed a woman once. But this is the third time! *Look* at her, John, almost no shine left, she's already decaying. She *has* to be Serviced. You can always take her out again, if you really like her."

"She wouldn't remember me, you know that."

Steve slapped him on the shoulder. "So what? So long as she remembers how to cook and clean and treat your cock like an emperor . . . !"

He was right, of course. Few men denied it was more pleasant if you liked the woman you rented, but it could hardly be considered indispensable.

"She's been reserved, in any case."

Steve whistled his surprise, and was about to say something when his new woman, followed by Maria, came into the kitchen, already looking anxious. They were all like that at the beginning, unable to be away from their men for more than a few minutes without something akin to panic setting in. While obviously not the same quality as those in the private sector, Steve's woman was still in very good shape, perhaps the best the Library – that was odd, why was it called a Library? he suddenly wondered – had to offer. He could have drawn her out himself the week before, he thought ruefully. W*hat's wrong with me?*

"Isn't this a lovely kitchen?" she said. Her voice was high, sharp, like a new kettle.

"It's the same as any other subsidised housing," Maria

answered coldly. It was clear she didn't much like her. Didn't want to remember what she had once been herself?

"But you've made it *specially* nice, I can tell! To keep John happy. Still, you'll see, I'll do even better for Steve!"

"I applaud your ambition."

"Oh, isn't it wonderful to be off the shelves? To be alive?"

There was the tiniest pause before Maria answered: "What does 'alive' mean?"

The other woman frowned momentarily, then giggled.

"It means making Steve the happiest man in the world!"

"Ah yes. Something only you could do, of course."

Nonplussed, the woman turned her attention to Steve. John saw, however, that his friend, though holding and caressing his woman, wasn't really listening to her at all, he was listening to Maria. *Steve has noticed it, too!*

That was satisfaction of a sort. A small recompense.

The visitors didn't stay very long. Besides, it was impossible to talk to Steve in private. He would arrange to meet him later.

Afterwards, Maria said: "Steve looks very happy today. Why do you think that is?"

She was deliberately provoking him. "I don't know. You tell me." The worst possible response.

"I don't need to." She was staring out of the window. The light picked out the tendons of her muscles. 'Flayed' was the word that came to mind.

He wanted to shout out, "Well, show some appreciation, then!" but held himself in check. It didn't help.

"What are you trying to prove?"

The injustice stung.

"I'm not trying to prove anything. But, God damn it, I'm doing it for you!"

11

She swung round, her eyes blazing.

"Yes, for *me*! That's just it! Not for *you*! Just for me! Oh, John, don't you see, it's almost worse this way, it's almost worse!"

"What's wrong with you! What more do I have to do to . . . ?"

To . . . what? The words went round his head like an echo, like another voice.

He stormed out into the dingy back yard. She followed him a few minutes later.

"Oh John, I'm sorry, it's the memories, that's what I'm scared of losing. I'm so scared of waking up one day, and there was no yesterday."

She touched his arm, and added:

"And there are things I've learnt that I know I wouldn't learn again, not with a different man."

There were many things he could have said then. He said none of them. The moment passed.

Such moments had never come in his life before. He didn't know how to handle them.

†

Who had reserved her? Some lover of the low life who had simply liked her photo in the catalogues, or – a chilling thought – the same man who had caused all that damage before? He was afraid of him, without knowing why. He felt – although he had no logical reason to feel this – that the reservation of Maria 8 had been a challenge to him personally. He sensed danger, as if he were a beetle lying helpless on its back on the edge of a sandpit, and the nameless man was the lion ant lurking beneath. If he struggled, the first grain of sand would start to fall in, then the second . . .

†

Watching her undress that night, he noticed more signs of decay. Where the gold had flaked off, bruised flesh was showing

12

through, and body hair was beginning to show under her armpits, and on the lower part of her belly. As she got into bed, he noticed a slight odour. For the first time it entered his mind that she might actually die.

He cursed himself for his own weakness. Here he was, with a woman becoming more unattractive day by day – even her hair now showed streaks of brown and black – when all he had to do was exchange her, like everyone else did.

It was ridiculous, there would be no point in renewing her for two more weeks. She would simply deteriorate more. He would exchange her tomorrow. It would be the best thing for her.

He woke up in the night, and found her curled up on the floor, naked and shivering, weeping silently, photographs of their early days clutched in her thin hands, smudged with her tears.

†

He took her to the Library the following day to renew her.

The Blueskin frowned.

"If you do insist on taking her out again, why don't you at least leave her overnight, so she can have a Service? She'll be ready again by midday tomorrow."

"Without any memories."

"Of course. That's the point. A Service deletes personal memories, egoism, desires. That's what we were brought here for, weren't we?"

"No, thank you. It's only for two weeks, anyway. I'll take her as she is, if you don't mind."

She stared at him with an unreadable expression, but proceeded silently to fill out his Library card. As she was doing it, he suddenly thought: since the Services are so vital, why do they even *allow* women to be renewed without one? Why give us the choice? It didn't make sense.

A lot of things, he was beginning to realise, didn't make sense.

As they were leaving, the Librarian said – and her voice was somehow less harsh than usual:

"Remember, she must be back by the thirteenth at the latest. To allow time for Servicing. We'll repair her, of course, make her as good as new, but we can't guarantee she won't be mistreated in the future."

Why had she said that? He turned round slowly, unwillingly, while a warning voice was telling him not to listen.

"What are you saying?"

"I'm simply reminding you that there are no guarantees for the future of Maria 8."

"Why should anyone harm her?"

"That's a question we often ask. Indeed, that's why we're all here, isn't it?"

"Are you saying this other man, the one who's reserved her, will harm her? *Has* harmed her in the past?"

"No, I'm not saying anything. I'm simply reminding you that there are no guarantees."

"But why are you telling *me*? Now?"

"It's a warning we give to all our . . . clients who keep a woman longer than is necessary or advisable. We assume that the woman has been renewed because the client is seeking more than sexual gratification. And might therefore have some interest in what happens to her after she is returned."

She paused for a moment, and for a moment he thought he saw something like pity in her eyes.

"I've been authorised to inform you, by the way, that the person who made the reservation was the Prime."

He turned away and walked out slowly, this time completely

unaware of the glittering women on the shelves and their vacant golden eyes.

†

The days fell away like the last leaves of autumn, fluttering away from his reach as he tried to grab and hold them.

Things changed with Maria 8. Not only because this was the final renewal, but because of the Librarian's last words, which buzzed round his head like disturbed hornets.

He told himself again and again that whatever happened to Maria 8 after the 14th, he was in no way responsible, there was nothing he could do. Yes, he might, or might not, have made the final renewal only out of a sense of guilt, or weakness, or sheer cussedness, or some incipient sense of loyalty – he didn't know himself – but he found himself worrying more and more about her future.

. . . Because he was beginning to feel certain that it was the man who had just reserved her who had inflicted the terrible wounds which were becoming more and more visible as her golden skin fell away. He had no evidence at all for this, it was as if the knowledge had always been with him.

The last traces of Maria 8's brightness disappeared. In bed, her breasts now flattened slightly when she lay down. He noticed that she had begun to sweat when he used her. Although she continued doing the household chores as before, she quickly tired, and sometimes didn't even finish them.

There was no logical reason at all to keep her now. And every reason not to.

But he realised with shock and something akin to fear that, even so, he didn't want to take her back.

He didn't want to exchange her.

He had no word for this unknown feeling.

15

But it was the day he realised this that he began to wonder whether there might be some way to avoid returning her.

But for the reservation by the Prime, it might have been possible. He could have invented excuses not to return her – forgetfulness, illness, and so on – and in the end the Library might have simply let the matter pass. It could hardly matter to them, he thought, which of the women were in stock, and which were out on loan.

But you didn't mess around with the Prime. His power was absolute. He owned everything. It was said that he could annihilate you with a mere thought.

Yes, the Prime's power here was absolute. But outside the City?

All his life, there had been rumours that the City wasn't everything, that there existed somewhere else, an outside, a magical place where women didn't have to be Serviced, where the Blueskins were unknown.

But no one who left the City, it was said, had ever returned.

He mentioned his crazy idea to Maria. The look she gave him then, the way she came across and folded herself in his arms, made the idea seem not crazy at all.

They made their plans.

And were arrested fifteen days later on the outskirts of the City, taken to the Palace, and hurled into separate dungeons there.

✝

After he had been lying alone for a few hours, shivering, listening to the sinister dripping of water somewhere, a bright light suddenly burst into the cell. No one was to be seen, but a voice boomed and echoed all around him.

"John, you've surprised me. I really didn't believe we had it in us."

16

"What have you done with Maria?"

"Your first question is about the woman. I'm learning a lot. But I can't answer that question yet, I'm afraid. Not just yet."

"Who are you?"

"And I, your King, your Keeper, only merit the second question. I *could* be offended. Thing really are so much simpler here. Me, I'm the Prime, of course. And the next question is, or should be, 'Who is the Prime?' However, for the sake of your sanity, I don't think I'll answer that question, either."

"Why am I here?"

"If you mean 'here', in this cell, why, the answer's obvious. You've been a bad bad boy. But if you mean – which, of course, you didn't, but never mind – 'here' as in 'in the City', why, to see what you're going to do."

"What do you mean?"

"Why do geneticists love fruit flies so much? Because they don't waste time hanging around, they live and die in a couple of weeks, things are speeded up, you can see what's really happening. The Big Picture."

"Why did you reserve Maria?"

"Hmm, the heretic interrogates the Inquisitor! This is a strange place, indeed! But I don't mind: even your questions are my answers. I just told you. To speed things up. Put you under pressure. See which way you would turn. Anyway, she isn't *your* woman. She's *ours*."

"Did you own her before? Was it you who damaged her?"

"Now *there* you've really hit the nail on the head! That's what I'm trying to find out. Was it *me* who damaged her? And if so, do I care? That's why I'm here. Or should I say, that's why *you're* here. Tell me, what were you planning to do?"

John didn't answer.

"You weren't planning to leave our little kingdom, were you?"
John remained silent.

"Ah well, I can wait, I'm not a fruit fly," the other said calmly. "Meanwhile, let's take a *really* close peek at your mind, shall we?"

They must have drugged him, because he began to have a crazy dream, or vision, he didn't know which. He thought he saw himself asleep on a bench outside a restaurant, and Tweedledum wandered by with Tweedledee, saying to Alice, "If that there King was to wake, you'd go out – bang! – just like a candle!" Opposite the restaurant, there was a statue of an eyeless prince, the tiniest sliver of gold leaf hanging from one shoulder, with a dead bird lying at its feet – whether swallow or nightingale, he couldn't be sure, but it was well and truly dead, stiff and cold, and somehow that seemed to matter. A frog hobbled out of the restaurant on crutches, accompanied by another Prince, this time a little one, who was wearing an elephant on his head. "They ate my legs, and didn't even kiss me!" the frog muttered. "Don't they realise how vital it is to kiss me?" It swivelled a reproachful eye back inside the restaurant. "I suppose, to be fair," the Little Prince was musing , "it was easier for me: I only had one rose on the planet, in any case. We're going for a stroll in the Garden of Forking Paths," he added, "where we might well see some butterflies, very educational, their life cycle. If you'd like to join us . . . "

The vision began to dissipate. He knew he wanted to go with them, that they had the answers, but . . .

"Not just yet. One final turn of the screw, to be sure."
The voice was his own. But he hadn't spoken.

†

He was taken to see Maria the next day. Her body lay on the floor in a corner. It was dull and heavy, a soggy, imperfect thing. There was blood between her legs.

18

He flung off the guards in a fury, knelt down, lifted her, and held her and howled, while his tears, the first ones he had ever shed, fell on the dull, lifeless flesh.

And where they fell new skin sizzled into existence, skin that gleamed and flashed and danced in the light, and the eyes opened, and the mouth smiled, and the tears bounced back, flickered all around, swirled like trillions of tiny glistening raindrops that rapidly engulfed him.

†

And the rain poured down but still the man – whose name might or might not have been John William Smith – walked. And walked. Lines of Robert Browning echoed through his mind like the ticking of an underwater clock:

My soul
*   Smoothed itself out, a long-cramped scroll*
*   Freshening and fluttering in the wind*

When, drenched with the rain, he finally entered the flat, he heard her in the kitchen. He laboriously took off his coat, dried himself in the bathroom, and stood for a long time staring down into the garden, puzzled. The sun broke out, and the water droplets on the leaves suddenly shone and shimmered in the light. Brighter than gold. He rubbed his eyes and frowned. As if trying to catch a memory. Brighter than gold . . . He went slowly downstairs and into the kitchen.

She was at the sink. Thin arms, so often holding a dishcloth or a Hoover, thin legs, so often dragging her back from the shopping, thin face, so often hardly even noticed, let alone kissed. Etiolate, because he had stopped giving her any light . . . how could anyone shine with no light?

As if in a trance, he went to her, lifted her arms out of the sink, and pulled her towards him, forcing her head against his

19

chest, and held her.

Just held her.

He had once, years ago, worlds ago, had words for this feeling.

THE ROAD TO DAMASCUS
†

The nightmare began again, although no one could have known it, when Hemera took her daughter to the pet shop to buy her a Betelgeusian squoggle-catcher for her tenth cloneday. But the last one, it turned out, had been purchased just a few hours before.

Little Maia burst into tears – those special tears that always induced thoughts of either suicide or girlicide in her mother. Even on recycled air, the child's squalling capacity was awesome.

"Are you sure you can't get one?" asked Hemera. She looked the owner straight in the eye. "I could make it worth your while."

The owner, who had not failed to notice the Venusian lava-serpent necklace and the equally priceless Ganymedean shawl, looked round cautiously. They were alone.

"We won't be receiving any more squoggle-catchers for at least a month," she said slowly, "but if you really want an exotic pet – I mean, *really* exotic – and you're able to pay, then perhaps I can help. Unofficially, you understand."

Maia, like everyone else on the Artemis Five trading colony, had learnt the art of negotiation very young. Mother and child looked into each other's identical eyes, and in a double blink the pact was sealed: Maia's tears went into provisional remission, and Hemera nodded to the young woman.

Twenty minutes later, they were in a well-hidden underground warehouse, where the faint peppermint smell of an Andromedan Polypod still lingered. That augured well: the Polypods had built up a fine reputation as audacious starfarers whose contraband goods tended to become collectors' items almost at once. But when she saw the new 'exotic' creature in its cage, Hemera's first impression was hardly positive. It was bipedal, malodorous, and unpleasantly hairy. It looked up when the two women and the girl entered, and began chattering away and gesticulating, and even threw itself on the floor in what in a human would have seemed a supplicating gesture. Maia whooped with delight.

Disinfectant sprinklers couldn't completely suppress a rather unpleasant odour. Hemera wrinkled her nose.

"Don't worry," the owner said reassuringly, "it doesn't usually smell quite so strong. The smell is easily cleared anyway by pouring almost boiling water over it. It makes strange noises when you do this, a kind of deep scream – it clearly finds it unpleasant – but it gets rid of the smell, and also makes its skin nice and soft – if a bit wrinkled. But try not to let the water boil completely."

"It's rather ugly, isn't it?"

"Well, it's not very pretty, I admit, but it *is* extremely affectionate, if treated well."

"Where's it from?"

"You know the Polypods never reveal things like that. But they did claim that it's one of the most primitive creatures they've ever come across, possibly predating even the colonisation of this segment of the galaxy!"

"That would explain its obvious lack of intelligence."

"Ah, but it's not completely unintelligent! Irrational and at times hysterical, yes, but not unintelligent. I've had it here for a month or more, and . . . well, you'll see what I mean if you decide to buy it. Indeed, it's this strangely warped intelligence that would make it such an interesting pet."

"What's it called?"

"The Polypods called it a gollub, but they said they made up that name because of the sound it makes when it drinks."

"Are you sure it's not dangerous? I don't like the way it's looking at us."

"It has little tantrums now and then, but that's no problem: I can throw in a neuro-whip free, just in case, which sends a disruptor beam straight at the pain centres."

"Oh, can I try now, Mummy?"

The owner looked doubtful, but a peremptory glance from Hemera resolved her doubts.

"Here, young lady, but only turn the dial just a fraction."

She handed Maia an oblong box with a red dial. The little girl pointed it at the gollub and twisted the dial as far as possible. She jumped up and down in ecstatic delight as the creature shrieked and hurled itself in agony against the bars, losing two teeth in the process.

Hemera gently took the neuro-whip away.

"Now you mustn't do that too often, darling," she chided. "You're only to use this thing if the pet's disobedient, or for training. Unless you're really, *really* bored." She recalled what Maia had done to the Rigan cloud-bat, which had necessitated repainting the whole apartment, and even part of the glideway outside. Still, little girls would be little girls.

"I'm sure you'd never need to use it," said the pet shop owner, as tactfully as possible. "As I said, the creature's usually quite obedient. In any case, there's an easier, less damaging, way to control it. You see those funny lumps of flesh hanging between its legs? According to the Polypods, those two things like dried apricots are called berls, and seem to serve no other purpose than to be violently scratched, but that other thing – I call it a twitcher – has some quite remarkable properties, I can assure you. At the moment, it's true, you can hardly see it, because of your daughter's . . . um, playful enthusiasm, but it has a quite unique capacity of expanding and contracting. Moreover, I've discovered that you only have to stroke it a bit to make the gollub instantly attentive and desirous to please."

"Can it communicate?" Hemera wasn't interested in the ridiculous twitcher.

"It seems to have a rudimentary form of speech. Mainly gibberish, of course. But I've managed to pick out a few sounds that may well be words. What's more, although I know this may sound like gynomorphism, the pathetic fallacy, it sometimes seems to show real, almost human, emotions, although that's clearly impossible. As I've already said, it has a strong desire to please, and will do almost anything for the reward of having its twitcher stroked."

She gave Hemera a significant look. "I might add that it could be much more than just a toy for young girls. Oh yes, it could definitely have other uses. But far be it from me to pre-empt your own discoveries." Her smile really was quite suggestive. Hemera pretended not to have heard: the woman clearly hoped to charge more by making the creature seem more interesting than it really was.

"There's one unfortunate thing I should warn you about." *Ah ha, here comes the candid I-wouldn't-want-to-mislead-you patter.* "When its twitcher has been expanded for some time, a rather unpleasant substance comes out, sometimes with considerable force. It's not dangerous, but it can be annoying."

"Substance?"

"Yes, you know, a bit like what snails and slugs leave behind. Luckily, there are usually warning signs when this is about to happen: the creature breathes much more heavily, its face becomes red and blotchy, its grunting becomes very rapid, and its eyes go funny. The best thing at this stage is to throw very cold water over it, or use the neuro-whip, although it might be better to just let this substance come out, since when it's repeatedly drenched with cold water it tends to become either very morose or even unusually aggressive."

"This . . . substance won't damage the carpet?"

"Oh no."

Hemera was still hesitating, but she knew Maia had already made up her mind. And the pet shop owner knew it, too.

"A few words on its care. It seems to do well on a liquid diet, alcohol is best, and seems to keep it quite happy. But always – always – make sure it's chained to something in the house. If it escaped . . . well, as you know, the authorities are getting stricter all the time. A woman was publicly flogged last month for possessing an inter-phasic Nebulan trunkfish."

"I saw the flogging! It was great fun!" Maia informed them, giggling.

"Maia likes to watch educational programmes," said Hemera.

"Well, I hope you enjoy your new pet. If treated well, it will undoubtedly become a warm, devoted creature, and you'll find there's nothing nicer than to return home in the evening, and have it come bounding up, licking your feet, and jumping up and down in welcome."

†

The following few days were indeed happy ones, for both mother and child. Maia would take piggyback rides on the new pet, pull hair out of its nostrils and eyelids, put gungy-slugs into its ears, set fire to the strange tuft of hair at the end of its jaw, and treat it as she did all her toys. At first, it was rebellious, and prone to gibbering too much, but the neuro-whip and the berl-cruncher (a little device that Maia herself invented) soon solved that small problem. It was the creature's strange twitcher, however, that gave her most delight. She would stroke it until it stuck up, pull it down until tears came to the creature's eyes, then suddenly let go. She liked to paint it, tattoo it, lasso it, and throw prickly Jovian ring snakes over it. Once, she managed to wind it up so tightly that when she let go, the resultant jet brought down a careless fly. Aiming for the opposite effect, she discovered that simply putting a Scorpius X-1 giant vampire spider near it caused it to retract to the point of invisibility. Sometimes, her friend Aegina, a merry red-haired girl a few years older than her, came round. Aegina, who never bothered with clothes, for some reason had a strong effect on the creature: upon seeing her, its twitcher would twang upright almost immediately, without any need for physical winding up. Both girls found this hilarious, but at the same time, unfortunately, the gollub would get noticeably agitated, and it was necessary to use the neuro-whip or berl-cruncher to calm it down.

If anything, Maia's mother seemed even more pleased with the new acquisition. Her best friend Hestia (they had been cloned in the same lab on the same day) soon noticed a new freshness about her friend's cheeks, a spring in her gait, a mischievous smile playing about her lips. When she pressed Hemera about this, the latter blushed, and said coyly:

"Well, the *burtee* might have other uses, you know."

"*Burtee?*"

"That's what it seems to call itself."

Hestia insisted on knowing more, so one night, after Maia had gone to bed, Hemera invited her round.

"You just have to experience this," she said, "it's like nothing I've ever felt before."

She was lounging in a chair, idly swinging her feet, while the *burtee*, with a white cloth tied round the front of its body, was standing at the sink washing up. Every now and then, Hemera snapped her fingers, and it would break off, bend down, lick her feet, and await orders. There were scorch marks on its shoulders, a sign that a certain amount of training with the neuro-whip had been

26

necessary.

"Has the cleaning robot broken down?" asked Hestia, puzzled.

"Oh no! Listen, I can't explain it, but just watching it slaving over the kitchen sink, occasionally kicking it or using the neuro-whip, gives me a most incredible sensation of well-being! Yes, really, I swear I'm not having you on! Just come and sit with me, and see if you feel the same."

It was hard to keep Hestia away after that.

But this innocent contentment was not to last long.

One afternoon, a grim-faced Woman in Black burst in, armed with a needle-gun, searched the house, found the naked *burtee* whimpering behind the toilet, and briskly clubbed it into unconsciousness. For some strange reason, she stripped and examined both the women and the girl very carefully (Hemera thought she heard her mutter 'steel in tact,' but that made no sense). After finding out the name of the pet shop, she warned them never to mention the gollub to anyone at all, on pain of an extremely protracted death, and took the plaything away, together with Maia's berl-cruncher and the neuro-whip. A little later, they saw the pet shop go up in flames, and not long after that, a muffled explosion came from the direction where the underground warehouse had been.

†

Where had it come from? Were there any others? If there were, there existed the terrifying possibility that the creatures might once again spread across the Galaxy – after all the bitter centuries spent eliminating them – and usher in a new Dark Age.

Galactic Watcher Boadicea, sworn to protect the Federation against the Scum of the Universe and uphold the values of The Great Purification, took off from Artemis Five, with the still unconscious gollub staked out on the cabin floor, and reflected on her good fortune. Without that tip-off a few days before . . .

Within half a day she caught up with the Andromedan ship, slaughtered the crew, and interrogated the Captain.

The quivering Polypod Pirate, after she had threatened to inject concentrated cod liver oil into its tentacles, had told a strange story. It had been hiding out with its crew in one of the bomb craters of Old Earth and they had come across some natives who claimed that a strange machine had just appeared one day out of nothing, and that the gollub had staggered out of it, uttered a noise that sounded like 'O sheet!', and promptly collapsed. The creature was so similar to the pictures of prehistoric devils they had seen that they had taken it back to their village planning to sacrifice it to their local goddess. The Captain, who liked to think he was a connoisseur of blood rituals, had gone to watch the sacrifice and had found the proposed victim to be so strange that he had immediately sensed profit. The Polypods had snatched the creature from the sacrificial slab, and made off with the antiquated machine as well.

When an order had come through from their underground dealer on Artemis Five, the gollub had been delivered there.

Boadicea already had a suspicion as to where the creature had come from, and when the Captain repeated some of the 'words' he thought he had heard: 'inkland', 'worta', 'bludiyell', and, above all, 'tymatcheen', she was sure.

'Tymatcheen'!

The Black Watcher waited only to take a single look at this 'tymatcheen' (it was still in the hold of the pirate ship) and then injected the cod liver oil into the terrified smuggler after all. It immediately spasmed into the Tentacular Death Frenzy which, battle-hardened as she was, still left her breathless with shock. And a pang of guilt: she didn't usually break her word, and the Polypod had clearly had no idea what a Time Machine was, but if it uttered the mere word in certain quarters . . .

Although not herself in the Time Division (where the learning of Ancient English, as well as the contemporaneous sub-dialect Bûshian, was obligatory), as a Grade One Watcher, Boadicea had a smattering of AE, and was well acquainted with the history of Time Travel. She knew, too, that despite the repeated warnings of the Ultimate Time Guardians, the Federation Council still secretly maintained a Time Travel capability, although they were wise enough not to attempt to make use of it except when their own existence might be at stake.

But this was not a Federation machine!

And it certainly wasn't from the future!

As the ship's robots transferred the artefact – which was vaguely wasp-shaped – into her own Starfighter, she tried to come to terms with what she had stumbled across. Something that had been feared more than anything else.

A Machine that had come from **the past** with a creature that had been extinct for thousands of years!

She looked down with an exultant smile at the gollub now finally beginning to recover consciousness at her feet. She suppressed a healthy instinct to destroy it at once. She had to deliver it to the Council first. She could just imagine the jealousy on the face of Her Greerness, who only the week before had publicly criticised her for her 'rebellious streak'. Honour and fame beyond her imagining lay ahead.

But there was something to be done before that. Like so many others who had dabbled in Pre-history, she had been disgusted by the accounts of what had gone on in those distant times. And yet a secret part of her had always wondered what it must have been like. She told herself that, before delivering the gollub to her superiors for execution or experiments, it was her duty to herself as a serious historian to find out once and for all whether the incredible stories were true.

She kicked the gollub for a few minutes to put herself in the mood – it certainly was just as exhilarating as she had read! – and threw off her uniform.

And that, though at the time she didn't realise it, was the beginning of her metamorphosis into the Abominatrix.

And of the Second Dark Age of the Galaxy.

JEANNE

†

Jeanne is dying. Her dying is returning my strength to me, so I no longer pretend to the others, but go openly into her bedroom and lie beside her, but not like before. All that was bad between us is gone, devoured as she is being devoured, as she would have devoured me, and she is now just a little girl who is lost and defeated and dying, and only half understands why. I lie beside her and rock her gently, and move the damp hair from her terrified eyes with rough callused fingers, and tell her lies, tell her that everything will be all right, and last night I'm sure she whispered, "I couldn't love you before, you know why I couldn't, but now I think I can. Is it too late?" And I lied – or thought I lied – again, and said of course not, and then she cried, the first time she had been able to cry in her whole life; silent, welling adult tears that trickled under my fingers as I stroked her cheek.

I know Alain will never forgive me for this, for robbing him of a part, just a little part, of his prey.

And I am afraid, yes: but the really wonderful thing is, I don't care. Mary, open the curtains again, and let our children look out, you don't have to hide me from them any more.

†

Among the so-called solitary wasps, the females confine themselves in most cases to providing food and a sheltered home for the development of their larvae. The normal pattern is for the wasp to make a nest of some sort. These nests reach their highest development in the elegant undivided nests of the potter-wasps (Eumenes), *each of which shelters a single larva.*

†

Jeanne's mother, Suzanne. Sitting outside a coffee-house in a village near Périgueux, in the Dordogne, simple yellow dress over a pale slim body, hair that really *was* the colour of corn, cut short and ovalling her face, large light green eyes that looked up at me as I passed, lips that almost curved into a smile. And I, instead of walking on, as I had intended, stopped to gaze at the avalanche of green hills falling on the village, pretended to wipe sweat off my brow, turned back, and took the table next to hers, and thought that *I* was the hunter.

I'd like to say we made love that same night in the old semi-derelict farmhouse she lived in, but that would be wrong: we did the things that adults do when they are making love, so I thought we were making love. A week later, I left my hotel room and moved in.

Of course, I now realise why Suzanne acted as she did: the duty of a mother is to provide for her young. Even at the time, I don't think I ever *really* believed in the miracle: I was fifty-five, muscle turning to flab, hair already grey and attenuate like smoke from a dying fire. From the beginning I paid for everything. When she told me, within a couple of weeks, that she preferred to sleep alone, I wasn't so very surprised, and neither, I must admit, did I really mind. It was still cheaper and pleasanter than the hotel, I enjoyed doing odd jobs, and I had the company of her twelve-year-old daughter, Jeanne.

The farmhouse had already been partly reformed: rooms had been partitioned off, a bathroom constructed with shower and heating rail, electric oven in the kitchen. Yet these things seemed oddly *extraneous*, like a picnic rug on the grass, like a monkey wearing a suit. The floor remained rough and uneven, the stone walls thick and ageless, it retained the smell of the soil and the country, reminding me of pictures of Mr. Badger's house seen as a child, in and of the earth. And Suzanne and her daughter gave the impression of being, like the house, things of nature, fixed, unchanging.

Jeanne. Wild blonde hair that made you ache to catch it in your fingers, the great, solemn green eyes of her mother, freckles like daisies dotting the fields around the valley, child's lips hinting at a woman's heat. Jeanne.

My destroyer.

My saviour?

The . . . *games* . . . began almost immediately. At first I took no notice when she somehow turned playful kisses on the cheek into kisses on the lips, or when she came and stood by me as I was sawing wood and flung her arms around my thigh, or buried her head between my legs when I sat on the sofa. After all, I had two daughters of my own.

Suzanne began spending more and more time away. It is easy to see now that I should have left. But the poison was already in me: that is why she was not afraid to go. I made excuses for her to myself. After all, could a man of my age really expect to monopolise a woman like her? At least I had a kind of home again. Though I tried not to, at times I remembered Mary in England, with little Sue and Jenny crying beside her, and the shock and loathing on her face, and the curtain drawn tight as if in shame as I started the car. No, I had nothing to go back to.

I really believed it was I who was making the decision to stay.

†

Confining itself to a class of victims particular to its own species, the female wasp hunts caterpillars, spiders, and other insects. These are stung so that they are paralysed and packed into the cells of the nest.

†

"Look," Jeanne would say, lifting up her T-shirt, "look how they're growing, come on, you can touch them, if you want to," and sometimes she would jump on me from behind and wrap her legs round my neck so that her thighs were pressed against my lips. I still tried to pretend to myself it was just playfulness (when she never smiled?) but soon I realised I was taking longer to tie my shoes just with the hope that she *would* ambush me, taking a shower without closing the door, looking up into the trees while she picked apples. And though she would sometimes laugh or giggle, she never really smiled: her laughter was strangely savage, it mocked me, clawed at me, tormented me. Her eyes, big strange eyes like her mother's, always looked straight into mine, never around me or beyond me, as in normal human intercourse, but deep into my own eyes, seeking a way, a path, to the vulnerable interior of my being. As if she *knew.*

And still I said to myself that she acted as she did in search of the affection she never received from her mother, even when she *was* at home, which was now almost never. As for her father, it was as if he had never existed. I had asked Suzanne about him, and she said coldly he had served his purpose, and refused to tell me any more, and when I asked Jeanne, she looked mystified, as if the concept of father had no meaning.

I tried to come to terms with what was happening. I sensed that in some visceral way Suzanne had weakened me, had stripped away my defences to leave me exposed to her daughter. My need to hold Jeanne, to rub my cheek against her tiny breasts, to kiss her hair and feel stray strands tickle my tongue, to follow her game, and then make it just that bit more daring – yes, that was already a sickness, but almost worse was the weakness I began to feel every time I was near her, and a growing apathy with anything that was not her. She was feeding on my desire, and on another thing I did not recognise at the time, and the exhilaration of our games slowly turned into something else, a debilitating fear that crawled around the edges of my mind, always there just beyond the reach of consciousness.

One hot August afternoon I found a pile of old books in a big filthy plastic bag in a corner of what had been the stable. Perhaps the owner had been a teacher or a student, because many were on biology, zoology, botany, and related subjects. One, called *Insect Life*, caught my attention, and I browsed through it, fascinated by the complexity and diversity of the subject, terrified by the pre-programmed cruelty of many of these creatures. It was only that night that it occurred to me that those old books should have been covered in cobwebs. I read the book more carefully.

When I accused Jeanne, she cowered away from me, and said I was crazy, and ran into her room, slamming the door on me. But then I hadn't expected her to admit the truth.

✝

The larva that hatches eats its victims alive, and is thus assured of fresh unspoiled food throughout its life; just enough victims are provided for the completion of its growth. Usually the mother wasp has no contact with her offspring beyond the egg stage.

✝

Monique saved me. Or was it Alain? Alain, who hates me because he knows there is a little part of Jeanne he will never have.

They arrived maybe a month ago. I was lying sick and torpid on the bed, and Jeanne's scream broke through the haze and the pain and the slushy greyness that was now my mind. I stumbled into the sitting room and, like a swimmer looking up at an object on the surface, made out Jeanne cowering in a corner away from the door. I crossed the room, put my arms protectively around her, and after a moment she stopped screaming, and subsided into a breathless sobbing. Only then did I turn and see a woman standing in the open doorway with a young boy beside her.

35

Monique had come, she said politely, from Rouen to see her cousin Suzanne, and wondered why we hadn't received her letter (we had no phone). She didn't show much surprise when I said I hadn't seen Suzanne for more than a week. She's like me, she said, loves to travel. I wasn't the first, she said, to have been left to look after Jeanne.

They had to stay the night, of course, and the next day I found I was feeling better than I had for many days. When Monique asked if I had any objection to them staying a few days, until her cousin returned, I said of course not, it wasn't my place anyway.

Jeanne started to change immediately. I sometimes seemed to catch her – it can't have been my imagination – staring at Alain (for Monique, like Suzanne, tended to disappear most of the time) with hatred and . . . how can I put it, despair. It was as if she recognised a stronger force, a force as elemental as herself, but fresher, more potent.

She became weaker day by day, rarely leaving her room, except sometimes to creep into the garden. I could feel that her power over me had been broken, and I knew why: she would flinch when Alain walked past, though I never saw any violence between the two. Indeed, by then I knew I never would.

Her force, her vitality, was diminishing, and she was fading into . . . a little girl. A little girl whose death was now as inevitable as the falling of leaves in autumn. And I, as I became stronger, began to feel something quite different towards her. Like I had felt, at the very beginning, for my own two little ones.

I saw her sitting in the garden once, just before the end, her tiny form hunched over the small pond, her shadow being stripped and sucked away under the water, and I went and put my arm around her – this time with none of that gnawing sexual tension – and, without looking up, she said:

"You must leave. Now. In between. After, it will be too late."

I asked her what she meant, and then she did look up at me, confused, her hair stumbling over her cheeks, and said, "What did I say?", and when I repeated her words, she said nothing, but began to tear off strips of bark from a twig with jerky, scrabbling movements, with a look of such terror on her face . . .

I believe I knew what she meant. I sensed that I had been given a reprieve, that there was one small moment, the moment when Jeanne was being destroyed, that I would be free. I even began a weak, pathetic letter to Mary, but I could not drive away the memory of the scorn and fury in her eyes, and knew that I would never send it.

†

Cleptoparasites, meaning 'thief-parasites', is the best term to apply to the bees and wasps whose breeding habits resemble those of a cuckoo. Indeed, they are often called cuckoo bees and cuckoo wasps. They lay eggs in the nests of solitary wasps and bees, and their larvae feed on those of the host species and on the store of food that has already been collected.

†

My Jeanne is dead. I watched the life force being sucked out of her, I saw it creeping through every pore, like early morning fog rising out of the Dordogne valleys. At the end, we were united, I and this little pale creature who had been trapped between two worlds, and she must have sensed my tears because I think she whispered, "It wasn't too late, was it?"

Maybe what followed was the rictus of death; I prefer to think it was – at last – a smile.

I could have left, before, while Alain was busy with her. I like to think she fought harder to give me that chance, and who is to say it was not so? Is there not sometimes more truth in what might have happened than in what did happen? For a time I had the strength to leave that house that had become too much a part of nature, and I didn't go, because she needed me – or I felt she needed me – or I needed her to need me – and at last I had the chance to expiate so many sins, done and undone.

I had found – no, I really believe I had been *vouchsafed* – the strength to do something greater than escape. *Let thy will be done...* The will not to leave her alone with her destroyers, and, by sharing her suffering, the power to wash away the stain and ugliness of everything that had gone before. Yes, she died, as she had to, and she shrivelled in my arms, but she had asked that wonderful question, she had smiled – please, please let me believe that she had smiled! – and I looked down on her tiny face, now so terribly *empty*, and understood at last what she had really given me. *And forgive us our* . . .

I felt a tingling, a touch, an icy sliver of movement inside me, and looked up weeping and proud and finally free into the merciless hunger in Alain's eyes.

THANK YOU FOR YOUR SUBMISSION
†

Dear Mr. Courtly-Pines,

Thank you very much for submitting your short story, *Battering Brenda*, which we have read with great interest. It is not, however, quite what we are looking for at the moment. Might we suggest that you read an issue or two of *Desperate Wails*, to familiarise yourself with the kind of stories we publish? We enclose details of subscriptions, and writer's guidelines.

Dear Mr. Courtly-Pines,

Thank you very much for your subscription. We enclose the latest issue of *Desperate Wails*, which we hope you will enjoy reading.

Dear Mr. Courtly-Pines,

I apologise for only responding with a form letter before. Your story, *Battering Brenda*, though excellent, is still not suitable, I'm afraid. You certainly write with unusual passion, but perhaps the story line is just a little bit 'thin'? But please do not hesitate to try us again.

Dear Mr. Courtly-Pines,

Please let me express our gratitude for both your generosity and your faith in *Desperate Wails*. It is not often that we receive a five-year subscription in advance. We appreciate the support, which will help us to ensure a bigger, better magazine (which, by the way, is called *Desperate Wails*, not *Nails*).

However, to answer your rather pointed – indeed, almost belligerent – enquiry, while we do read submissions from our own subscribers with unusual care, a subscription *per se* does not guarantee publication. Your story, *Battering Brenda*, does indeed show promise – we were reminded of *The Duchess of Malfi,* and certain paintings by Bosch – and there is a raw fury to the work which certainly caught our attention. Perhaps if you rewrote it, with a little less gore? The torments suffered by the eponymous Brenda at the moment constitute the whole story, and while extremely imaginative, you do not explain *why* the aliens should wish to abduct, beat, and torture her for ten days. Also, might we suggest a more varied style? A sentence such as 'And then they ripped out her tongue and re-implanted it in her anus, and then they turned her nostrils inside out and coated them with her own steaming faeces, and then they pulled out her pubic hairs and threaded them through her nipples with jagged rusty needles, and then they hung her from the ceiling by her nipples, and then . . . ", while delightfully colourful, does tend to become a trifle repetitive.

Dear Mr. Courtly-Pines,

We liked your joke about our being 'scoundrels, cads, and bounders' who need 'a good horse-whipping', ha, ha! How the power of the word can bring back the lost charm of a bygone age!

We have read with the utmost interest the revised version of your story. Once again, however, we regretfully feel unable to accept it for publication. Your explanation that the aliens torture Brenda because 'they didn't like the way she answered back', and 'the nagging shrew deserved all she got', is original, but not sufficient. And the addition of that last line ('*Now* will you remember to put sugar in my tea!') while providing a certain motivation for the events in **Battering Brenda** – a kind of inverted **Stepford Wives** scenario, with aliens thrown in – still fails to remove a certain unnecessary *unpleasantness* from the story. Neither do we feel that changing the title to **Bloodily Battering Brenda** is any great improvement.

Dear Mr. Courtly-Pines,

I must ask you not to phone the office again. When I returned this afternoon, I found my secretary almost hysterical. We have had to give her the week off.

The reason I did not answer your last two 'letters' was because, quite frankly, they were in extremely bad taste. In our business, we expect – indeed, encourage – a certain amount of healthy criticism, but your letters advising me to publish *Bloodily Battering Brenda* or end up like her, while clearly intended to be slyly humorous, have become a trifle wearing. I have tried to be tactful, but since you push me into it, I have to say that your 'story' is obscenely and obsessively misogynous and sadistic, with not a hint of literary merit to redeem it.

Dear Mr. Courtly-Pines,

Your subscription is hereby, as you so forcefully requested, returned.

PS We were somewhat puzzled by your inclusion of a reproduction of Edvard Munch's *The Scream.*

Dear Miss Courtly-Pines,

I confess I was rather surprised to receive your letter. I assure you we have nothing whatsoever against your father. I understand your commendable desire to help him, and the lengths to which you are apparently willing to go are a credit to your filial instinct, but regretfully both myself and my co-editor are gay, and so will not be taking up your generous offer.

Dear Mrs. Crinkly-Oaks,

Thank you for your letter, and we hope you enjoy your hundredth birthday next month. We had no idea that your son by your first marriage, Mr. Courtly-Pines, was nearly seventy, and we are sincerely sorry – although not particularly surprised – to hear that his relationship with his wife Brenda is not a particularly happy one.

Yes, your son's hobby is indeed quite fascinating, and we naturally share your delight that last year he was finally able to complete his collection of amphibian heads with the rare (perhaps the last?) Costa Rican emerald glass frog. As you say, boys will be boys.

It is refreshing – almost comforting – to know that he has taken up a new hobby at this stage of life, and we would like nothing better than to 'warm an old lady's heart', as you put it, and run his story in our magazine, to coincide with your birthday. This, unfortunately, is impossible, as we are very short of staff since the suicide of my secretary, but we enclose a list of magazines which are aimed at a slightly older readership, although, as the list is last year's, I cannot guarantee that all the editors are still alive.

Dear Mr. Courtly-Pines,

Perhaps you have not been informed that we are now in the third millennium, and double-barrelled names of sadistic septuagenarians, thank God, no longer carry any weight. Do you really believe you can *frighten* me into publishing your senile ravings?

My dear Mr. Courtly-Pines,

That was an excellent joke, ha, ha! about double-barrelled names and double-barrelled shotguns – a nice *double* meaning, if I may say so! I have always had the greatest admiration for the SAS, to which you inform us you belong. We have taken another look at your father's quite remarkable story, ***Battering Brenda***, and it is now obvious that we misjudged it terribly the first time. We shall we more than pleased to publish it in our next issue, and so there will be no need for you to pay us, as you so kindly suggested, a midnight visit with your friends.

PS. I have to admit – ha, ha! – that the damp scalp you included with your witty letter gave us quite a fright!

My Dearest Mr. Courtly-Pines,

We will be extremely honoured and delighted to publish your

new story, ***Battering Brenda All Over Again*** (we especially enjoyed the pun in the title!) in our very next issue – which may well be our last, but not to worry, ha, ha! We find the idea of the protagonist of the first ***Brenda*** story being abducted again, one year later, and being subjected to a further series of horrific tortures, an original and fascinating one. By the way, quite a lively lad your son, eh? A real chip off the old block, ha, ha! It is refreshing to find such determined loyalty in a family.

Dear Mrs Crinkly-Oaks,

We were sorry to read that your son has been arrested for the murder and dismemberment of his wife Brenda. We naturally share your opinion that he never really intended to kill her (as is proved by the fact that he chose to dismember her alive) and that his trial is simply the vindictive revenge of the lower, illiterate, classes. We also share your grief that your grandson was cold-bloodedly shot while gallantly attempting a commando-style raid, with biological weapons, on the prison where his father is being held. Our thoughts are with you at this difficult time.

We wonder whether you might have any of your dear son's other writings – stories, diaries, poems, childhood jottings – anything at all. As you know, ***Desperate Wails*** was the first magazine to recognise and encourage his unusual literary talents, and to have the courage to publish the two ground-breaking ***Brenda*** stories, half a million copies of which were sold less than a week after his arrest. Perhaps you would like to read through the enclosed contract – don't worry about the extremely small print, it's really nothing of any importance – and allow us to help you to manage his literary estate.

PHANTOM VERDICT

†

Ah! Que du moins, loin des baisers et des combats,
Quelque chose demeure un peu sur la montagne,
. . . Car qu'est-ce qui nous accompagne,
Et vraiment, quand la mort viendra, que reste-t-il?

(Verlaine)

The knife in my hand clearly announces my intention, and what he has become stares up at me, fearful and uncomprehending, thin white fingers feebly clutching the sheets like asparagus sliding over the rim of a tin. Death has refused to issue a prospectus, to enable him to make adequate provision for his own eternity, so he hangs on, and leaves me no choice.

That other girl so long ago, the one who got away, the one I should have learned from. I spotted her in the college bar once. Hair that swirled dervish-like across her face in a chaotic dance of life, and eyes that flashed with the glint of a magpie's wing. Too much life: he flinched away – even then – scuttled away to safety like a cockroach when the light is suddenly turned on. When she lost patience, and soared away on the thermals of her own vitality, I foolishly picked up what I thought were the pieces, and patiently set myself to weld them together again.

His breathing is ragged, jerky, like the last drop of greasy water being sucked down the plug hole. The fear that has always been there, hiding under the guise of erudition, civility, respectability, is now engulfing him. An old Financial Times is still on the bedside table; I want to wave it in front of him, let the forecasts and figures that he worshipped shower down on him and suffocate him with their merciless banality, but I realise he has to die a different way, so that the other may live again.

I was never very pretty. Sensitive boys would tell me what wonderful blue eyes I had, relieved to have found an honest compliment. Others simply lunged straight for my over-developed breasts. Oh yes, I see now why he chose me: safety — who would bother to attack a gold prospector who came back only with silt and mud? And yet . . . and yet, he was different. Under his touch, my breasts felt as delicate as bluebells, as fragile as a hint of honeysuckle. But those early embraces were the clutches of a promise doomed to wither, and the decades have since shuffled out of their tombs to scatter dry bones over the memories.

I often dreamed that the young man of those days simply stumbled into another dimension, that he was there waiting for me.

No more waiting.

The rain is thrashing against the window, anxious to burst in and flush away the final droppings and husks of our lives. The rasping of his breathing is the sound of someone cracking open walnuts. Is that what his heart will look like, inside? Only smaller, more wrinkled? Will his ceasing to breathe really change anything for him? Is lack of all movement really so much different from every movement planned, analysed, nervously given permission?

I now know that J. Alfred Prufrock never did finally dare to eat his peach.

But I, I will dare for him. For us.

We were walking through a park one afternoon and saw a couple of boys, no more than thirteen or fourteen years old, pushing and tormenting an old black woman on a bench. They looked round when they noticed us, and tensed as if to flee. But something told them the truth that I had yet to learn, and they casually turned their backs on us, and spat at the old woman. He walked on, dragging me protesting with him, explaining how it was wise not to interfere in these cases. Would only have made things worse for the

45

woman, in the long run. I was in love with his learning, his knowledge, his reasonableness, so I persuaded myself to believe him. But that night I dreamed the old woman's body was hanging from the ceiling like a halalled sheep, her blood dripping between us and creating a torrent that snatched him away from me.

I foolishly ignored the Cassandra within me.

It is surprisingly easy. I look into his terrified eyes, and then I stab the knife down into his sunken chest – not too far, if he dies too quickly all is lost – and then twist to make a space for the other to escape. All I am doing is snapping a lock, and his cries of agony are to me only the welcome screech of dungeon bolts being drawn back.

He became a university lecturer, specialising – what else? – in ancient history, where the clash of armies was distant enough to be unreal, the echoes of pain deadened by time, the smell of blood long gone. I watched him shadowshuffle through the lives of the dead, while in between what was left meticulously filled in insurance and tax forms – with absolute honesty, because dishonesty might bring retribution – and fretted over pension funds, and low-risk stocks and shares, and minute scratches on the bonnet of his safety-featured Volvo, and the right amount of red wine to reduce the risk of a heart attack, and the shocking manners of his students as they slurped noisily at life.

A life without a single misdemeanour, a single crime. Except that of denying life itself.

'A man needs a little madness', said Zorba the Greek, 'or else he never dares cut the rope and be free.' In the film, at this point the music of Mikis Theodorakis cuts in with a beautiful violin melody like the rising sun.

In the film.

But I have cut the rope for him and he will be free and the music will cut in again and I – and he – will dance again.

There! There he is! Like the ectoplasm you see in horror films. Squeezing through the hole I have made, raising himself, rearing up like a male orgasm filmed in slow motion. A tiny face, an unformed pinched face, almost that of a foetus. The features are glowing, evanescent, inchoate. The head is twisting from side to side, stretching, trying to drag its body after it, but it seems trapped in the old man's chest, as if invisible hands are grasping it, holding it back.

Of course! He will not let go, even now! He is too afraid of the fury of what he might have been.

We didn't have children, though we did occasionally have sex, since that's what respectable couples are supposed to do. His well-behaved penis would politely doff its cap and slide in and out of me like a metronome, and he always seemed slightly ashamed after orgasm and quickly withdrew, though on good nights he would stay there beside me for all of a minute, before, with a kind of crabwise furtive moment, slipping out of bed and going to wash himself. All those nasty germs we keep inside our vaginas were something beyond his control, chaotic, something to be avoided.

The tiny eyes turn towards me. What is the colour of non-being? What is the colour of that which never was?

"Where have you been all this time?" I whisper.

And the answer comes back like the wind strumming a broken lute on lonely Andean peaks, as the condor silently circles. *Aborted, aborted, aborted . . .*

The head is still swaying from side to side, straining, and finally a wispy, insubstantial body begins to emerge, but not completely, as if it is still stuck in slime. In his final weakness, it has found the strength to try to resurrect itself, to clamber out of him into existence, but what he has become will not let go so easily.

The eyes look at me, and in their emptiness I am able to see clearly the plea for help, and perhaps for vengeance, too – vengeance for never having been allowed to live.

In a frenzy of blighted love and longing, I stab and twist, frantically clearing away the debris of bone and flesh. The glow of the tiny face is now stained by spurting blood. But no matter, he is free, and he sways towards me, gazing at last into my own soul, searching for his companion of so long ago. I rip open my dress, baring my now withered neglected breasts to him, I feel him beginning to enter me, I am preparing to go with him, wherever the journey – and then he gives a moan of despair and recoils from me and starts to dissipate . . .

And I know at once that he cannot forgive me for having accepted his own incarceration, the treacherous veneer of all those years, the gaudy replacements and trappings of respectability I had been offered. *"I had no choice, I did it for you, I had no choice!"* but I know that this is the eternal lie, must always be a lie, as I scream in utter despair, throw myself forward, my hands reaching out, to catch and hold the meaning of this death, but he is withdrawing back, back, into his jailer's body, with nowhere to escape to. At the end, there is just the naked face again, twisted with grief, and then that too begins to disappear, and all that remains is a mutilated old man's body.

And my own tears looming larger and larger until I drown in them.

SANCTUARY

†

"The only thing stopping many doctors practising euthanasia in Holland was a fear of prosecution. Research suggests that Dutch people have been leaving hospices and hospitals and moving abroad to avoid the possibility of euthanasia – this legalisation will make their fears worse."
(*Ruth Davies of Pro-Life Alliance,* New Scientist, *December, 2000)*

Ah, how prophetic that was!

A mere ten years have passed, and yet here we are, my sister and I, on a small Spanish fishing boat, our father hidden under a tarpaulin, watching the pitiless English shore recede – oh, so slowly! – into the distance. How the spirit of Francis Drake must be, no longer 'dreamin' arl the time o' Plymouth Hoe', as the poet would have it, but weeping in its hammock for shame, to see that it is now only the old enemy who brings a beacon of hope to darkest Albion!

For tonight the cargo isn't fish, but something infinitely more precious: the emaciated body of our ailing father. An innocent man whose only crime is to have grown old.

In an hour, we should be picked up by a Spanish naval patrol boat, and within twenty-four hours be in Spain – and Sanctuary at last. A lot of risks have been taken, a lot of palms well greased to get us this far – never have I been so glad that father is a wealthy man! – and we've been assured that there'll be no problem getting him into the Programme.

I stare into the black waters, and recall how the horror all began . . .

†

As early as 1991, the Remmelink Report had already sounded

49

a warning, showing that even then, over 5% of Dutch deaths were caused by euthanasia, voluntary or otherwise. A mere couple of decades later, the country which once spent more on its health services than any other in the world now spends that money on a cruel and repressive state police whose chief victims are the old and the sick.

To be fair, that wasn't the original intention. No, at first, the Dutch used euthanasia to allow people to die with dignity, and later in an honourable, if misguided, attempt to *improve* conditions in their hospitals by saving money. The steps that led to the present Abomination were, however, as inexorable as they are well-documented.

First, it was incontinent patients, and a draconian 'three shits and you're out' policy, a measure initially very popular with patients in adjacent beds (is this not how all tyrannies begin, by turning neighbour against neighbour?), with the lethal injections usually being carried out with shameful – and shameless – alacrity by the nurses whose olfactory senses had last had to combat the pungent results of the patient's sphincter's *laissez-aller* attitude.

Soon, however, even the most tight-lipped sphincter was not enough to save you. Since the law still required the patient's consent as well as two doctors' signatures, the 'good doc-bad doc' technique became commonplace. The 'bad' doctor would twist the patients' arms (if they had any), or thrust terrifyingly clear photos of a naked Japanese *sumotori* in front of their eyes (same proviso as above), while the 'good' doctor would whisper things like, "The pain is going to become unbearable soon", or "Surely you wouldn't wish to become a burden on your dear family?" or "We want them to remember you as you are now."

If these methods failed – as they sometimes did, since old people are notoriously stubborn and cling to life like nuns to their chastity – the doctors could take advantage of a new law and claim either 'incurable dementia' (defined as the insane desire to go on living in such an imperfect world), or 'clinical irreversible selfishness' (the deliberate waste of public money which could be used to help younger patients, and fund doctors' pensions and pieds-à-terre). In neither of these cases was patient consent necessary for euthanasia.

Thus began the reign of terror in the Netherlands. In the beginning, it has to be admitted, the medical profession tried to maintain its high standards, and the really conscientious doctors would insist on giving the lethal injections themselves, while others with a less comfortable and relaxed relationship with their patients would use the services of a trained anaesthetist.

But from this it was but a small step to realising that it would be cheaper to strangle the patients than to inject costly drugs. At first, again, the strangling was performed, as was only right and proper, by the gentle healing hands of a qualified doctor, but many felt that this was wasting too much time on manual labour, and the strangling soon came to be farmed out to immigrant *thuggees* from India, who could thus make their peace with Kali.

The rot, then, began in Holland. Britain, however, wasn't slow to follow, inspired by the shocking example of King Charles III himself, who, fed up with waiting for the crown, decided to 'assist' his mother to die. She nearly got away, making a last-minute break for it, but was unlucky enough to scoot out of the Palace Gates just as they were Changing the Guard. She got trampled by an ambitious horse whose distant ancestor had done away with William III. It was much to her credit that she never once lost her stern expression or her hat during this ordeal, and was even able to gasp, "We are not amused by that horse – shoot it!' before she expired. Inspired by this example, and the sprightly truncheons of the Mayor of London's New Metropolitan Police, the Lords in Parliament all signed a Living

Will, and within a few months only the most colourful were left, in order to attract American tourists.

Those early years are full of horror stories. Our own poor mother was just one victim among many. Neither my dear sister nor myself was able to be there at the time, but her last moments were secretly recorded by a cleaning woman who hoped to sell the tape to *Goodbye* magazine.

The first part of the recording relates, not to my mother, but to the patient beside her; it gives a chilling insight into the sheer callousness of the doctors.

(Doctor to relative) "How long has she been in a coma?"

"Two years."

"Has she worked at all during that time, contributed in any way at all towards the wellbeing of society?"

"But how could she?"

"That's not the point. She is a burden on the country. Move aside, the revised guidelines are quite clear."

There followed the sinister 'squelch' of tubes being taken out.

Then, a new voice, our mother's:

"But I'm only here to have a cyst removed! I'm not terminally ill at all."

"You are now!" was the response. "We don't want you to feel pressured, but you'd better sign this consent form, or else!"

"But what about your Hippocratic Oath? You've sworn not to take life!" Our mum was a sharp old dear. She'd been a barrister.

Of course, she'd got them there, which might explain why there was no more discussion, only the sound of breaking bones, the ominous scratching of a pen on paper, then gurgling sounds. Poor mum! It's too late for her now, but at least we'll be able to save our father from such an ignominious end.

Things went from bad to worse. Even Jack Kevorkian, Doctor

Death himself, in England to receive an honorary knighthood from King Charles, got a bad stomach from the food, and was forced to endure Physician-Assisted Suicide. Apparently, he put up quite a fight, which just goes to show that it's sometimes difficult to live up to your beliefs when it really counts.

And the next step was, I suppose, inevitable. Why wait till the old people were actually in hospital? Why use up more bed pans and linen than was necessary? Why pay for the hospital transport? King Charles, it must be said, made a rousing speech against this latest horror: "One didn't pursue one's mother from the Royal Domicile with a pack of out-of-work fox hounds just to see this kind of aberration creeping in!" he protested.

In vain the royal fulminations. The story of how the Terror spread out of the hospitals into the world outside is too well known to bear repetition. The British Secret Services lent their equipment to the cause of medicine, devices so sensitive they could detect the faintest creak of arthritis, the smallest clack of testicles in desiccated scrotums, the most furtive plopping of dentures in water. To reach sixty was to fear for your life. The 'proofs' of senility multiplied faster than bacteria or politicians' evasions. You forgot to put a stamp on the letter? Bam! You wore different-coloured socks? Wham! Even the inability to spell the name of the small Welsh village 'Llanfairwllgwyngyllgogerychwryndrobwllllantysiliogogogoch' backwards was used (in Scotland, moreover), as evidence of impaired mental faculties.

We have all seen the shameful scenes on TV: columns of geriatrics, too sick to leave their beds, trundling down the roads leading to the coasts, while whooping doctors in land rovers pick them off one by one (it has been estimated that more old people now die on Britain's roads than hedgehogs); fights to the death for pitifully cramped spaces in the false roofs of long distance trucks once used to smuggle in immigrants; wrinklies mown down as they try to storm gangplanks to escape by sea, or swarm over runways to cling on to the wings of aircraft.

A particularly bloody episode, which made the world headlines, was what has come to be called Turnbull's Last Totter, after the name of the leader of a rebellion in a leading Scottish hospital. The geriatrics there, many of them trained in the killing fields of Glasgow in their youth, managed to take control of the hospital, holding a group of consultants hostage for three days before the troops were sent in. Over a hundred people died that day, ten of them from heart attacks. Turnbull and a hard core of his Totterers, however, were able to escape. I often wondered what happened to them, not knowing then that I was soon to find out.

The terror spread all over Europe, and then over the rest of the world. Nowhere was safe anymore. For a time, it seemed that North Korea was a secure haven, but then someone did tests on their dog food . . .

In the end, it was clear that only Spain was able to provide real Sanctuary.

†

We did it! We reached Gijón, on the northern coast of Spain!

We had chosen the long sea route because the roads through France were one long bed-jam. A few *real* oldies, who retained wartime contacts from the French Resistance, stood a good chance of making it, but my own father had no such contacts, having only served in the Falklands, before becoming a dot.com millionaire selling musical condoms to parliamentarians and accountants.

It hadn't been cheap getting out of England, but we two sisters had earlier agreed that we didn't mind how much we bit into our inheritance if it helped to save our father. We've always been a close family.

Ever since they chose a soldier instead of a sailor to lead the Invincible Armada, the Spanish have been sorely underrated. But that quixotic sense of chivalry immortalised by Cervantes has never quite left them. Maybe too, there is a feeling that the wrongs of the Inquisition can be somewhat rectified.

Whatever the reason, we were treated with the greatest respect at all times, especially when they learnt that my father was an ex-soldier. In Spain, patriotism still has meaning, I'm pleased to say, as does respect for *sabiduría*, the wisdom of age. In Gijón, we were put up in a comfortable *pensión*, and driven down to Madrid the very next day. We knew that there were places of minor Sanctuary in almost every town in the country, but our father deserved only the best.

At last we reached Sanctuary in the Ventas district of Madrid, in what had previously been the *Plaza de Toros*, one of the most famous bullrings in the world.

Sanctuary was An Idea Whose Time Had Come. Almost everyone now sees that. But there still appear to be many misunderstandings, and occasionally even wilful misrepresentation of the whole concept. The words 'barbaric' and 'sick carnage' have been casually bandied about by those who know nothing, when in fact it is a clear case of genuinely ethical Physician-Assisted Suicide, officially defined as 'when a physician provides either equipment or medication, or informs the patient of the most efficacious use of already available means, for the sole purpose of assisting the patient to end his or her own life'. This is exactly what the Spanish do — before the refugees enter the ring, the authorities provide them with the 'equipment and medication' (poison-tipped walking sticks: merely sharpening them is not enough as the patients often don't have the strength to impale their enemies), and inform the patients how to make the 'most efficacious use' of these means — namely, by allowing themselves to be pricked by their opponents. If the patient chooses instead to assist the *opponent* to commit suicide, this simply shows how innate is the human desire to aid others.

Originally the '*gerontolodores*', as these doddering gladiators are affectionately called, had been wheeled out into the ring on their beds, so that they could conserve the energy they would need to fight. However, up to an hour could pass before some of them were able to actually rise from these beds, and some shamefully took the coward's way out, and expired before doing so. This was not likely to please the demanding Spanish aficionado. It had also been found that having only two combatants fighting at a time could take far too long, with or without beds. Allowing half an hour for them to be able to even catch sight of each other, a whole afternoon might well pass before they were near enough to enter into combat. So ten beds were now wheeled out simultaneously, pushed into the centre of the arena, and, at the sound of a trumpet fanfare, upended, spilling the combatants on the sand.

Although the former *toreros*, bullfighters, had lost their jobs (given their skill in arrogant strutting, they soon got employment on the catwalk modelling beachware), there was still a place for the old *banderilleros,* who would sometimes have to use their streamered darts to chivvy reluctant combatants into getting up to fight. Sad to say, some old people are so set in their ways (as well as into plaster) that they have to be goaded this way. Not often, thankfully. The whole point is to give these people the opportunity for a worthy death.

The system, as I say, has been terribly misunderstood by some. It has two overriding aims – to allow the patient a brave and dignified death, and at the same time to bring in money to treat other, younger, patients. It has frequently been compared to the old sacrifices of virgins to the gods for the good of the community. But that system was manifestly unfair to virgins, who, by definition, had never enjoyed the best that life has to offer. No, our gladiators (and notice the 'glad' in gladiator) have already had a good long life. It's only right that they are now given the opportunity to contribute something for those who come after.

For the Spanish had made an extraordinary mental leap, and comprehended that the real purpose of euthanasia should not be, as in the rest of the world, merely to *save* money, but to **earn** it! Instead of hospitals using up taxpayers' money, they could now make a profit and contribute to the general good, since all profits from the converted bullrings went into the health service. With the popularity of these contests – and what more noble spectator sport could there be than to watch people die with dignity, not hidden away in some foul-smelling hospice, but indomitable under the life-giving gaze of the Iberian sun – the Spanish *Seguridad Social* was now bringing in as much money as the National Lottery.

All new Spanish hospitals now have a small bullring (the anachronistic name has stuck) attached, since the tournaments have proved an excellent boost for the morale of the other patients. Instead of having to witness the slow deterioration of their fellow patients in the wards, a depressing sight for even the flintiest of hearts, they now have the tournaments to look forward to, with all their colour and splendour and pageantry. Studies have shown that these spectacles have such an uplifting effect on the other patients that the average stay in hospital has decreased by between three and four days per patient. The more enlightened have been known to stagger off the operating table in order not to miss a tournament.

It was very gratifying to find that British prestige, which had fallen so low in the Lager Lout-Marbella Mafia years, had been fully restored by the exploits of Turnbull and his kilted Totterers, who had found their way here a year ago. Indeed, some of the Totterers had been among the very first to earn the right to an honourable death in Sanctuary. Moreover, more than a dozen of them, due to the ferocious blood and whisky running through their veins, had won their contests, and, as with all the victors, are now being treated with the most modern medicine and equipment, and may well live to celebrate their sesquicentenary birthdays.

Which, of course, is one of the main side benefits of the system, and this return to pure Darwinism may turn out to have profound implications in evolutionary terms.

Some have found it odd that a Catholic country like Spain should be so progressive in these matters, bearing in mind the previous record of the Church in questions of euthanasia. But the Opus Dei had come to understand that Jesus himself had openly made use of Assisted Suicide (it was so obvious once pointed out), as had most of the early martyrs.

And what, some say, about aged pacifists and conscientious objectors? They are not forced to fight. They can opt out without any loss of dignity provided they offer themselves for vivisection, an equally honourable way of paying their final debt to God and Society.

In view of all this, you can imagine our surprise and sadness to hear that we – yes, my sweet sister Goneril and I – have in some quarters been accused of sacrificing our beloved father for private gain!

Our accusers have pointed out that with all that money, our father could have paid for the best private treatment in England. Of course he could have! But my darling sister and myself had too much love and respect for him to allow him to choose to rot away in some bed, humiliatingly dependent on others, subjected to cruel aggressive medical treatment. Cordelia didn't agree, of course, but she's always been a bit of a simpleton, too sentimental to see the wider picture.

Which is why, since we are both doctors ourselves, we signed the consent papers for him, and also why we tied him up and brought him to Spain. The poor man's mind had been affected and he could no longer be trusted to make the correct decision.

We have never hidden the fact that we each inherited a million upon his death. But that had nothing to do with our decision. We wanted him to go out with dignity, and by God he did us proud! No, he didn't manage to win – believe me, we would have been more than pleased if he had since, as I say, the money means nothing to us – but he did put up a sterling fight before being impaled on the poisoned point of the walking stick wielded by Turnbull the Totterer himself. As the Totterer, awarded what I found out to be his tenth '*oreja*' by the ecstatic crowd, cut off our twitching father's ear as his trophy, I felt a sense of pride bursting through me. What an honourable death!

In that moment, his eyes filming over, he turned his head towards us, struggling to say something.

I like to believe he was giving us his final blessing.

EXPIRY DATE

✝

The calendar arrived on Christmas Day, and that in itself was odd. Was the Royal Mail or whatever it now called itself doing long-overdue penance for the year's dismal service? Hardly likely; someone other than the postman must have stuck it through the door of his house, although the large envelope did bear a stamp with an illegible postmark. On the back of the calendar was a mysterious message in bold handwriting: *From Jennet D to her man of clay*. Peter had no idea who 'Janet' was – he tried not to associate with women who couldn't even spell their own name – and 'man of clay' sounded decidedly insulting. As if he were a lifeless ancient Chinese terracotta warrior, or a brainless golem. The 'her' seemed to imply some sort of relationship, but a quick run-through of recent lays yielded no clue.

It was a typical nature calendar, about twenty inches square. There was a page for each month, with a main picture on top, and small circular paintings in the corner of each day. These were the usual boring idealised rustic scenes; what did a town-lover like himself have to do with snow-covered copses, newly blossoming trees, soft-focus haywains, ploughmen who didn't even have the decency to seem weary? He didn't bother to look at most of the pictures, and indeed only stuck the silly thing on the wall in the kitchen because... well, that was the strange thing: he didn't really know why.

He hardly even glanced at it again until late on Thursday January the fourth – he had good reason later to remember the date – in order to check a dental appointment. Yes, the seventeenth was a Wednesday, no problem. The day's picture, he noticed, was of a crowd of happy skiers at the top of a slope. Daft fuckers! Freezing your arse off, and probably breaking your leg! Good chance of getting screwed afterwards though, he'd heard. He was about to turn away when the picture for the first day of the month caught his attention. Something odd about it. He looked more closely.

The scene was indeed unusual for a 'Seasons' calendar – a group of small boys playing in a graveyard, presumably by moonlight. Only what made it even more unusual was that . . .

It couldn't be! And yet . . . No, impossible! An illusion. He hurriedly fetched the magnifying glass he had inherited from his father.

It only confirmed what he thought he had seen: one of the boys was urinating on a grave. Not only that; the detail was so fine under the lens that he could even read the name on the headstone: Alice Newton. The boy's face was turned away so that he couldn't see it.

He didn't need to. Even after three decades he could still remember the incident. He had hated Miss Newton, the form teacher, with the dazzlingly pure hatred of a ten-year-old. Peeing on her grave after her fatal car accident seemed in retrospect a small revenge for the countless hours of boredom and tellings-off she had inflicted on him, but at the time it had been both exciting and satisfying. He remembered imagining her fleshless jaws open inside the coffin, and her eye sockets, waiting to receive his last disrespects...

Peter's smile faded as he realised that what he was seeing was impossible. His eyes flicked right. The next picture, too, was a scene from his own boyhood, this time a couple of years later, showing Carol Blair's spluttering face as she spat out bits of live spiders which he had imprisoned in her lunchtime tuna sandwich. Well, the fat cow had deserved it for being not only fat but spotty and swotty as well, always putting her podgy hand up in class. The third picture showed him pouring red ink on to the bicycle saddle of that red-haired snot who'd called him a 'cretin'– he never could remember her name, Clare something or other – and then showing everybody, having already spread the word that she'd had her first shag with a Paki shop-keeper the night before. In the fourth picture, still in his early teens, he was pushing some frightened protesting girl, he had no idea who, against the back of some shed while trying to grab her tits. The fifth picture . . .

The fifth picture – tomorrow's date – showed a dream cottage under a bright blue sky, with gleaming snowdrifts piled up against one wall, and two red-cheeked girls throwing snowballs, watched by some sheep. A happy, innocent scene. As were all the others for the month.

Peter sat down. Heavily. Not before grabbing a whisky bottle from the cupboard. What had Sherlock Holmes said? Once you eliminate the impossible – wake up, you old fart Watson, you're supposed to be taking this down! – whatever remains, no matter how improbable, can only be solved with generous quantities of the good stuff. He passed the next hour alternately standing up and examining the four pictures, and sitting down with his increasingly addled head in his hands wondering whether mad people knew they were mad.

It must be hellishly difficult to replace four pictures in a calendar without leaving any sign of interference or alteration, but he supposed it could be done if you were involved in the manufacture of the calendar, or had friends who were. But how had that Janet known about his innocent youthful pranks in the first place? Yes, there were old school companions who might have known about one or two of those events, but certainly not all four. And even if someone *had* found out, why would they play this trick on him nearly three decades and a paunch later?

Janet D . . . Janet D . . . man of clay – a pottery class? It was no good. As far as he remembered, he'd never met a Janet in his life.

The whisky and sheer exhaustion had their effect, and he overslept the following morning till nearly eleven. Fuck! His boss just loved it when he screwed up; gave her the chance to lord it over him, indulge in a bit of femdom; probably made her wet her oversize knickers. He tottered down into the kitchen, three-quarters convinced that the whole business of the calendar had been a particularly potent dream. But, shit, no! There were those four scenes from his schooldays.

No. Five.

The picture-postcard cottage and the obnoxiously happy girls and uneaten sheep had disappeared, to be replaced by the image of a dishevelled teenage girl staring out of the picture with disbelief on her tear-stained face. It was only when he noticed the pile of rocks behind her, which he recognised as one of the many tors on Dartmoor, that he recalled who she was; after egging him on, the bony bitch, supposedly his 'girlfriend', had refused to let him go all the way, and, furious, he had told her that it was all over, and that she'd have been a piss-poor shag anyway.

And so it continued through the whole of January and February. Each morning, a harmless bucolic scene had been replaced, in chronological order, by some episode from his life which could easily lead an outsider to think he was a bloody misogynist, for fuck's sake! He wasn't at all: he'd just been unlucky enough to have come across more than his fair share of slags, dogs, and ball-breakers.

He tried to catch the moments of change, of course, more than once sitting up all night staring at the next day's untainted picture, but inevitably he would nod off for a few seconds – and when he jerked himself awake his bleary eyes would be greeted by yet another questionable episode from his life. The calendar began to resemble a portrait gallery of what those bloody rabid feminists would have called mistreated women.

He often thought of getting rid of the blasted holier-than-thou calendar, and once even got as far as putting his lighter to the corner of the February page, as a warning to it. Somehow, he wasn't at all surprised when it didn't even singe, let alone curl up in shame. But most of the time he felt a morbid curiosity as to how it would all end. What would happen when the images caught up with the present date? Would the calendar just give up, and confine itself to yucky scenes of yokeldom? Would the mysterious Janet D finally make herself known?

He got part of his answer on the last day of February.

After two months of the impossible, he had become, if not exactly blasé, at least accepting. All right, so he had a muck-raking magic fucking calendar which didn't seem to have a very high opinion of him, but so what? Just because it was magic didn't mean you had to necessarily take any notice of its petty prejudices. Hadn't the bloody thing ever heard of moral relativism? On the other hand, it wasn't harming him. Why, he was sleeping almost normally these days, and without the need for pills. OK, he'd given up bringing women back to his flat for the time being, fulfilling his needs at *their* places or in hotels, but this did at least free him from having to wash up and keep the bedroom clean.

So that Wednesday morning he was already on his third cigarette and second coffee, and had even put some bread in the toaster, before he thought of looking to see what other thing from his murky past his Wall Confessor had decided to shove in his face.

Shit! He'd been trying very hard to forget that particular incident.

The three witches. Or rather, one in particular.

The Halloween trick-or-treaters had come at a bad time. He'd been having a slight erection problem (the erection was slight, not the problem) with a lady who was going to her husband's funeral the following day and clearly needed comforting, and at the very moment that navel discipline had finally been instilled, the children had rung the doorbell – and rung it and rung it, almost as if they knew what he was doing, and had already decided on the 'trick' option. The erection expired and moved on to a better, or at least more spiritual, life. Furious, Peter yanked on his trousers, stormed downstairs, filled a bowl with water, opened the kitchen door, and hurled the liquid at the three little girls dressed as witches standing outside giggling. Two fled wailing satisfyingly, but the third leapt back with a scream of pain, clutching at her face. She finally looked up at him – fuck, it really looked as if she'd just walked through a fire! – and stared at him with her little face twisted with rage – and pain?

"Just you wait till I reach puberty again!"

"Bah, you'll still be just as ugly!" Peter yelled, but her enraged gaze made him feel strangely nervous, and he slammed the door shut. He went upstairs to find the mourning lady getting dressed and looking so angry that he was careful not to go within her Roche Limit. He drew back the curtains and looked out of the window, which was above the main door, and saw the little witch had crossed the road, but was still looking at his house as if memorizing something. It was only a few hours later, lying in bed alone, unable to sleep, that he wondered at her use of the word 'again'. And since when did little girls go around using words like 'puberty', for fuck's sake? Didn't they just say, "When I've got titties"? At least, that's what his niece had said the other day, and she was about the same age.

The parents of the other two girls came round to complain, of course, and one of them fortified the complaint with a punch that left him with a black eye for a week. But no one came round to protest about the third girl . . .

Now, months later, seeing the image of that girl's crumpled face once again, he felt a deep unease, almost fear, and he deliberately kept himself very busy the whole day, in order not to have time to think about it.

But that night he couldn't sleep, and about three in the morning, the first of March, he gave up and stumbled into the kitchen. The calendar had moved on.

There were no more rustic scenes. Instead, there were smileys. Fat and sickly and yellow. One for each day: thirty-one of them. Each with a squiggle below it, and each one bigger than the one before. Indeed, the last one almost completely filled its circle, another day and probably . . .

A sudden premonition. He flipped over to April. Yes, the smiley for April 1 completely filled the circle.

It was also the last one.

The rest of April was blank! No circles, no idyllic scenes, not even a numerical date. Nothing. He turned over the page – May wasn't even there, just a completely blank page. And the rest of the pages were blank too.

On *this* calendar, his own special calendar, time ceased to exist on April the first.

April Fools' Day.

He glared outraged at the calendar.

"Fuck you! I've put up with you sniffing around my past, don't think you can get away with this! I can always burn you, you know. Well, all right, I can't. But I can turn you to the wall. See how you'd like that day in day out!"

It was bluster. His mind was still really on the girl with the crumpled face. Unwillingly, he flicked back to the February page, looked again at the last scene, then took down the calendar and reread the message on the back: *From Jennet D to her man of clay.*

Was 'Jennet' perhaps not a spelling mistake, after all? With a very unpleasant feeling in his stomach, Peter did something he knew he should have done long before, but had always put off doing, perhaps unconsciously afraid of what he might find. He went into the tiny lounge, turned on his computer, and went a-googling.

The very first entry that came up, after wasting his time with small Spanish horses and donkeys and mules, produced a last throw-away line that made him start with fear:

Jennet is also an old English girl's name, derived originally from John. Jennet was the first name of the daughter of one of the Pendle Hill Witches.

An hour of frenzied web research later, he thought he knew who had sent the calendar.

And also why her parents hadn't come to complain.

When you've been dead for centuries you tend to let things be.

In 1612 ten people, now known as the Pendle Witches, were hanged at Lancaster Castle, accused of having caused the death of seventeen people by sorcery. Five belonged to the same family. The grandmother, known locally as Mother Demdike, aged over eighty, died before she could be hung, but her daughter Elizabeth Device, known as Squintin' Lizzie, and two of her grandchildren, Alizon and James, were all hung.

And they were hung mainly on the basis of the accusations of the third grandchild, who was herself acquitted. Her name was Jennet. Jennet Device. Jennet D. She was nine years old. Many years later, she was again accused of witchcraft, convicted, but reprieved by King Charles I.

There was another Jennet, Jennet Preston, also accused of murder by witchcraft, and hung in York at around the same time. That might explain why the sender of his calendar had signed herself 'Jennet D', to let him know which Jennet she was.

His researches also gave him more than a hint of what the dedication to 'man of clay' really meant.

In those days, effigies of people who were to be made ill or killed by sorcery were called 'pictures of clay' . . .

He went back into the kitchen and stared at the last smiley. The squiggle below it was also much larger. No, it was more than a squiggle. ‏سامراء‎ He vaguely recognised the shape as some sort of language, Arabic, he thought. Perhaps it just said 'April Fool!'. Perhaps the whole thing was just a game. All children liked playing games, even four hundred-year-old witches, didn't they? Well, easy enough to find out: look for the Arabic alphabet in the 'symbols' files of his Microsoft Word program, find and insert the letters under the smiley into a blank document, copy that, and then paste into Google Search, and with any luck . . .

Yes, the squiggle *was* Arabic. It said, in proper civilised letters, 'Samarra'.

What the fuck did a Lancashire witchlet have to do with Iraq? He googled a bit more, and soon came across the old story of the merchant's servant who believed he had been threatened by Death, in the shape of a woman, in the Baghdad market, and who fled immediately to nearby Samarra to escape her. But she hadn't threatened him, only started with surprise at seeing him there, because she didn't have an appointment with him until that evening – in Samarra.

Well! That was a threat if ever there was one! It implied that whatever decision he took to escape whatever fate awaited him, it would be the wrong one. How could he *not* do something which she had almost certainly already seen him doing?

He had to give it to her. He had attacked Jennet on *her* day – Samhain – and the implication of the last smiley was that she

planned to return the attack on what she had decided was *his* day —
April Fool's Day.

"Very funny! Sarky little bitch!" he muttered. "Nasty
underage croneling!"

It didn't help that by April 1 exactly *thirteen* weeks of the
year would have passed!

He flung open the bedroom window and screamed out into the
Exeter night:

"For fuck's sake, you humourless little brat, it was only a bit
of bloody water! You don't have to take it so fucking personally!"

But then witches, he quickly found out, were a bit touchy
about water. Either they drowned in it, or if they managed to float,
they got burned at the stake for not drowning. And look what
happened to the Wicked Witch of the West: poor cow just melted
away. He remembered how the little girl had clawed at her reddened
face. And this particular witch at the age of nine had got her whole
family strung up just to save herself. Fuck!

"All right, fuck it, I'm sorry! I didn't know! All right?".

The night mocked him with its silence. Branches of a bare
tree across the street waved like slender broomsticks yearning to fly.

Perhaps if he could find the little brat and buy her an ice-
cream? Donate money to a coven? "Sugar and spice and all things
nice," he cooed hopefully into the menacing night air.

Damn it, how did you placate a four hundred-year-old witch (a
bloody northerner, to boot!) who apparently had just reincarnated,
judging from her comment about puberty again? Why had he been
unlucky enough to bump into her just at that dicey age? There was
nothing crueller on this earth than a pubescent girl, my god, he
remembered what his sister had been like, and what his niece was
like now! Unbearable! Hormonal horrors!

What could he do? He had read about enough cases of

improbable deaths to see how impossible it was to prepare for every contingency. There was the fanatically healthy vegetarian in South Africa who was killed while jogging by a frozen leg of ungrateful lamb which fell from a third-storey window. There was the veteran mountain climber who fell off the ladder while changing a light bulb, banged his head on the sink, and this time climbed his highest ever – straight to Heaven. A chap in Cyprus accidentally set himself on fire, ran out of the house and jumped into the nearby reservoir – and drowned.

He fell asleep over the kitchen table.

†

The days of the third month marched on by with the speed and determination of the Japanese sneaking up on Singapore through the Malayan jungle.

At the beginning, he tried to cheer himself up by reflecting that at least all those smileys meant he had a guaranteed month to enjoy life. Worldwide, hundreds of thousands of people would die during that time. Some perhaps even by witchcraft or voodoo. He had a whole month. By fuck, he'd enjoy it! Damn it, he'd shag and discard women like he never had before. So there, black and midnight haglet! But that was a non-starter. With the little witch's face filling his consciousness all the time, he was too nervous and distracted to manage even the corniest chat-up line, and when he did manage to pull a really desperate old dog, that same ever-present face put paid to any hopeful uprising.

And every day the smileys seemed to smile more broadly; at times he was sure he saw ghostly snaggle-teeth growing from them. Whether awake or asleep, nightmare scenarios of his own death played out in his feverish mind. He became jittery and jumpy, trembling and hollow-eyed. Even the sound of his own groans frightened him.

The calendar – he might have known! – proved to be both faithful and indestructible. He could take it from the wall, examine it, even curse it – but he couldn't harm it, or escape from it. It wouldn't burn, melt in acid, die in the microwave, decompose in the toilet. Testing possible escapes from whatever fate awaited him, he went to his favourite Parisian *pension* one weekend – this time alone – and the first morning that he woke up, there it was, hanging smugly, and impossibly, on the wall.

That little experiment put paid to any vague idea he'd had – despite the strong 'Samarra' hint that it would do no good – of hiding in another part of the world before or on the fateful day. Desert island? Tsunami! Alaska? Polar bear! Tibet? Yeti! Mountain top? Lightning! Underground bunker? Explosion! Church? Impecunious mutant monster mice! Who knew what powers a witch might have honed over four hundred years?

The appointed day finally came. He found suddenly that he was strangely calm. He hadn't intended to even get up. There was no point – he'd finished the last of the dozen bottles of whisky he'd bought the last time he'd had enough energy to struggle out of the flat. And if he was to die let it at least be in his own beloved homely stinking bed. Becoming maudlin, he wondered who would mourn him.

The women he'd slept with, or tried to sleep with? Hardly. And perhaps, just perhaps – he could at last admit it – they'd have a point.

The calendar, then? Would it miss having him to torture? For some reason he sensed a need to look at that last giant smiley. He almost felt a sort of twisted affection for it. It had subjected him to terror for a month. Stockholm Syndrome? He didn't care. At least it smiled at him, which was more than anybody else did!

He staggered out into the kitchen, collapsed at the table, and stared at his nemesis. As he did so, the April Fool smiley grew bigger and bigger, expanding right out of the circular frame. It was so big, so all-embracing he knew he was smiling back. He felt a surge of affection for the little witch. At least *she* hadn't forgotten him! He thought, too, of Jerry Cornelius' mother's dying words: "Yer got ter larf, incha?" Bigger and bigger the smiley became, so big that its curve was no longer noticeable, until it, and the man's heartbeat, flatlined out together into a final statement of eternal absurdity.

FOWL PLAY

†

(A humble tribute to a master parodist, Rhys Hughes)

When I woke up in a cage that, judging from the smell, might have just come from a poultry farm, my mind was at first completely blank. I knew I had never before been in this room, illuminated by hundreds of candles, and with walls decorated with unusual and somehow sinister-looking symbols.

And I didn't recognise the woman staring in through the bars, or the blindfolded man sitting beside her, with an expression of malevolent triumph on what I could see of his face. I had a feeling, though, that I might have seen them both before, perhaps even recently.

Could the woman be my wife? Had I perhaps rashly refused to do the washing up? Or performed my conjugal duties too perfunctorily? I didn't want to ask her directly because, if she *were* my wife, she would surely be offended that I wasn't aware of the fact, and might nag me: a mere cage is no bar to a woman's tongue.

Perplexed, I scratched my cheek. As I did so, I felt a deep curved scar gouged into it, and I noticed that my lips were terribly hard and swollen. So bad had been the wound that some skin was still hanging loose.

Ah, this might be a clue to my identity! The scar pleased me. It showed I had lived dangerously. I felt a tremor of excitement. Perhaps I had fought a duel. Could I conceivably be Robin' Darktree, the notorious unforgiving highwayman? Or Spermicidal Whiskers, the infamous pirate whose one-eyed glare could unman the most virile enemy? Perhaps I had fought *many* duels, in which, due to my speed and uncanny dexterity, I had never so much as received a scratch. Except for that one occasion, I suddenly seemed to remember quite clearly, when I had been challenged by an enigmatic, deadly, and mercilessly sensuous woman – much like Catherine Zeta-Jones in *The Mask of Zorro* – because of some classically tragic misunderstanding. My code of honour, of course, wouldn't allow me to raise my sword against a poor defenceless woman.

"Never," I had declaimed, my voice liberally sprinkled with nobility, "will I raise my sword against a poor defenceless woman!"

"Villain!" cried the feisty daughter of Don Diego de la Vega, "hiding behind a fictitious code of honour when what is really holding you back is my deliciously decadent décolletage and the flashing-dragonfly-wing flimsiness of my attire which, in this rather charming clearing in the forest sloping gently down to a crystalline sea, in the pristine early morning light, with the frost glinting on the bark of phantasmal beech trees like a poignant memory, and the sun straining to sneak round the trees in order to caress me intimately with its lascivious rays, barely hides my maddeningly provocative curves from your marvelling if lecherous eyes! *En garde!*"

Yes, surely it was chivalry which had stopped me defending myself when she had lunged with her delicate rapier.

Or had that sun jealously and deliberately got into my eyes?

A sudden wild idea brushed me, like Kandinsky having an afterthought: there was something about that woman sitting in front of me, watching me from behind those dark glasses, something about her stance and fulminating figure . . . Could she be the same one who had given me my scar? Could she be Elena de la Vega herself? Had her heart been won by the way I had stood there, my grey eyes calm and ironic, ignoring the blood gushing from my left cheek?

But immediately that memory was submerged by another.

I was actually an astronaut! Captain Pilchard Stopdrooling. Yes, now it all came back to me. My god, that had been a tough life!

Defending Earth from the scum of the universe is not all buddy quips, noises in a vacuum, and petrified hair styles. I remembered those sadistic bastards Kuiper and van Allen giving our ship a damn good thrashing with their pitiless belts; catching a hacking cough in the Oort Cloud and then falling into a coma; getting slimy diseases in worm holes; developing suppurating accretion discs; suffering from an excess of trapped solar wind.

But, on the other hand, the things we had seen! Pulsars, quasars, binaries, gas giants, blue giants, red giants, red dwarfs, yellow dwarfs, white or 'degenerate' dwarfs . . .

I felt a flush of fear! Of all the degenerate dwarfs, Engelbrecht had been the worst. There was so much bad blood between us that people slipped and slid in it if they came near. A sinister squat pugnacious interstellar assassin born to keep his head low and his ear close to the ground, a real heavy who came from a dwarf star with a ridiculously eccentric orbit which had rubbed off on him, and who had vowed never to be eclipsed by lesser luminaries. He'd had to change his somewhat right-wing politics after an acute red shift in his adopted star system. His first exploit had been to capture and cork a Betelgeusian ghost, which had greatly aided spectral classification. He'd just returned cock-a-hoop with one of the rings of Saturn, but the lack of oxygen there hadn't gone to his head, and, drunk on sidereal time and spiritual vacuum, he told tall stories and boasted that there was nothing he couldn't do. So he had been challenged to bring back a mythological creature, so that it could be stuffed and put in the Sages Hall of the Surrealist Assassins Club in Smallsphere, his home planet.

But then that memory was replaced by another. No, I must have been confused. At last I realised who I really was: Squeeze Thews, the Welsh Hemingway, the international sportsman and celebrated breaker of records, wind, and hearts, with a ransom on

75

my rakish testicles that increased with every balcony successfully and swashbucklingly scaled. I deliberately sported a rum-hither look to intrigue and intoxicate the maidens. I had melancholy muscles and terminally romantic toes and tendencies. Ladies nipped at my lip, and napped on my lap, and complied when I implied. Other adventurers cried out, "Kiss my steel!", but *they* weren't naked. I preferred to miss meals and steal kisses. I climbed trees and had epic conker fights with Baron Cosimo while Calvino wasn't looking. I dived and goggled at mermaids as they passed by with the fluidity of elusive dreams, and pursued them with pumping thighs and frantic flippers. I hunted down universally infamous villains and, now and then, wrestled leap years to the ground. For relaxation, I challenged disabled snails to races, or tramped mountain ranges looking for lost valleys and mythologies, and fairies shyly embracing inside four-leafed clovers or snuggling up in old boots. I nibbled nuts gingerly where the condor flies, and sipped *carajillo,* and curried favour with spicy South American ladies.

Yes, yes, and I now remembered I had a half-brother, Hymen Simon, who used music and poetry and romantic tales where I used muscle and endurance. His weapons were languorous lutes and impetuous mandolins. He minstrelled his way into women's hearts and parts with a broken harp dropped by a weeping Fallen Angel. He ardently pursued women round the world, a tireless retiarius seeking to ensnare them with nets woven from the fervid fibres of his poetic soul, hoping to bring them down with lassos of whirling words and lariats of lush swirling compliments! He promised nights of passion in Vienna, Sienna, Torquay, Paris, Bangkok, Mecca . . . But one night he was arrested in Rio, and accused of being a Troublesome Troubadour. They cunningly paraded Copacabana beauties in front of him, and when his frumious golden tongue was hanging out far enough, snipped it off, snicker-snack, hoping to turn

76

his soaring *cynghanedd* metres into plodding feet of iambic clay. They used the gold to make rings, one of which now adorns the delicately shy finger of a sleeping princess. But the words and music still gushed relentlessly out of his eyes, so they had to pluck them too, notes, motes and all. They left him writhing on the ground, in pain as they thought, but a passing entomologist pointed out that the man's seemingly random movements suspiciously resembled a bee's courtship dance. He was therefore further charged with 'Apiarian Aping Without Due Authority', and had his legs broken. He now had neither honeyed words, glances, or tics.

As I shuddered at the thought of those twitching limbs, I was suddenly jerked back to the present. The blindfolded man moved the malevolent triumph from his face to his tongue.

"Ah, Mr Isk," he said, "I suppose you're wondering what's happening. People who find themselves in cages at the beginning of second-rate stories often do that. Well, you are the victim of a fiendishly convoluted plot hatched up by myself and a wench I was generous enough to tumble a long time ago, Catherine Meaty-Zones here, now a powerful witch, whom you mistook for a lady of similar name and bosom. You're in a cage because you've been turned into – forgive me, I really don't know how to break this more gently – a chicken, destined to be my dinner for the next few days. Spermicidal Whiskers, Pilchard Stopdrooling, Squeeze Thews, Engelbrecht the Degenerate, and so on, are all characters I've invented. Like Claudius, I poured the stories into your ear while you were drunk, so that you would forget who you really were, and therefore be unable to resist a Transformation Spell. Still, they have also helped you to forget your predicament for a few hours: dreams to help you pass the time; it's quite an Aboriginal idea, you must admit."

"I'm a chicken? Then I'm not a writer or a lunatic?" I wasn't sure whether to be relieved or not. So what I'd thought was an enormous scar was in fact part of my beak and the loose skin my wattle! I scratched my comb in dismay, producing a rather tuneless twang, like Bob Dylan on a foggy Monday.

"Pah, you have the desire without the fire, the quills but not the skills. Your stories creak more than Mr Flay's knees in **Gormenghast** or the Queen's smile after a right royal eructation during her Christmas Day Speech. Your most rounded characters are still as flat as old beer. *I'm* the only decent writer around here. My name is Stark Antonym Zanahoria, as I'm sure you now remember. Everywhere I am lionized, and roar my appreciation. I thrive on contradictions, and glow with red hair, crude wealth, and logical impossibilities."

"A chicken?" I tried to stop bobbing my head.

"Yes, Cat here did the Spell, and put you in this cage. Remember that article you wrote in *Rhondda Quarterly* last month? Saying that my work wasn't worth chicken shit, and that more nuggets were to be found in a dilapidated McDonalds than in the whole of my work? Didn't you wonder why so many of your 'memories' concerned ships or spaceships? It's because you had unknowingly taken my ideas *on board*. But brilliant ideas in the head of a hack are like listeners to a Fidel Castro speech: they get bored and shuffle towards the back of the crowd, and in your case they've reached the edges, and are slipping out through your comb! You've come a cropper, bach! The few ideas of your own that you still have are hopelessly half-baked, so it's time to wring your neck, I'm afraid, and then finish cooking you. Though your prose is notoriously indigestible, I'm hoping your thighs are not."

"But why? What have I done to deserve this?"

"Written so badly, so predictably, so unimaginatively, that there was a serious danger that *you* might have got elected to the Swansea Literary Academi instead of me, since the last thing they want is internal competition. That's why they praise Dylan Thomas so much, so no one will notice the new poets and novelists. I intend to murder you, to make sure I get the only vacant seat, and because I've never liked you. But murdering humans, even ones as mortally tedious as you, is frowned upon, and punishable by law, even in Wales. There's no penalty against killing chickens, though."

"Why are you wearing a blindfold?", I squawked, playing for time.

"It was Cat's idea. She knows I'm a sensitive soul, and so she suggested I put it on before you woke up, in order not to see myself spilling your blood. It is easier to live with oneself when one does not witness one's crimes. I'm surprised more murders aren't committed by blind people, or at least cross-eyed ones. I know I'm a toad, but I'm not going to risk you crossing me, or pushing me into a hole. Proffer me the plump or scrawny neck of that chicken-livered coward, please, Cat, that I may kill, cook, slice, and dice him."

But now, suddenly, I really did remember everything. The poor fool didn't know that the *real* conspirators were Cat and myself!

I gave an evil laugh, and curled my beak with contempt.

"Ha, Zanahoria! Your commination I have allowed, but comminution is going a midge too far! Cat, remove his blindfold!"

"Just a minute!" cried the witch imperiously. She reached behind her, and produced a thick manuscript, which she held under Stark's head. She then tore off his blindfold while I stuck my head through the bars of the cage.

Stark Antonym saw me, was immediately sick all over the manuscript, and staggered around in agony before collapsing to the floor.

"Take that, carrot-face!" I cried. "I am no broody rooster, but a moody monster! Didn't you notice my name? Basil Isk? I am a cockatrice!"

"O clucking shell!" he groaned. "But that's impossible!"

"Not logically, only empirically so!" I crowed.

"Mendacious meretrix!" gurgled he, fixing his seared eyes on Cat. "May slugs beget bugs in your double-D dugs!"

"Silence, loquacious loony!" she snapped back, glaring at him with scorn and fury. "In my youthful innocence I worshipped you, Stark Antonym, and your writing, full of flame and fantasy and frowning opposites: I grew giddy with desire chasing after twists and turns in your stories, where juicy metaphors lurked in silk-bed ambush behind every sensuous simile. My only desire was to surrender my tender flesh to you and live with you for ever; I even loosened my virtue a little bit beforehand, so that you would have no difficulty finally relieving me of it. But when the moment came, all you did was furtively fumble me on the Mumbles, breathlessly bugger me on the Brecon Beacons, and then abandon me to pursue and bedazzle rich *salon* hostesses all over Europe. Had you left me anywhere else, the sandpaper of time might have smoothed away my spleen and filed down my fury, but you left me in Swansea! Swansea! I vowed then not to simply measure out my life with coffee and love spoons, but to take revenge on you. It took a long time, but eventually I became a witch.

"Knowing that both you and Basil Isk would be in Swansea to present your latest works in the hope of getting elected to that seat in the Academi, which rightfully belongs to another, I arranged to meet you both for a drink in *The Englishman's Severed Head*. I pretended I had forgotten your crime against me. My whole object was to get you at my mercy – which, by the way, is also a fictitious quality, but in this case a winning one!

"Of course, you and Basil pretended, in front of me, to be delighted to see each other, and claimed you had only really come to Swansea hoping to have the pleasure of witnessing the election of the other to the vacant seat.

"But before we met, I had told Basil my plan: to pretend to turn him into a chicken, but in reality to turn him into a cockatrice. He confessed he was too afraid to lay a hand on you himself, but that he felt he could see his way to *looking* you to death! Just as you, Stark, said you feared to murder a man in cold blood, but that killing a chicken, especially when blindfolded, was no crime.

"So when we met up, and while you two were smiling with false camaraderie, slagging off all the other Academi members, we got Basil drunk, as he had already agreed. You filled his head with your stories to take away his remaining personality, and then you helped me carry him back here to my home. I sent you off to the kitchen to prepare the cooking sauces and mix the stuffing, while I did my Transforming. I told you that after eating him, and keeping back a bit of chicken soup for our souls, we could then recline together on a soft luxurious bed made of his plucked feathers. "Yes", you joked, thinking yourself very witty, "as the bluesman Mississippi John Hurt almost sang, 'Make me down a pullet on your floor'."

"But instead of a chicken, I really created a cockatrice – my contact lenses and rather sexy *Dolce & Gabbana* glasses protect me from its gaze – and now its hideousness has, as I planned, caused you to vomit all over your manuscript, which you dare not now present to the fastidious Academi judges. In any case, you are unlikely to live more than a few hours."

As my rival groaned and shuddered in the corner, I cackled with delight.

"That'll teach him! Now you can transform me back like you promised, Cat, *I'll* get the Academi seat, and then we can marry in church and live happily ever after, and have two children, maybe three, and send them to a good school where they wear respectable uniforms, and bring them up properly to learn their catechism and know their place, and then we'll have pretty blue-eyed grandchildren and a garden and poodle and lace curtains to hide behind while we watch the neighbours."

I fluttered my wings and waggled my wattle suggestively, and stuck my beak through the bars to give her a little peck on the cheek.

"Back, hack!" she shouted, "or I'll break your drum sticks! You will never lay a hand on me, or an egg *in* me, either! Away, fowl creature!"

"But what's this? What about our agreement? What have I done?"

"What have you done? Stark Antonym just told you! You have less imagination than an undarned grey sock! Oh, if you knew how I suffered at school because of you! Your insipid *Liking Among The Dandelions* was a set text, as was your eye-closing *Behind the Scenes in Milton Keynes*. Three teachers resigned, rather than have to teach it, and another actually died of a fatal yawn in front of us while trying to explain the hidden significance of Ethel's daily shopping trips. We girls read Richardson's *Pamela* in the toilets for a bit of excitement, and underlined the naughty bits in Jane Austen. Your soulless works ruined romance for me, delayed my first period by a year, and gave me inverted nipples! My life was meaningless until I met Hymen Thews at a fencing class."

"Hymen Thews? You mean Hymen Simon, don't you? Or Squeeze Thews?"

"No, I don't. Stark Antonym has a strong imagination, that I can't deny, but his soul, like yours, is devoid of romance. Only rabbits and turnips really excite him. On principle he is all negative, nihilistic. Hymen Thews on the other hand is a *real* writer who not only never got the recognition he deserved, but is also the most romantic man alive, the only one worthy to lay his craggily exciting head on my savage Welsh breast. So much larger than life is he that

Stark in his fiction unconsciously divided him into two, the Cloven Lover: Squeeze Thews the man of action and Hymen Simon the poet-musician. And so great was his jealousy that in his stories he always had them bumped off – in one novel, Squeeze died of gingrene from too many biscuits, and Hymen, while his legs were still broken, was tied down in the sun until his back was bright red, and then, naked, forced to join in the Pamplona bull run."

"But . . . you're saying all my 'memories' were real, then, even though they weren't my own? But Captain Pilchard Stopdrooling can't be real! Or his arch-enemy Engelbrecht the Degenerate Dwarf!"

Her smile was more sinister than a chess board in a badly-financed operating theatre.

"Oh yes they are! After countless skirmishes, they decided to fight it out once and for all, man to dwarf. They stared each other up and down – Pilchard finished first – took deep valiant breaths, and were dropped in the local Grudge Crater on the Moon. But Engelbrecht, coming from a dwarf star, was so heavy, even there, that with each movement he sank more and more into the lunar surface, and as for Pilchard, he didn't dare get too close to the dwarf for fear of being trapped in his gravitational pull. They were too intelligent not to recognise zugzwang, so they agreed to a stalemate, and were taken back on board the Referee's spaceship, where they took another deep breath and to each other, expressed mutual admiration for a gallant opponent, and became the best of friends.

"Which is why I chose to take my revenge in this ridiculously recherché way. Since Pilchard just happens to be my uncle, he asked me if I had any ideas on how to help out his newfound chum. Engelbrecht was finding it difficult to locate any mythological beings in his part of the galaxy – apparently, they're a delicacy on certain planets, and have been hunted to extinction – and was in danger of being thrown out of the Smallsphere Surrealist Assassins Club.

Which is more serious than it seems; the back-stabbing there takes place *after* public exposure and expulsion, and all members, friends or foes, are expected to join in. That's another reason why I turned you into a cockatrice instead of a mere chicken. But you should feel honoured: I told Pilchard to tell Engelbrecht that I had hatched you from one of the *fatal eggs* laid by Bulgakov. So, although it is obvious to all you are not a great writer, you can at least claim to be the progeny of one."

"Oh vile villainess! But I'm not afraid. You said yourself Engelbrecht is too heavy to move even on the moon, so here he'd be as helpless as a boiled foreskin on a hook in a damp vestry."

I realised I was still infected by Stark.

"That was some time ago. Engelbrecht went on a diet for this mission. First he tried losing electrons, but found after a week his weight was just the same, of course. So then he cut down drastically and pluckily on carbohydrates and protons, and after losing about 300 septillion of the latter — that's a good 300,000,000,000,000,000,000,000,000 amu — he found he'd lost about a pound. Which, being a dwarf, was a fair percentage. He tested himself out last week in a boxing match, and clocked up a resounding victory against a remarkably sprightly grandfather clock. I don't think a mere cockatrice will give *him* much trouble. I'm pretty sure your lethal gaze won't work on extraterrestrials, though I've bought him a few pairs of short contact lenses, just in case.

"Anyway, I'm only keeping my promise to you: I told you that I had influence in the Academi, and that if you helped me in my plan — since Transformation Spells only work if the subject isn't resisting — I would make sure you went far. Well, so you shall! Out of the solar system, with Engelbrecht! He should be here soon. If you're lucky, he might get here before Stark starts to reek."

So saying, she picked up my cage with one hand, and hurled

me through the door behind her. A moment later, Stark Antonym's still-twitching body landed on top of me.

I looked up, and then had to squeeze shut my eyes. Oh horror of horrors! It was a hall of mirrors! If I so much as opened my eyes for a second I would be violently ill at the sight of myself. Trapped in a cage, and as good as blind, how could I hope to resist capture?

I had one last hope. If Engelbrecht and Pilchard and Hymen Simon and the rest were all real, then that meant Spermicidal Whiskers and Robin' Darktree also existed. I could expect little help from the former – he would be useless against women, except unborn ones – but if *I* hadn't been the one to receive the enormous scar from Catherine Meaty-Zones, then I must have been reliving the memories of Darktree the scandalously pitiless highwayman. He might, faced, fazed and amazed by her décolleté, have forgiven her in the chivalric heat of the moment, but when he got home and tried to shave, he would almost certainly have painfully nicked his underlying pitilessness. What if he were on the way here now, seeking dire revenge? If he killed Cat, her spell would be broken, and Engelbrecht would see that I was just a hapless hack, and leave me in peace.

A poultry hope, it is true.

At that moment, triumphant laughter came from the other side of the door, followed by what sounded exactly like a particularly treacherous witch being passionately kissed by a man with melancholy Machiavellian lips and a Brazilian-sounding limp.

And pretensions to literary respectability.

EPIPHANY IN THE SUN

†

The dog lay crumpled in the deserted road, which sliced like an old scar through the barren terrain, the fierce early afternoon sun beating down on it. All around, white limestone glittered, interspersed with patches of tenacious vegetation seared and bleached with the heat, stunted, thwarted. In the distance, the glint of water – the Aegean carving a great arc against the city of Izmir staggering up from its shores. But here was only rock and aridity, and the flies and midges which had settled like minute vultures on the dog's protruding tongue and shapeless jowls splayed on the scorching tarmac.

A car approached from Izmir along the other side of the road, suddenly slowed and stopped. The driver twisted round to stare at the dog through the rear window. The woman beside him fidgeted.

"What are you looking so shocked for? It's horrible, yes, but it's only a dead dog."

"I think it's still alive. I'm sure its head just moved."

"I didn't see it. Anyway, what can we do?"

"At least move it out of the road before any more cars come."

She frowned, then nodded. "Yes, could be dangerous if anyone was driving really fast."

"You mean, for the dog, of course?"

She glanced sharply at him. "Of course, that too."

He made a U-turn, and stopped the car on the verge beside the dog. It whimpered as he got out and approached it cautiously. There was no blood, no tangible sign of pain. Just a paw scratching on the road, and flanks heaving in quick jerks. He stretched out a hand tentatively, almost as if offering a benediction, and when the dog made no movement, half carried, half dragged, it to the side of the road, where he stayed looking down at it.

86

The woman came and stood beside him.

With the featureless plain stretching behind her, she was like a bright accidental flash of colour on a faded canvas, the gleaming yellow of her blouse and the cheerful blue of her shorts leaping out from the tired greyness of the surrounding landscape. She pushed a fly from her face, a face framed by long blonde hair, a face clearly used to loving and laughing and living, a face that, like her body, was healthy and vibrant and young, somehow out of keeping in this harsh ancient land.

"Has it been run over or something?"

The man, a few years older, muscular and tanned, yet with thin, almost ascetic, features, looked up. "I can't tell. There's no blood." His voice was strangely tense.

"But how did it get here, miles from anywhere?"

He didn't answer, just kept on gazing at the dog.

"Well, there's nothing more we can do," the woman continued after a moment, "even if we'd got the time."

He didn't look up. "We can't just leave it like this."

"We have to. What else can we do?"

"Look, we're only just out of Izmir: why don't we take it to a vet?"

"What about Ergün?"

"Oh, he'll wait for us. And anyway, it wouldn't take long."

"Oh no? Your 'just out of Izmir' is more like twenty miles, and you'd still have to find a vet when you get there. Do you really think we'd still get to Ergün's in time!"

"So we miss a trip in his boat. Is it that important?"

"Yes, actually, it is!"

A small silence. Perspiration trickled down her cheek, pooled at the base of her throat. Then she suddenly smiled. "But not as important as keeping my future provider and bed-warmer happy! If it really means so much to you . . . In the boot, though. I've heard some of these Turkish dogs have rabies. I don't want you to start dribbling at the mouth – any more, that is, than you already do over the girls in your classes."

He evidently decided she had earned that small victory, for he made no rejoinder, just tweaked her nose affectionately.

Sweating profusely, he clumsily deposited the unresisting dog in the boot of the hired Anadol. He tied the boot partially open, making sure the gap wasn't wide enough for the dog to jump out. He lingered a few moments, stroking its head.

The journey was an almost silent one, the woman showing a determined interest in the orange orchards floating hazily by, and the occasional glimpses of the sea beyond them. The man, too, seemed lost in his own thoughts, until he finally slid a hand over on to her cheek. She took it and pressed it and traced its brownness with her fingertips. But neither of them spoke, as if aware that the presence of the dog carried a subtle threat with it.

On the outskirts of the city, he stopped several times to ask where a vet could be found, and was finally directed to a dingy building in a poorer outlying area. It stood opposite a small patch of wasteland, in one corner of which tottered a dilapidated *çayhane*, or teahouse, with the usual smattering of men lounging around – men who suddenly became alert when the couple got out of the car, like cats that have spotted movement in the grass. They stared openly, blatantly, at the tall blonde girl, so different from the dark-haired women of their own race.

She looked round nervously, suddenly conscious of her bare pale legs, of her blouse clinging to her in the heat.

"I'll come in with you. All those gaping men, they give me the creeps."

"Oh, they're harmless, really. But in places like this, they do tend to twitch a bit when they see foreign women. Especially women as unbelievably scrumptious as you! But we won't be here long."

She took his arm, urging him forward, and they entered the building. Within five minutes they were outside again. He was almost shaking with anger, while the woman, looking bewildered and frightened, clutched his arm, a gesture he seemed unaware of. He leaned against the car, hands gripping the roof-rack.

"But, John, what happened?"

He didn't answer, just stared over the roof of the car, a vein pulsing on his forehead.

She burst out with sudden anger: "At least have the decency to tell me what's going on — or am I supposed to have learnt Turkish in five days?"

He finally answered, his voice distorted with fury.

"That bastard, that *stinking* bastard . . . and I'm a fucking idiot, too! I should've known . . . "

She waited, looking at him with a compound of apprehension, sympathy, anger.

"He said he could arrange to have it shot. *Veteriner* doesn't mean what you'd think it would, fuck-all to do with *helping* animals. They just check for disease in livestock. Turks don't keep pets, animals are for eating or kicking. OK, my mistake, but he could have *looked* at the dog, I was willing to pay the bastard. But no, he wouldn't even *look* at it!"

He was oblivious to the group of men already gathering round them.

The older men looked eerily alike — tough, sun-battered faces, crinkled eyes, carious teeth, beards or stubble on their chins, all wearing dirty stained vests, grimy baggy trousers, some tied with string at the waist, dusty strapless sandals — but there was kindness in their eyes, dignity seared into their faces. The young men were different, drenched in cheap eau-de-cologne, hair slicked back, black moustaches aggressively curled, tight chest-hugging shirts, their dark strength vitiated by the desire to be modern, to nourish themselves on the husks of western civilisation.

The woman spoke anxiously, urgently:

"John, let's talk about it after, please! Let's get away from here first."

He became aware of the knot of men around them, took a deep breath to calm himself, and nodded. Before he had time to open the car door, however, one of the older men said something, pointing at the dog, whose head was now thrust out of the boot. At first, the Englishman answered only with curt politeness, but a conversation developed, with more and more of the bystanders joining in, and he quickly became animated. A small boy left the group and ran down the street.

"They say it's probably been poisoned," the man explained , "but that if we force a mixture of garlic and *ayran* – you know, that yoghurt-like stuff you tried yesterday – down its throat, it might be sick and bring the poison up. Could just work, too!"

"You're not going to do it here, now!"

"Of course. The sooner the better."

"What about Ergün?"

"Oh, a few more minutes makes no odds now."

She gazed at him with astonishment and dawning anger.

"Look, John, if you don't care about keeping Ergün waiting, you could at least think about me."

"Cathy, come off it, just a few more minutes, that's all!"

"While I get stared at by all these filthy men? And in this stinking bloody heat, too!"

"Those filthy men, as you call them, at least care about the dog – which is more than you seem to do!"

She glared at him. "Don't try to take it out on me: it's your precious Turkish friends poisoned the dog, not me!"

He made an obvious – too obvious – attempt to speak calmly.

"Cathy, I'm sorry, OK? I know you're hot and tired and fed-up, I don't blame you. But now we've got this far, we may as well see if this *ayran* trick will work." He glanced at the dog. "That's if it *has* been poisoned. Maybe we should've left it where it was. But we didn't. We can't just dump it here now."

"And why not? Let your new friends work their miracle cure. I can't see it makes any difference whether we're here or not. Or do you think that dog will recover just because *you're* near it? I just want to leave. Now."

The tension that had been in him since they had found the dog flared to the surface.

"Bloody well leave then! Take the car! Have your bloody boat trip! Have Ergün as well, since you're so keen to see him! Christ, you're no different from that stinking vet!"

She looked at him incredulously, tears of humiliation springing to her eyes. Her hair was sticking to her face with the heat and dust; she tried to fling it back with a furious shake of her head, but only a few stray strands moved. The pathetically futile gesture dissipated his sudden rage. He reached out, pushed her hair from her eyes and cheeks with remorseful tenderness.

"Cathy, I'm sorry! That was stupid. Oh shit, what can I say? I wish we'd never found the dog, not when it's coming to this. But . . . it's . . . it's as if . . . at first, I thought all we had to do was find a vet. But now there's no-one else, now it's just the dog and us. Don't you see?"

Her eyes flicked to the men around them. He understood.

"Oh, these people are good with advice. I daresay they care in an offhand sort of way. But they won't actually touch the dog themselves, oh no. If *I* don't make the dog sick, no one will. So you see it *does* make a difference, it really does." He was almost pleading.

She turned away, her face set. "I'll wait in the car."

He stood back as she got in, his face taut with indecision. Just then, however, the boy returned with a bottle full of a whitish liquid which he thrust, grinning, into his hands. He hesitated, then swung round and moved to the boot of the car.

The dog's condition was worse. As he carried it awkwardly across the road to the patch of wasteland near the teahouse, it hung limply in his arms, and when he put it down, sank immediately on to its stomach. It breathed raspingly, moaning and twisting its hind legs as if seeking to escape the jaws of some metal trap.

He lifted its head and began to force the liquid down its throat. It yelped, struggling to turn away, but he gripped it tightly under the jaw and continued to pour. Most of the onlookers had followed him across the road, offering vociferous advice. But the man seemed oblivious to them, to his surroundings, to the heat and the smell, to the liquid staining his arms and clothes. There was a manic concentration in his actions, something desperate, almost brutal, in the way he jammed the neck of the bottle deep into the dog's mouth. As if it were an enemy, rather than a creature he was trying to help.

By now, the woman was back in the car, which had both windows wound down. Two of the younger Turks sidled across. One of them offered her a cigarette, and laughed rudely when she shook her head. He rested his elbow on the open window on the passenger side, looking in at her. She shrank away, but her defensive gesture only emboldened the man, who now leant his head, darkly handsome in a coarsely sensual way, on his elbow, and stared openly at her exposed legs, making comments to his friend, who now joined in the game – which was already ceasing to be a game – and moved round to gaze in through the other window.

She glanced helplessly behind, but the small crowd across the road was now fully occupied with the drama of the dog. With the movement, her blouse tightened over her body. This – and her fear, the sense of having her trapped – excited the first man beyond control. He thrust out his hand, pushed it brutally, frenziedly, inside her blouse, grabbing and twisting at her breasts. The second man started to put his arm through the other window. With reactions speeded by near terror, the woman grasped the door handle on the side of the first man, pushed the door outwards with terrified strength. His head and shoulders trapped in the window, the man was jerked off balance before he could extricate himself. She stumbled out of the car, lurched a few feet, tripped, twisted her head round in panic. But the men were running off down a side street. She half knelt, half lay there, her breath ragged, before pushing herself to her feet and staggering across the road.

The reason nobody had noticed the assault was now apparent: an ugly pool of white flecked with yellow was seeping into the ground in front of the dog's head. The man, still kneeling, looked up as she reached him, excitement and triumph animating his face.

"It worked! Look, look, it seems to have brought up everything that was in its stomach. We'll have to wait for . . . "

"John, please, John, get me away from here!"

He noticed her expression. "Cathy, what's happened?"

Her face was disfigured with humiliation. "Just get me out of here, for Chrissake!"

Before he could answer, a loud cheer went up from the onlookers. He swung round. The dog was getting up. One hind leg still dragged on the ground, its breath still came in great rasping gasps – but it was almost on its feet. It tottered, would have fallen again had the man not caught it with a swift movement. For a second, the dog's great head clasped in the man's arms, cheek touching jowl, the two seemed like one single shapeless creature newly spawned from the ground itself, a weird hybrid that did not belong in this time and place. Then the dog slipped to the ground again, its tongue scraping weakly over the vomit already drying on its mouth. Panting, again oblivious to everything around him, the man tore off his tee-shirt, and wiped the dog's face.

The woman had remained where she was, like some gaudy hollow scarecrow that would topple in the first gust. Even the younger men found their eyes drawn to the crumpled despair in her face rather than to her body. A fly walked unfelt over her cheek. Her arms dangled at her sides, a bruise discolouring one of them. Her eyes followed the man's movements with the dull intensity of the victim mesmerised by the glint of the sacrificial knife.

The man finally rose, and shook his head, as if suddenly remembering where he was, who he was with.

"It's looking a bit better, isn't it? This has buggered up your afternoon, but I'll make it up to you, I promise." He looked down at the dog again. "But now what? I don't want to just leave it here. What if we took it to Ergün's place? In the orchard, yes! The dog could stay there till it's recovered."

"Yes, John, you do that." Tonelessly. "Leave it at İnciraltı."

"Cathy, are you all right?" With sudden concern, "Why, what've you done to your arm?"

"Nothing, John. Nothing for you to worry your head about. Can we go now?"

He looked at her distractedly for a few seconds, then turned back to the dog. He carried it back to the car, not noticing that the passenger door was wide open, and once again with difficulty lifted it into the boot.

Ten minutes later, they were heading back out of the city. With both windows open, it was almost cool in the car. The man, who had not bothered to put on another tee-shirt, was beginning to relax. The sweat had dried on his face, and his hair straggled over his forehead, giving him the tired appearance of a swimmer just emerged after a long time in the water. The woman was slumped in her seat, head thrown back, eyes staring at nothing.

The man didn't speak for some time, lost in his own dark thoughts. But finally he shook his head as if to dislodge some unpleasant memory, glanced at his companion, and became aware of her alienated expression.

He took one hand from the wheel, rubbed the back of his fingers down her cheek, leaned over to kiss her. She didn't move.

"Hey, not sulking, are we?"

No reply. He turned her face towards him, his fingers pulling on her cheeks, which momentarily became a shapeless blob, like the jowls of the dog when its head had lain in the dirt.

"Cathy, you're crying!"

She tried to blink the moisture away, but it was a final effort. The next moment, she was frenziedly pushing him away, sobbing convulsively.

He slewed the car to a halt, tried to comfort her. She buried her head in her hands, recoiling from his touch, her body shaking uncontrollably. Seeing the uselessness of trying to stem the flood, he waited until it should subside, his face a mosaic of contradictory emotions – love, pity, exasperation, surprise, shame.

His attention was fixed on her, but even so, once or twice he glanced, almost guiltily, towards the back of the car, towards the boot and its strange cargo.

When she had sobbed herself to exhaustion, she seized some tissues from the glove compartment, wiped her eyes and cheeks slowly, roughly, distractedly, as though it were not her own face, staring ahead through the windscreen. When she finally spoke, her voice was tiny, quiet, as if it came from far away.

"We've been apart too long. Maybe we knew each other once — I like to think we did; or is that just a trick of memory, too?"

He knew no answer was expected.

"I was being selfish, you think I don't know that? Wanting nothing to spoil my day. Wanting to hog you all to myself. And why not? You came here for a year, then it became two, then yet another. And all those lovely young university students adoring you. How many of *them* did you take out in Ergün's boat, I wonder? But I had you each summer. Enough to give me memories, to keep me faithful. *Faithful!* How's that for old-fashioned? But because it was you, I respected your quaint religious principles. And it all seemed worth it until a few days ago."

He began to speak, but she cut him off.

"So what's wrong, you're going to ask. And you know what? I can't even tell you. I've been here five days, and I still don't know what's wrong. There's something . . . different about you, about us. Perhaps that's why I was a spoilt brat going on about Ergün's boat. I was wrong, I admit that."

"No, you weren't. I should've thought how it was for you in all this heat."

She smiled bitterly. "Always fair, that's you. The vicar's nephew. That stubborn belief in justice." The smile faded. Abruptly, harshly:

"When you told me to piss off back there, would you have tried to stop me if I had?"

"Oh come on, Cathy, you know very well I didn't mean it. I was upset about the dog, that's all."

"Yes, of course, the dog. How could I forget the dog? You really wouldn't have tried to stop me, would you?"

"All right, at that exact moment, maybe not. But it's not

worth getting . . . "

"You don't even *want* to understand, do you? When I was in the car, did you stop one minute to see if I was all right?"

"I was busy with the dog, for God's sake! Or would it have satisfied your vanity if I'd just abandoned it?"

"My vanity! Good God, he thinks this is all to do with my vanity!" She was staring at him with wild disbelief. "Oh yes, I'm vain all right! So vain I loved it with all those men leching at me, oh yes, I just lapped it up when those two bastards tried to rape me! I really only ran across the road to you so they could get a better look at my arse!"

"What the hell are you talk . . . ?" Sudden remembrance, shock in his eyes. "Oh Jesus, of course, when the dog was sick! But you didn't say any . . . Cathy, what . . . ?

" . . . what happened?" Her voice cold and flat again. "I already told you. Nothing. Not really. Just mashed my tits around a bit, that's all! Hardly worth mentioning, happens to thousands of women every day. What's one tit among so many?"

He gazed at her helplessly, horrified.

"John, don't look so concerned! You just didn't notice, that's all. But, by God, it hurts to find you can just . . . not even *see* me like that!"

He shook his head in bemused, silent negation of her words.

"I love you, Cathy," he finally said simply, factually. "What happened back there must've been awful, I know . . . "

"No, you don't know! Don't say you know when you don't, *can't* fucking know, damn you!"

He winced at the fury. His face took on an expression of irritation, alienation.

"Jesus, if you won't even let me speak . . . !" He restarted the engine.

"Suddenly remembered the dog, have you? Sorry, I didn't mean to take up so much of your time."

In his anger, he pressed the accelerator too hard, and the car jerked forward.

Moonlight. The same road, the same spot. A few months earlier. Driving back half-drunk from Ergün's place with Lâle. Leaning across to kiss her, one hand on the steering wheel, the other stroking her thigh. Lipstick mixed with the strong aniseed taste of rakı. A movement in the road, his foot fumbling for the brake. The thud. The young Moslem woman, terrified of being found with her English language tutor, urging him not to stop, it had only been some wild animal, it would be all right . . .

He drove in silence before finally turning off the main road into the tree-arched track leading to Inciraltı, the nearest beach to Izmir proper. A gang of fishermen, their wiry weathered bodies glistening in the hazy light, were hauling in a net, as if in a tug-of-war with an invisible opponent. They shouted out friendly boisterous greetings as the couple slowly drove past. The woman flinched.

A creaky hut stood only a few yards from the water's edge, beside an orchard straining with orange and apricot trees, and aubergines lying bloated and ugly on the ground. A light breeze was coming in from the sea, ruffling its surface like the hair of some shaggy leviathan, and mixing the smells of sand and soil and sea, of fish and fruit and debris.

The man got out of the car, called Ergün's name. No answer.

"The boat's not here, either. Perhaps he took some other friends. Why don't you have a swim till he gets back?"

She ignored his suggestion, sat impassively in the car. He moved towards the boot.

"Oh shit!"

She swivelled round at his exclamation. He was dragging the

dog from the boot, laying it beside the car. She heard its low moaning, saw it writhing on the ground, its belly grotesquely distended. The hind legs jerked frantically, the filthy fur matted like long-dried seaweed. A mucus-like substance had congealed round the corner of the eyes, and a pungent fetid smell came from the mouth, which hung open, tongue splayed over the lower jaw, coated with dried saliva. The head snapped up, the eyes stared straight at the man, and it howled, the sound rasping the nerves. The sound ceased as abruptly as it had begun, but the head remained erect, and the eyes still open, open through all the agony, focussed on the man crouched over it, pleading from the other side of hell.

She stumbled out of the car.

The man looked up at her, and it was as if she were looking into the dog's eyes. Screaming, too, for release.

"Three more hours of pain, that's all I gave it, oh God, three more hours of . . . this."

Then, his eyes wild, his face suddenly twisting: "And I really thought I was being given a second chance! Get back in the car, Cathy. I don't want you to . . . see."

She followed his gaze to a rock a few feet away, half embedded in the ground. It took her a moment to understand.

"No," she whispered, "no, not after all that."

"*Because* of all that. A job to finish." His voice was almost unrecognisable.

"John, it's dying anyway. You don't have to . . . Jesus Christ, no, John! John, only a few minutes, maybe, and . . . "

"No, not a few minutes. Not this one! An eternity, this one! Cathy, please . . . get in the car."

Driving back, sobering up, the awful doubt, was it dead, or was it still lying there broken and bloody, in needless agony, waiting for the next vehicle to break off another piece of its body? Too late to go back now . . .

. . . Only it hadn't really been too late, had it, but the girl had promised to spend the night with him, and he'd resisted temptation so long, and the mystery of a Moslem girl, and Cathy was so far, far away . . .

He moved to the rock, scrabbled frantically to wrench it free, staggered back to the dog. She turned away, stumbled towards the water's edge, gazed out unseeingly at a seagull bobbing indolently on the glittering surface. Long minutes passed before she heard the first sickening crunch, then another, and another, and another . . .

*But why did you have to punish **her**? I was the one you wanted.*

A sharp gust of wind lifted her hair. A sudden wave splashed over her feet. The seagull flew off screeching. She turned. Where the dog's skull had been was now only the rock with bits of bone and blood and tissue sticking to it. The man was crouching over it, sobbing uncontrollably.

She shivered in the August heat, then went and knelt beside him, wept on to the back of his bowed head, cradling him like a baby.

THE HEISENBERG MUTATION

†

Charles Algernon Soames, who occasionally lent money to the Sultan of Brunei, first noticed something was seriously wrong just before his eighty-fifth birthday. It was a freezing mid-January day, so his wife had thoughtfully opened all the windows and turned off the heating before she went out. He had been rubbing his arms to alleviate the frostbite when he noticed that from the shoulders to the elbows there seemed to be a sharp ridge. Icicles? He was about to call one of the servants, remembered his wife had insisted they take the week off, so slowly struggled to remove his shirt – his pullover had been left just out of reach – and saw that his arms seemed to have flattened out into something resembling cricket bats.

His wife had carelessly forgotten to cut the phone lines, so he called his doctors. All five of them.

"Perfectly normal," they pronounced, switching to *soothe* mode after secretly exchanging astonished glances, "a bit bony, it's true, somewhat aggressively scapular, but you can't expect to be built like Schwarzenegger at your age, can you?" They overcharged him by the usual amount, and added on thirty pounds for the joke. Funny jokes cost a lot more.

The next day, it was his legs. Lying on the bed, he heard a *Ping! Ping!* and felt his buttocks and belly rush to meet each other. He looked down and saw that his legs too had come together and flattened out into a rectangular shape, rather like a gravestone, with his feet hanging over the edge of the bed like overgrown indecisive spiders.

This time, the doctors, who had, for a trifling five-figure sum, kindly stayed overnight, made no jokes. They even allowed unsightly creases of doubt to distort their professional smiles, and finally

101

admitted that, although they were of course quite confident that nothing was seriously wrong, it might be a good idea to call in a specialist. When the old man irascibly reminded them that he had been paying them specialist's fees for the last decade, they coughed, adopted pained expressions, and said they meant a specialist in *Flattened People.*

By the time the specialist in Flattened People arrived, Soames had lost the power of speech, as his trunk and head had followed the geometrical example of his limbs. He was now thinner than a Communion wafer in a cost-cutting church, resembling one of those cartoon characters flattened under a bulldozer. He was also clearly suffering from severe dehydration; his skin had become drawn and dry like parchment, his fingers and toes yellowing and curling up like paper.

"Indeed, when you come to think of it," remarked the Flattened People specialist meditatively, "he looks for all the world like a man-sized document. Yes, definitely a document. Do you realise he has perfect A4 ratios?"

He was taken to a private hospital – *very* private, since the mere millionaires, the pre-multi ones, were dragged out of their beds and expelled, if not exactly unceremoniously – a million was still a million – certainly expeditiously, into a nearby annexe. The doctors laid him on top of what they claimed was a state-of-the-art raised bed specifically designed for Flattened People, though it might have been suspected, from the faint nail polish odour, that it was simply one of the secretary's tables. The hospital, however, clearly could not charge the same prices for a table not specifically designed.

After exhaustive tests, it was shown that the specialist's diagnosis had been remarkably accurate – but then he *was* the recognised world authority on Human Flattening. There could no longer be any doubt.

Charles Algernon Soames had changed into his own Last Will and Testament.

"I have to confess," said the specialist, trying unsuccessfully to appear modest, "that this is not the first case I have come across, although it *is* the most pronounced. If you think about it, the man who bought out Bill Gates with some loose change was almost bound, as he grew older, to be regarded more as a source of possible bequests than as a human being. We are here dealing with a classic example of Heisenberg's Uncertainty Principle, the influence of the Observer on the Observed, but at a supra-quantum level: in this case, so desirous were people to get our patient's money, they all saw him as nothing more than a kind of walking will. The potency of their greed finally shattered the molecular structure of his body, and . . . well, here's the result." He tapped Soames lightly on the watermark which was just appearing.

The doctors all shook their heads sadly at this extreme example of human greed: they could only take their cut while the patient was alive.

"If you could give me Dr Heisenberg's phone number, I'd like to discuss his theories with him," said a young intern, anxious to impress his superiors with his willingness to learn. "But surely, if they had all wanted him to die, his death would have been more likely than this transmogrification."

He was disappointed that they all took this very impressive word in their stride.

"Ah, yes," said the specialist, " but, with a few rather . . . um, noticeable exceptions, most of these people didn't particularly wish for his death in itself – that was incidental – they simply wanted his money. So he turned into a Will *without dying*."

At that precise moment, as if to confirm the remarkable diagnosis, one of Soames' toenails broke off, and what looked like part of a signature was revealed on the inside.

The specialist nodded sagely. "Just between us," he said, "I do believe the Queen of England is showing indisputable signs of the disease, too. You may have noticed that she has already taken to wearing envelope-shaped hats."

They called in the family, and explained – tactfully, they hoped – that Charles Algernon Soames was now high quality vellum instead of flesh and blood. (This was not exactly true, but you do not tell the potential beneficiaries of billions of pounds that their loved one is like Manila paper or decayed papyrus.)

Mrs Soames, in particular, despite her previous life as a starlet in *Baywatch*, showed herself to be a strong-minded woman not to be bowed, or even ruffled, by adversity. "Let's open him and read him then," she said impatiently. "The sooner we contest his Will, the better!" Her sons looked at her admiringly.

The doctors coughed as doctors do and pointed out that, although her loved one was now clearly and irrevocably a document, he was a *sealed* document. To 'open and read him', it would be necessary to break the seal. And since the seal was an integral part of the new-look Mr Soames, this would be tantamount to dissecting him.

"Well?" said Mrs Soames. She really was a remarkably strong woman.

She was eventually made to see that her darling husband couldn't be dissected without an official death certificate, and (in answer to a second 'Well?') that they couldn't issue such a certificate for the moment since they were getting definite EEG readings from his . . . well, something.

In other words, Mr Soames might no longer be flesh and blood, but he wasn't dead.

When Mrs Soames tornadoed out of the hospital, her two sons

swept along in her wake like tumbleweed, the doctors cursed themselves for their scruples, realising that now their only chance of retiring young was to somehow reverse their patient's condition. There was little help to be had from the available literature on the subject. Dr. Jekyll had destroyed all his notes, Alice had been suspiciously vague about the technical aspects of the Duchess' baby turning into a pig, they hadn't even heard of Kafka because of the education cuts of the Thatcher years, and the physiology of bats, frogs, selkies, and serpents was obviously quite different.

They all looked at the specialist in Flattened People.

"I really do believe," said he (and to think his tutor had advised him against doing a doctorate in FP!) "that our only chance is to find someone who regards Mr Soames as a human being rather than as a walking Will, leave them alone together, and this might reverse the process." Probably, he thought privately to himself, it would have been easier to find ten good men in Sodom and Gomorra.

Albeit with misgivings, they began with Mrs Soames, but even after politely relieving her of a blow torch, Stanley knife, and jemmy she had hidden under her dress, after just a few minutes the Will began to smoulder and rustle in alarm, which was not a good sign. The same thing happened with the two sons from a previous marriage, the grandchildren, *and* the two charming pretty little great-granddaughters. Business colleagues, Golf Club partners, ex-mistresses achieved nothing more than to make the Will rustle and groan faintly. A couple of friends from his schooldays induced something like an ear to sprout from its top left-hand corner, but this soon transmuted back into paper, as these same people, who had more or less forgotten Soames, began to wonder whether *he* had forgotten them, and whether, even if he had, he might not now include a little something in return for their help.

They called in a medium. This move didn't restore Mr Soames

105

to his bipedal form, but it did let his doctors learn something about his state of mind. His voice, somewhat thickened by ectoplasm, emerged from the medium's contorted mouth: "Piss off, the lot of you!"

"This is only to be expected," said the FP specialist, who was a very understanding man, despite being a doctor. "It can't be very comfortable being squeezed into a few sheets of paper, even if they are man-sized."

Mrs Soames, claiming that only the dead spoke through mediums, adduced this as an additional reason to have her husband buried or cremated, and his funds as well as his soul released. The SAS were called in to remove her from the hospital.

By now, despite precautions, the case had become public, and even shared headlines in the tabloid newspapers with the exclusive revelation that a leading politician was about to 'come out' as a hermaphrodite, and in the broadsheets with the news of the invasion of the United States by Liechtenstein.

The Church, of course, having nothing better to do, soon joined in against the doctors' humanitarian decision, once Mrs Soames had promised to make certain donations. As one of God's blessed creatures, proclaimed the General Synod, Mr Soames had the right to a Christian burial immediately. And for once the pro-euthanasia lobby agreed with the Church: if people in irreversible coma had the right to a dignified death, surely the same should apply to people in irreversible wood pulp – or goatskin, or onionskin, or whatever.

"Let me help him pass on to a better life through a shredder anointed with holy oil," thundered Dr Kevorkian, "rather than linger ignominiously in a filing cabinet."

The case was referred to the High Court. Crowds gathered outside. "But, good God, man, he must be dead!" muttered a hundred champagne voices whose owners felt they might have been included in the Will; "Open him up, and then let him rest in peace!"

"He isn't dead!" retorted a thousand beer-and-plonk voices, whose owners knew they were not included in the will; "Let him be!"

One hundred rich voices against one thousand poor voices was obviously a draw, so the question went to the International Court of Justice in The Hague – Holland, after all, was *the* place to experiment with euthanasia laws – but they passed it on like the hot potato it was to the UN. This decision would probably have sealed Mr Soames' fate – and *un*sealed Mr Soames himself – since it had long been the dream of many of the duskier UN members to slice up a colonial capitalist or two. But before they had done more than salivate a little, developments overtook them.

†

Charles Algernon Soames, as it happened, fully shared the desire of the duskier UN members that he be unsealed and his pages cut open, even if he might not have agreed with their motives. He was as interested as anyone else in finding out what he, as his own Last Will and Testament, actually said. His great fear, indeed, was that if he never regained his human form – which would enable him to write a nice, normal will – his silly squeamish doctors wouldn't open him up and let the lawyers execute him – as a will, that is, not as a human being.

His physical form was the result of the way others had regarded him, that was clear, but were his contents their *desires* – or their *fears*? If a haruspex were to come and read his entrails, would he find that his wife had been left everything, as she wanted, or nothing, as she feared? He didn't know himself. What he did know was that if he died intestate (a bit ironical, considering he was a Will now), his family would get everything – give or take a few billion that the State would snap up.

Although his odd metamorphosis had deprived him of movement and sensation, it had replaced them with a new sense. The pressure and influence of others' thoughts and desires had turned him into a Will because of a latent telepathic gift, and that gift was now more than just latent: he found he could read the hearts and minds of everybody, not only those around him, but everybody who had even remotely impinged on his life.

He wasn't completely surprised when he looked into his wife's mind, once he'd worked his way past the maggots: the open windows in winter, the bars of soap left on the top stair, the mosquitoes hidden in his underwear, Julio Iglesias coming constantly from speakers just too high to be reached except by a wooden stepladder just beneath which he happened to notice a pile of give-away sawdust, the sending of three extremely athletic and mettlesome young prostitutes to his bed (simultaneously) – all these things had more or less prepared him for the discovery he now made: that she visualised him as a sticky slug-like creature blocking the slot to the world's biggest piggy bank because he wouldn't do the decent thing and die. He recalled sadly the idyllic early months of their marriage, which had led him to write a will leaving everything to her. One afternoon, however, he had discovered her disporting herself on the altar in their private chapel with a dildo in one hand, and the open will in the other. This was, to say the least, unusual so early in a marriage, and he had taken advantage of her moment of orgasm to snatch the will away from her, and burn it.

The rest of his family and acquaintances, too, had all looked at him, to differing degrees, not as a frail old man, but as a potential dispenser of bequests. And deep within himself, he suspected that perhaps this was all he really deserved. Had he himself ever really given love, apart from that infatuation with a wife a quarter of his age? How had he ever deceived himself into believing he wasn't buying her?

There was, as far as could judge, only one exception, one creature which had loved him totally, absolutely, unfalteringly.

Not his two-year-old great-granddaughters, who had early been taught by their parents to sit on his knees, and always to bear in mind that 'smelly farty old man' really meant 'lots of sweets for ever and ever'. Not even his dog, which, behind all the lickings and welcome-home barkings, had never really forgiven him for having had him 'doctored' just after he'd met the very willing new young Pekinese from next door.

No, none of these. The only creature that had ever really loved Charles Algernon Soames had been his goldfish.

He was amazed. All those years when he had believed his goldfish had been aimlessly opening and shutting its mouth, staring out stupidly from its bowl, it had in reality been *blowing him kisses*! In the goldfish's stolid mind, like the sixpences in the old Christmas puddings, shone just three elements – a memory of when he had come home one day and just managed to save it from his wife's new (and suspiciously hungry and savage) cat; the vision of his hand pouring food into the bowl; and a mass of love for him as thick as the Antarctic krill beds had once been.

Soames felt a tear on his cheek: in that soulless world of power and finance, something had really loved him.

Felt? His *cheek*?

He was beginning to change back again, he felt warmth and tingling returning to him, he felt . . . but then came all those other voracious minds, wresting him back into their fears and desires. They were too many, too lusting, too strong. He fought back, lying there quietly, shutting them all out, receiving and **returning** the love of the goldfish. He felt a calm strength building up inside him, and with that strength, his mind reached out for the specialist in

109

Flattened People, while he concentrated on growing back the only thing he needed.

Three hours after that, except for a single hand, he was nothing but yellow, decayed parchment, breaking into pieces and fluttering and floating tantalisingly to the ground while his wife looked on furiously, and tried to snatch a piece of paper from the specialist in Flattened People and the lawyer with him.

†

The family disputed the new Will, of course. They went to the best lawyers, promising them a percentage of whatever they got. But the new Will left a huge sum to the Law Society, with the stipulation that if even one of their members were to dispute it, the donation would not be made. Of course, there were still one or two who were lured by the enormous sums promised by the family if they won, but after they had had a leg or two bitten off, they realised that their colleagues were quite prepared to live up to their reputation as sharks.

The money that didn't go to charity went to found the Charles Algernon Soames Humano-Goldfish Friendship Association. Here, in the biggest aquarium in the country, with walls decorated with waterproof paintings of cats – cats on racks, in Iron Maidens, on gridirons – went to live *the* goldfish, cared for by over a hundred well-paid ichthyophiles. The specialist in Flattened People, who was really quite a romantic, would go there sometimes, and recall that strange scene of the newly-formed hand writing the new Will, and the way it had then seemed to wave a strangely peaceful goodbye, and he would smile and shake his head and watch the goldfish. Once he thought – but no, it was as if someone, something, else put the thought there – of the Ancient Mariner who suddenly loved and blessed the water-snakes, and how in that moment

> *. . . from my neck so free*
> *The albatross fell off, and sank*
> *Like lead into the sea.*

When he was sure that no-one was looking, he blushed and returned the goldfish's kisses.

CIRCE'S CHOICE

†

'Sooner shall foliage grow on the sea, and sooner shall sea weeds spring up on the mountain tops, than shall my love change while Scylla lives.'

(Glaucus to Circe, Ovid's **Metamorphoses**)

What will it be like, after hunting her for so long? I would prefer to kill her as the old Scylla, with the teeth of my hounds tearing her body into chunks while my clawed fingers scrabble inside her chest and yank it out. What will it look like, her heart? Tiny, black, withered, putrid, the same as my own? Or will there be, as I suspect, nothing?

But my hounds are dead. A knife will have to do.

As long as I remember why I am here. I must remember. Sometimes, it's so difficult, my lives all merge into one eternity of hate, and years pass before I become even momentarily aware of who I really was. When I am near the sea, it is easier to remember.

My fear is that when I destroy her, my meaningless lives will have even less meaning than before.

But no, that *is* the meaning of my life: her destruction.

Yet . . . why did she return there, to the Island of the Dawn, where she must have known I would find her?

†

I sense you, Scylla! Ah, you are now so near! Your bloodlust is carried here on the sea spray. Instead of being able to draw comfort from each other for the annihilation of our world, one of us must destroy the other. My skill and my fierce magic, that proved more powerful even than the dark night of the gods, made you immortal. Or was it the force of your hatred? Yes, your hatred and my magic. Together, they will bring our bitter story to a close.

112

†

Should an eternity be built on a single mistake? Yes, I ran from him. He began to emerge from the water, so glorious, so godlike, his hair a waterfall frozen in verdant silver, it was as if he and the water were but one substance, and the water simply curled into his shape. But then he hauled himself on to a rock, and I saw that below the waist he was no longer a man, but a true denizen of the sea. I was young then, and beautiful and vain, and had always been sheltered by the water nymphs, so although I wasn't really afraid, I turned and ran away. A part of me hoped and believed he would come again the next day, and he would continue to woo me, and I would relent, and he would perhaps take me to the secret chambers of the sea. I thought of him all that night, never suspecting what had happened – how he had tried to drag himself after me over the shingle, how the sharp stones and shells opened up a dozen cuts on his chest, and how my thoughtless laughter coming from behind the trees drove him to despair and he hurled himself back into the sea, and swam to cursed Aeaea and sought the aid of the evil sorceress living there. Circe! The unloved goddess, for all her beauty, she who could only gain the feigned affection of lions and wolves tamed and emasculated by her foul magic. Blinded by his sudden passion for me, Glaucus recklessly paid no heed to her own lust, her own vile cravings; she offered herself to him, and he carelessly rejected her, and Fate looked up astonished at his rash words, and then smiled, and twisted her Threads, and from that moment I was doomed.

And he, he never came to see me, he never came to weep or curse over my fate. His youthful hot words, that had roused the fury of the sorceress, and condemned me and all who came within my reach, in the end were empty and meaningless.

Words that might have kept a little part of me alive . . . empty and meaningless.

✝

Ah, Scylla, who turned all heads while I languished alone on my island, banished there by Zeus himself on a whim, why did you have to pretend to run away? A childish caprice that has brought us to this moment. If you had stayed, just a single smile, he would never have come to me, and I would never . . . He came to me, and I thought . . . I still see the look in his eyes when I, myself feeling no more than a little girl, offered him the untested body and love of a goddess. He dared to turn away from me, and, unbelieving, uncomprehending, shrivelling in my own shame – I, a goddess, had offered to take him even after you had spurned him! – I raised my wand, so rightly feared . . . but he had already dived into the sea and was beyond my reach.

But not beyond my vengeance.

The stench of my own tears and vomit, as I lay huddled into myself and broken on the beach for day after day after day, must have been what finally brought me to my decision.

Perhaps if I could explain to you now . . . but it is too late. You need, and deserve, more than explanations. As do I. Soon, very soon...

A sailor took me to the bay where you always bathed. A sudden wind lashed my fine useless robes like whips against my scorned virgin's body, stung my eyes, almost hurling me to the ground, as if to warn me, to prevent the crime. If only you had been there, with your adoring water nymphs twisting and turning about you like dolphins made of sunlight! Perhaps they would have calmed my anger, perhaps they would have called Poseidon himself to intercede for you.

But you weren't there. I recited my spells and dropped in your pool the potions that would turn you into a monster.

114

And when Glaucus found out, and dared to curse and rail against me, I who had offered him all . . . that was too much.

I compounded the crime.

†

Just an old woman, said the fisherman who rented me this boat, living in a stone cottage inside the ruins of what must once have been a palace. But I look across at the island, and I know.

This time I will have her!

Once . . . once before I was so near! Odysseus was within my reach!

Oh how sweet that revenge would have been! To snatch her lover, perhaps with her foul fluids still drying on his body like spittle, dangle him over the ship, and then snap his writhing body in two, devouring the lower half, letting the organs that so pleased her slither down my throat, and throwing the other part, the torso and head, high into the air, high high so the wind could catch it and carry it and send it crashing down to her cursed island! And she in her palace would glimpse something falling and maybe yawn and stretch her satiated limbs, limbs that have known love as mine never have and never can, and wander out curious to see what it was . . . Ah, then her shriek would have reached me even above the roars of my insane companion across the strait, frenziedly sucking down the currents in a meaningless whirl!

But I didn't know then how, unlike the hot-headed Glaucus who had blurted out his deadly folly, guileful Odysseus had feigned love to save his skin – for who could *really* love so vile a creature as her? –so that tiny part of me that was still human simply admired him as so many others had done, and at the last moment I turned away, and took another of the sailors instead.

When I learned who he was, whose bed he had just come from, how I had let him escape . . . then, even my monstrous hounds

115

cowered before my rage!

†

You think Odysseus tired of me, that I could not hold him back from Penelope.

The truth would have given you even more satisfaction. But for you, I could have held him forever. I only turned his men into swine to make him, proud captain, set foot on my island. And he, frothing with fury, came running, as he believed, to their rescue! I played my little pantomime, and he held his ridiculous sword at my throat, as if mere iron could ever have harmed me, and I willingly allowed the phallic blade to enter the lonely recesses of my godhead, making him believe that *he* had conquered *me*! And he famed for his cunning!

It was necessary to heal the wound made by Glaucus. But I came to really love him.

For a time, he loved me too. But never the way Glaucus loved you . . .

And you, Scylla, as you jump from your puny boat, splashing through the waves, full of the accumulated fury of centuries, knife already clenched in your hand . . . what if I tell you that your vengeance began a long time ago?

One afternoon, as we lay in the shade of the red pines, he said that his men wished to leave the island, though he himself would stay, and I considered the sea course they would have to take.

And remembered you! I warned him of the danger of Scylla and Charybdis, and he noticed the change in me, and asked me why you had such hatred of the sailors passing through the straits, why you were as you were, why at your waist you turned into six snarling hounds with serpent necks. I pretended ignorance, and indifference, but I know he suspected, remembering what I had done to his men. I looked into his eyes and saw the terrible doubt . . .

116

Ah, Scylla, how you would have gloated to see how I shrivelled up then, how my juices became drier than the bones of rats, how his suspicion flushed through my body like the Hydra's bile and poured into our place of pleasure!

Odysseus finally left with his men. Because of you.

†

My hounds. My beautiful sea-blue hounds. Six of them. The very mention of them would fill sailors with fear and loathing.

And yet . . .

They never ran after butterflies, never shook snow off their glistening fur and stretched out beside a warm log fire blessed by Hestia, never followed the enigmatic delights of scent. Trapped in our hellish cave half way up that smooth cliff face overlooking the Tyrrhenian Sea, where no man could attack us, they lived, with me, less than a half life. Hunger forever gnawing at us, gazing out ceaselessly for seals and dolphins, and sometimes human fare. We devoured screaming victims in order to live. We killed through necessity.

At first I hated them, oh how I hated them! In the early days, I tried to destroy them, scraping sharp rocks, or even the bones or teeth of victims, across their throats, despite the pain that I ineluctably shared with them. One I almost did succeed in killing, though I was screaming from the agony for hours. When I stopped screaming, there it was, stretched over my waist, panting, blood still trickling from the gashes I had made, looking up at me in agonized incomprehension, and then it was that I first knew love, first began to fully understand what Circe had taken away from me forever. Until then, I had never shed a tear that was not for myself. I collected leaves and made them soft in my mouth, and covered the wounds, and my hound slowly recovered.

Century after century they were my only company, they were

117

my lovers, my children, my enemies, my friends. Yes, Charybdis might have moments of lucidity and look across and up at me, but the moment would soon pass, and she would sink back, trapped forever in her unthinking inhalations and exhalations, probably not even knowing, and certainly not caring, how much she was feared. So I had only my hounds. When hunger pangs were not driving us wild, for the mariners learned to avoid our strait, when an autumn evening would lay itself around our cliffs and slowly, tantalizingly, draw back the veil and give us the gift of the stars shining over the Ausonian Sea, then, sometimes, we would know a moment of peace, and instead of howling and snarling, the creatures that were now me would gaze up at me with sad eyes full of questions, lick me and lay their heads on my unkissed breast.

And then – when was it, a century ago, ten centuries? – Circe's spells began at last to lose their force, and one by one, my hounds died and fell away from me.

But, no, they didn't die, they are now within me, forever a part of me, and that is what all men fear. Even with the waning of the magic, Circe has managed to make men afraid of me! Inside, I am still Scylla!

†

And when he left me, you let Odysseus escape from your hounds. And do you regret that? Oh, how I soon wished that you had devoured him! Seven long languorous years he spent in Calypso's perfumed sheets, while I wailed and mixed my potions in loveless futile fury, because Calypso too was a goddess, and too powerful to attack.

Seven years.

I would like you to know that.

But I dare not. It might make you hesitate.

†

I seem to have so many memories, although I don't know if they are mine or another's. Usually it is water. More than a hailing, it is a summons. Many seas, many oceans, as though I have moved from place to place in search of something. Apart from seeking *her*. Though since I have become human again – almost human – I have sought out the company of other outcasts. Twisted faces that reflected my soul in a leper colony that closed half a century ago on a tiny island in Guadalupe (so why am I still so young, if her magic is dead?), and I remember more mud-brick leper houses in Karakalpatkia in Uzbekistan, south of the Aral Sea, where the poisoned land and water might almost have been the work of Circe herself: I, who once had too many limbs, have always been drawn to helping those with too few. The truth is, I flee from 'normal' people. I flee from them before they can flee from me.

But one day, working at the Leprosy Hospital in Istanbul, I caught her scent, borne up the Aegean coast!

✝

And what would you say if I told you about Telegonus, our son, as brave and astute as his father Odysseus? I had long ago forgiven Odysseus for his enforced years with Calypso, and his return to his wife, and I sent Telegonus to Ithaca to bring him back to me.

Oh yes, he brought him back.

But no breath in his body, no light in his eye, the worms already making him their home. His own son, my son, *our* son, had slain him in error. Though was anything ever really in error in those days? Weren't we gods just as much victims of Fate as the mortals? Did I *really* have a choice when I approached your pool?

Would *that* appease you, Scylla? No, it is too late for that. Your face is carved into one single murderous purpose, as you move away from the beach, and towards my dwelling, clutching your puny

119

knife. Wouldn't you like, though, just once, to taste *my* despair, instead of your own? Let it swirl round your mouth – so pretty, yes, so pretty, you were always more beautiful than me, oh, you never knew! – and then spit it on to the point of your knife, and make sure you twist as it enters my body? Come, Scylla. For this we have lived, you and I, and this day it must end.

✝

I sometimes try to convince myself that my memories are false. I can't see the scars any more; where my hounds lived, and were finally loved, and died. Perhaps, in a certain glancing light, I can make out, or imagine I can make out, lines of skin that are just that little bit rougher, can see the hint of a shape that has not been seen in this Age. Again, too, there may sometimes be an echo of a limb, an acute feeling of something *missing*. But I would, if I could, put all this down to fancy, to a quirk of my mind, which people say is too knowing, too mature, too bitter.

If it weren't for the men.

The men, *they* sense my hounds, without knowing what they are. They look at my face and flowing hair with open admiration, they draw in their breath when they see the perfection of my breasts, they become hurried, they frantically try to undress the rest of me as quickly as possible, they rush to enter me . . . and then, always, that look of uncomprehending surprise, nervousness, fear. And afterwards, each according to his character: some laugh at themselves and apologise, and some lie there unspeaking, sad, puzzled, and others roll over and find some excuse to leave the bed, and some, many of them, choose to blame me.

Which would be so very contemptible if it were not, just this once, the truth.

In that other life, I did not have sexual wants, although my hounds did. They would mate with each other, and I would sense something of their compulsion. Now I have my own body and a need, a terrible need after so many centuries, to achieve my own fulfilment. But the urgency is too great, I know. Men sense it, fear it.

But it isn't just that. My hell hounds *are* still here – there – as though phantom teeth lurk within me.

One of the oldest fears known to man: Circe's final cruelty.

That is why I force myself to remember, why I am moving now towards that clearing among the trees. If ever a creature deserved no pity, she is the one.

✝

Do you really believe I cannot see you? Have you forgotten who I am? *What* I am? With nothing but the strength of your hatred, and a weapon I could once have deflected with a simple Word of Command, you dare to enter an enchanted place where even the plants and insects have always obeyed me.

He came back, Scylla. Glaucus came back. My furious magic, which had entombed him in rock at the bottom of the sea, allowed him to survive the passing of the gods, just as it saved you. With its weakening, he finally freed himself.

And came for me, as you are doing.

But when he saw me, saw what I had become, the fury and the scorn slid off him. He gazed at me for a long time, then he knelt before me and took my hand and said: "Circe, let it be, it is over. Your time finished long ago, but you do not die because you are trapped in the tyranny of your own magic."

And I said to him: "One thing, only tell me one thing: *could* you have loved me? If you had not seen Scylla first?"

In his answer – and I knew *he* could not lie – was some of the comfort I craved.

So I asked him for one last thing in exchange.

You need never know the price of your freedom.

121

Of *our* freedom.

✝

At last! I see her! But . . .

Is *that* a goddess? That ancient *thing* slumped there on the balcony, like the remains of some huge insect? My hound senses bring to me such a smell of decay . . . as if she has been rotting on the inside all these centuries. I am used to ugliness and the snarl of disease with my lepers, but this is a decay more horrible, more *final*, than any I have seen.

Of course, she is the last, the very last, of her kind.

But all I feel is even more rage. Rage that even *she* could not extract any good out of her evil, which might at least have revealed a *reason* for all my suffering. That translucent deformity I see is only what she has always been inside, a creature who cannot feel, cannot love, a vileness, an eruption of pure evil.

But although the dying of my hounds can only mean the dying of her magic, that does not mean she – it – does not retain enough to destroy me.

She has seen me! She was already looking in this direction. And is that grotesque expression a smile? So she is, after all, prepared. It does not matter. Either way, there will be an end.

✝

A chill autumn breeze is rustling through the trees that surround me. I never felt the cold before.

From where I am, I can see Mount Olympus, far away to the west, in what is now another country. Another time.

Such hatred! It is buffeting me, overwhelming my senses. Magic contains its own mysteries, and is not so easily overturned. Although the visible form of the terror has gone, the terror itself remains. Wherever you go, whatever identity you take on, whatever language you speak, the horror will go with you.

122

Unless I fulfil my promise to him.

You move towards me. I fear that I am still too strong, that the goddess in me will lash out, despite everything, and I will lose this one chance. But I have broken the wards around this dwelling, and brought sleep upon the animals that have always guarded me. I have broken my wand, too. It resisted, as I knew it would, because I *am* my magic. It fought back, it made the very hands that twisted it seem to glow with strength and youth and beauty, the deceitful promise of always, but this time I had a memory to aid me . . . . it finally snapped, and in that moment the centuries, too long frustrated, hurled themselves rabidly upon me, searing, gouging, crushing me.

I have already given you your vengeance, Scylla. Now it is your turn.

If only I could speak with you at the last. Perhaps try to . . .

But I know there will be no words.

No.

Only in the Sacrifice will be the Purification.

A sudden shower of rain, that has stopped almost as soon as it began, and now the raindrops huddle in the grass like fallen stars. A final shaft of sunlight, and I think a part, a small part, of it, is touching me . . .

✝

She is walking along the shore, head down, twisting the white sand with her toes as so many have done through the ages. She feels peace. She has washed the blood off her body in the cold waters that embraced her in sudden recognition, and the sea has taken away her final memories and mingled them with the blood of the sorceress. She doesn't know where the blood came from, or remember how she got here, or even where 'here' is. It doesn't seem to matter. Peace. She is walking along the shore, and she feels as if she has always done this. The memories are gone, but they rise and fall with the swell of the sea, she knows the answers she isn't seeking are there.

Obscurely, she senses a new mortality.

She looks up, her fingers instinctively moving to hide scars that are not there, as in the distance a swimmer begins to emerge from the waves. It is a man, lithe and strong, luxuriant hair clinging to shoulders and back, rising from the water as if it were his kingdom.

Her instinct is to turn away, to hide among the dunes that quietly resist the sea's dominion. But Circe's blood sends final urgent murmurings with the cresting of each wave, and she walks on.

Towards the meaning of the sacrifice.

TWO LEGS BAD:
A Love Story
†

(Warning: contains unusual sexual practices; not recommended for the squeamish)

I was in the supermarket when I knew they'd found me.

I was waiting for Billy outside the check-out, using the opportunity to glance through the papers. I saw him wheel his trolley towards the aisles, sizing them up with a practised eye. Murphy's Law of Supermarket Queues, he once told me, could usually only be broken with the aid of an assault rifle. But he'd studied maths and physics at university, and prided himself on having a firm grasp of probability theory.

When he settled on the third queue from the left, I silently applauded his choice. It wasn't the shortest, but taking everything into account – apart from the obvious, like the number of trolleys and whether they were attempting to double up as delivery vans – I saw greater potential dangers in all the other queues. Aisle One included a customer with clear signs of senility feebly clutching a wad of out-of-date '10p off' vouchers, Aisle Two a harassed mother with a screwed-up-face-about-to-cause-serious-havoc child, and Aisles Four and Five were infested with smug credit card payers, half of them with loyalty cards and arthritis. For a moment I thought Billy had missed a rather promising Aisle Six, until I noticed the whip marks across the shoulders of the checkout girl. She must have been in training: competition from other chains was fierce these days.

It was only because I was watching Billy that I also peripherally noticed a completely unattractive woman dressed in a black suit who reached the checkout aisles at the same time. She walked straight to the back of the queue that happened to be directly in front of her, Aisle Two, without even glancing at the other queues. Odd, I thought, but then forgot about it. Something about the woman *was* instantly forgettable.

However, strange things at once began to happen in that aisle. A young man suddenly had a coughing fit and left the queue in embarrassment and a cloud of rumbustious mucus, while the harassed mother gave the child a willow-on-leather clout, stunning him into silence and nipping the rebellion in the thud; goods which had earlier filled trolleys to overflowing seemed to have diminished in quantity and size; and as for the check-out girl . . . I swear I've never seen fingers move so fast, except my own on my zip when Patti had first said yes – well, she hadn't exactly said yes, but where I come from if you don't say no very loudly . . . Yet, when I looked at the cashier's face, it was even blanker than is usual in these cases.

The result was that Billy was still three complete old dears away from the finishing post when the woman arrived at the head of her queue

Gripped by panic, and suddenly sweating even more than usual, I looked into her face, hoping I hadn't blocked out my emotions too late. She must have sensed me looking at her, because she glanced across at me. I had my dark glasses on, to protect my swollen eyes. She looked at me for a moment, sneezed, then turned and marched out. And the moment she was gone, I couldn't remember her face. It simply didn't seem to have any distinguishing characteristics.

That, combined with her lightning passage through check-out and the sneeze, could really only mean one thing. No human would have possessed the mental powers needed to break Murphy's Law. One of the Septinians must have survived and got through after all.

Target: me.

By the time Billy came through, I had managed to compose myself.

His freckles were heaving with excitement.

"Did you see that?"

"See what?"

"That woman. Christ, she blew through that queue like a tornado!"

I looked round vaguely. "I don't see who you mean."

"She's gone now. That woman! The gorgeous one!"

"What woman?"

"But I saw you looking at her!"

I hesitated. "Oh, I must have been just staring into space."

"I could've sworn . . . Never mind, I'll tell you about it over lunch."

I'd only met Billy a few weeks before – it hadn't been easy for me to make friends here, quite apart from the risk – but we'd got on well from the beginning, helped by our shared interest in astronomy. Today we'd planned to have lunch in a restaurant by the river.

"Er . . . Look, Billy, small change of plan. Patti's just phoned, wants me to pick up her mother or something. Had some sort of fall. Nothing serious, bloody nuisance, but . . . Can we skip lunch today?"

"Oh, OK." He sounded disappointed. "But you've time for a quick half, come on. Or maybe a brandy, good for that cold of yours. Are you *never* going to get rid of it?"

"Sorry, Billy, I promised. Must dash. I'll give you a call."

I felt his eyes on me as I walked towards my car.

Goodbye, Billy.

That afternoon I resisted the impulse to catch a train out of town – it would only postpone the inevitable – and instead tried to relax by doing some gardening. I loved the sheer magic of making things grow; Billy once said I had green fingers, which was truer than he thought. But even gardening couldn't help me to relax that afternoon.

Part of me had always been prepared for this moment.

But not so soon. I hadn't had time to make any arrangements for my child. I would have to tell Patti the truth.

†

It had been more for her sake than for mine that I'd never told Patti about my previous life or my marriage. Though I admit it also made me sad to think about my wife. Dark she may have been and golden-eyed, but her jealousy!

"You'd go after anything with a skirt and two legs!" she'd yelled at me, all her eyes flashing fury. "What's wrong with four?"

Well, nothing, I suppose. But a new fashion had hit Mars. It was my perhaps immature fascination with bipedalism which not only ruined my marriage, but led to my being exiled on Earth.

The Abductions of Earth people had been at first simply for amusement or vivisection practice for medical students. Terrans were so much more fun than the boringly globular off-pink Venusians, who barely exuded a *glerk* when you opened them up. But then someone had the bright idea of adopting a few, and taking them to underground parties. They immediately became all the rage. Mulder's sister was an absolute sensation, and as for Scully . . . ! So popular did they become that many Martians decided to temporarily undergo limb removal to take advantage of the Four Legs Bad Two Legs Good fad, since some of the Abductees seemed to have a problem *interacting* with us, or even refraining from screaming, in our own form. I myself – perhaps as an overreaction to a violent argument with my wife, during which she had viciously bitten a deep chunk out of one of my tentacles – was one of the earliest to be *simplified.* I chose a human male form, in order to be able to *interact* with Scully. Well worth it at the time, let me tell you! And even after we Returned her, I decided to keep my new shape a bit longer, partly just to annoy my wife, and also because those who say two heads are better than one have never had double migraine, or tried sleeping on their sides or shaving in a hurry. It was also nice not to have your tentacles gnawed away during copulation.

But fashions, like the aurora borealis, change. Mars had never been infected by religion before, but the Head of Government, besotted with one of the Abductees, fat and podgy and senile and dressed all in scarlet with a funny hat, who claimed never to have *interacted* (!), picked up on something he had said and suddenly proclaimed to our astonishment that seven-limbed Martians were made in the image of the Creator of the Universe, and that to alter that image, as we newly-formed bipeds had done, was a Sin. Quite definitely a Sin. A Big one. Quite possibly even an Original one. He didn't quite know what a Sin, especially an Original one, was, but he claimed he had been informed in a vision by the newly-discovered Septinity that we quatentacles were an abomination that had to be destroyed. At once.

Luckily, we had friends in the Fleet who quickly smuggled us into life capsules, and dropped us at random over the nearby Earth, to make it difficult for anyone to find us. We Martians had never really been a warlike race, and we felt fairly sure no one would bother to mount an expedition just to find us: that nonsense about Sin would soon be forgotten, and the same loyal friends would pick us up when the fever was over. And indeed, within a very short time, that Head of Government was ousted by another who claimed that it was a deadly insult to the Omnilimbed Creator to limit Him to a mere seven tentacles: having once discovered it, the Martians took to religion like Glaswegians to whisky or bowels to bacteria.

However, all movements have their diehards, and we were warned that there was a hard core of Septinians brandishing something they called a fatwallah, which apparently gave them divine (the seven-limbed variety) permission to hunt us down, even on Earth, and even if it meant losing three limbs in order not to stand out too much on their arrival. Luckily, the new Multinians also issued something very similar called an out-of-office buwallah claiming that the *real* Deity (the zero-to-infinitely-limbed variety) had specifically stated that He wanted the remaining Septinians burnt and dismembered, especially the fatwallah-waving ones. Our friends advised us to stay on Earth until these earnestly eccentric groups had wiped each other out.

Of course, it wasn't easy settling in on the blue planet – the enormous gravity alone made me feel, and be, pretty low at times, and I was unlucky enough to land, not in a pleasantly warm place like Antarctica, but in what I took at first to be the tropics, a boiling hot island called Britain, sweating my new balls off! And horribly allergic to the pollution. But with time I got accustomed to it. And when I met Patti, and she moved in with me, I began to live an almost normal Earth life.

I must admit, though, I frequently stared up nostalgically at the night sky, thinking of my fiery impetuous wife. My copy of **Norton's Star Atlas** was nearly as well-thumbed as my **Phantom Limb Pain Treatment**. And though I was very fond of her, sex with Patti was not really satisfying. Simply not tentacular enough. Oh yes, on Mars, with Scully, it had been amazing, but that must have been either because of the thrill of manipulating my new unencumbered body, or because the Earthwoman had some nebulous quality, some mysterious X-factor, that Patti didn't. Once the novelty wore off, I felt vaguely let down. I suppose I still hadn't really got used to the scarcity of orifices in the human female.

But all that was now irrelevant. My assassin was close to finding me. I needed a shoulder to cry on, and, more important, a favour to ask. I resolved to tell Patti everything when she came home that evening. I was sure she would understand

✝

And she did indeed take the fact that I was a Martian in her stride. Well, almost. With the help of many brandies laced with hysterics. Even the admission that I was already married only caused me to lose a few slices of facial skin. It was the other matter that caused a slightly more serious rupture between us.

"What the fuck do you mean, 'you're pregnant, and will I look after your child if it's laid before they get you'?"

Odd. She didn't usually swear. I explained.

"'Oviparous'? What the fuck's that?"

"Um . . . it means I lay eggs."

"Oh, my Christ! And just where do you lay them from?"

"Er . . . perhaps you don't really wish to know . . . "

I could see by her attitude that she felt that was a pretty bum remark. I decided to try to put her mind at rest.

"It's not yours," I said. "Our gestation period is two years, it must have been my wife's." I smiled reassuringly. "So it won't be a hybrid."

To my surprise, this failed to placate Patti.

"So you're saying I've been sleeping with a . . . thing who's really just the left-over bits of some fucking great green monster who's already pregnant from some other fucking great green extraterrestrial squid!"

I forgave her for the demeaning 'squid' reference – my news was perhaps somewhat unexpected – but I did have a sudden feeling of protectiveness towards my wife, who wasn't really green at all: more yellowish than green.

To cut a lot of unnecessarily bad language short, Patti was quite unreasonable, and moved out the same evening. "Think I'm

131

going to hang around to breastfeed a giant bloody spider?" she yelled in parting. After she'd gone, I found she'd torn out half the pages of my beloved John Carter books, and thrown all my boxes of Kleenex in a bathful of water. Disappointing and disillusioning, I have to say.

Still, perhaps it made things easier.

With a supreme effort of will- and sphincter power, I managed to lay my egg round about midnight. I wrapped it in cotton wool and placed it lovingly in a twenty-pence-off Nescafe jar. This I slipped into my pocket, and then walked out of the village and, after peeing vigorously against the wall of the BNP clubhouse, climbed the small hill behind it.

There, I released the blocks on my mind, and called my assassin to me.

†

Assassination Martian-style is a venerable and civilised affair. It is, for example, completely unthinkable to kill someone from behind or by surprise. A Martian would rather kiss a Venusian than commit such a dishonourable act. No, even the most pitiless assassins will openly face their proposed victims and offer them the same kind of weapon that they themselves are going to use.

Of course, it is invariably a weapon that the would-be assassin has practised with for months, years, decades, or even centuries, and the victim will often find himself with a weapon without the slightest notion of how to use it. Well, you wouldn't be much of an assassin if you didn't kill your victim at least ninety-nine percent of the time. But in theory, it was a fair contest, which is why assassination was both ethical and legal: even the costs of medical treatment for any wounds received by the assassin were tax-deductible.

For me, the important point was that assassins were usually just normal Martians doing a job that most Martians didn't want to do. They were not necessarily cruel or unfeeling. Yes, this one was most likely a religious fanatic, but I still hoped that I could persuade her — assuming I lost, which was only realistic — to take my orphaned egg back to Mars and give it to my wife, together with my final noble words.

I saw, but didn't hear, the tiny flying craft appear a dozen metres away. As I expected, the woman from the supermarket emerged. It had only taken her a few minutes to arrive. This suggested that she had known where I was all the time. My last hope gone; I'd thought that perhaps my opponent would be a rookie but I was clearly up against an experienced professional. It surprised me that such a person would have joined the Septinian sect.

The moon cut her out in silhouette as she approached me along the path. She was still wearing the same black suit. Would I be the first Martian in more than a century, I wondered, to die beneath an alien moon?

I couldn't see her weapons. So at least it wasn't going to be the huge Thark three-handed sword. That was a relief — I'd never been able to even lift it.

She stopped about three feet away, and gazed steadily at me. I waited for her to release her own mindblocks and allow me to know who she was, as etiquette demanded.

When she did so, the shock was so great I could hardly move or speak for a few seconds.

Hidden behind that unappealing exterior I detected the swirling fractal neural patterns of a mind I knew if anything even better than my own, since the owner had spent decades giving me pieces of it on every possible occasion.

I had never felt so hurt, so betrayed. Yes, we had quarrelled, but somehow I had always thought that we would eventually come together again. My voice not quite steady, I asked:

"Do you really hate me so much you were willing to be simplified just in order to pursue me here and kill me?"

My wife smiled. "I thought that's what you might think! That's why I waited a bit."

She was smiling even as she planned to kill me! A large purple Martian tear fell down my earthly cheek. Yes, maybe I'd gone a bit over the top with Scully, but after what my wife had done to my tentacle . . . Did our ninety-three years together count for nothing then?

She took a step towards me, but seeing me flinch and raise my arms protectively, she stopped.

"I didn't come to kill you!"

Had I imagined those delicious words?

"Say that again."

"I said I didn't come here to kill you!"

"You mean you're not here because of that fatwallah?"

"Of course not. Most of the Septinians were caught and burnt at the stake anyway. And recently, it's been discovered that what had happened was that some toxic agent had got into our Canals, which is what caused all that religious disease to spread in the first place. Everyone is cured now. The troublesome abductees in the long white or scarlet dresses have had their crosses inserted in their rectums, and been sold to ransomed Venusian captives for their weekly orgies."

"So why did you come then?"

She looked into my eyes. "I'm about to lay our egg."

"But . . . but . . . you can't! I've just laid it myself!"

"Impossible. I can feel it when I walk!"

"I tell you, I've just had it. Less than an hour ago!"

I took the coffee jar out of my pocket, and held it out to her. She opened it, sniffed, tipped the egg carefully into her palm, wiped off the grains of coffee, held it against her cheek, and then ran her (now pitifully innocuous) tongue over it.

"It's ours, yes, it's ours! But how . . . ?"

We stared at each other.

"*Bitharkinos* . . . " I whispered.

A small silence. We blew our noses.

On Mars, both male and female are able to bear young – we define the sexes not by child-bearing ability, but by level of hysteria and irrationality – and both produce normal healthy cute seven-limbed nippers. But only one at a time. And until the egg is laid, usually after two years, neither partner can conceive again. (That's what had surprised me most on earth – the frightening distance between partners, their essential *separateness.*) But every once in a while, male and female conceive simultaneously – *bitharkinos* – and this is considered immense good fortune, and festivities are held all over the neighbourhood and unransomed Venusian captives gleefully sacrificed on glowing spits. But because of our tiff, neither of us had told the other we were pregnant before I'd had to flee Mars.

There was no need for more words. I looked at her, in my mind's eye seeing not this rather unappetising creature with long slim silky legs, tight buttocks, flat stomach, narrow waist, pert breasts, full glistening lips, elfin nose, blue eyes, and flowing blonde hair she had been simplified into, but my beloved sensuously squamous wife of Mars. I remembered how her multi-faceted eyes would turn from gold to purple when she was angry, and would thrash about in a pink and blue frenzy when she was excited. I recalled how in lovemaking both her heads would arch back and ululate with pain and pleasure, while her spiked tongues would lash and sting my writhing ovipositors, and of the hours we would have to spend untangling ourselves after a coupling on those wonderful nights when both Deimos and Phobos were at the full. I had repressed those memories in loyalty to Patti, but now . . .

No, we didn't need to speak. She put the egg – *our* egg – back into the coffee jar, and advanced on me with obvious lascivious intent. I found my clothes being telekinetically torn off.

"Wait!" I cried, "wait until we're back on Mars with our own bodies. I want it to be the best ever. Let's not spoil it using these pathetic excuses for real bodies."

It was a test. I could sense the effort it cost her. But she too must have remembered how it had been between us before we'd had our silly misunderstanding. She nodded towards the spacecraft, and held her hand out to me.

I felt unusually optimistic as I joined her. Patti's hurtful attitude had cured me forever of my bipedalphilia, and my wife was at last learning to control her impatience. And we could now at last look forward to the double scritch-scratch of tiny claws and our babies' first hisses.

There's no place quite like home.

GOING BACK

✝

"You see, Jenny, I never did forget you, I remembered you longer than you can ever imagine. And you are fine now. Ah, but the price I am paying, the price!" I hear the voice, but I can't see the face in the dreams, or I see it as one might see an image from beneath waves in the sea, bobbing, flickering, distorted. But I know, I sense, who it is. And I sometimes wake with tears on my cheeks, and it seems as if they are not my own.

✝

When they woke him the first time, Simon Brent went to visit her grave. It was in one of the few cemeteries left in the country, preserved for tourists. It was still just possible to make out the name: Jenny Smith. Such a common name then. Jenny Smith: 1989-2008. Not even twenty years old. A living, suffering creature mashed down into two trite words: Smith, Jenny.

Two words that could still accuse him after a century. And would probably accuse him for many more.

The tombstone itself was crumbling and decayed. And inside the grave, would even bones now remain?

And would it serve any real purpose to disturb the memory of bones?

But it was something beyond logic, something he had to do, though they had told him it was still impossible, that it always would be impossible. He should enjoy the miracle he had been offered. Many of the Returnees, they told him, died soon after they were taken out: 'cured' of the disease which had killed them, but instantly attacked by others that had been patiently waiting their turn, like polite persistent worms in a queue. Or was it Time itself that was killing them? That was why they had revived him, before

137

the stipulated moment. If they put him back . . .

But at least his greatest fear had proved unfounded – he still had a 'soul', whatever that was, his emotions had not been frozen out of him.

He knew because of the tears that blurred that common name. Smith. Jenny.

He returned to the Centre annexe and turned down the brave new life they offered him. He would wait. Wait for the impossible.

†

Jenny Smith is preparing for the disco. The fashion this year is the nano-skirt, and she's pleased, because she knows her legs are her best feature. She isn't exactly plain, and with her unusual height and rich black hair cascading down as it does, she doesn't go unnoticed. But she's never been able to compete with the really pretty girls.

She wonders whether Simon will be there tonight. She senses that he's a bit different, though he tries to hide it, to act like the louts he hangs around with. She can tell he's interested, too, but so far she's put him off. He's a bit young, and she's slept with enough boys to know that it doesn't gain you any respect – or even a decent orgasm, most of the time.

And anyway, she always hopes that one day she will meet someone really special, someone to take her away from the drabness of life in a small seaside town.

Perhaps tonight will be the night. She says this each time she goes out.

Everyday dreams of an everyday girl.

†

The second time they woke him, the impossible had become possible. In a way.

"You don't *look* two hundred years old!" was how Alex

138

Feynman, the Director, greeted the man whose drive and money had founded the Centre. The man who had set one condition: that he be cryogenically stored, and revived to see the end result of what he had set in motion.

Feynman tried to explain the science to him, but how do you explain a guided missile to a man used to a club? A word processor to a person scratching on rock? After the brightest brains had battled with the ideas current in Simon's time – time travel through distortion caused by spinning black holes, tachyons, time slippages, exotic matter, chronons – two hundred years later, as is the way with science, it was none of these. All Simon Brent understood – or really cared to understand – was that the time traveller – if you could call him such – could now double back on himself, as it were, like a knitted jumper unwinding back into its original ball. It would be a journey of the mind only, the body remaining as an anchor on reality. The traveller would be an onlooker, only able to see what he had already seen before, do what he had done before. It was a very limited form of time travel, a literal trip down memory lane. The past could not be altered, because of the Paradoxes involved.

Simon Brent almost gave up then. But he sensed that Feynman was holding something back. He probed and pressed until finally he learnt what it was.

✝

Am I going mad? Bloody schizo? I keep seeming to catch echoes of voices, well, *one* voice, in my head, or rather, not even a voice, because there are no words, more like a presence, like a fine mist slithering into the cracks of my mind. For no reason I suddenly feel disgusted and angry, somehow terrified of myself.

I saw Jenny Smith in the street today, and that's when the presence seemed strongest. I felt a sort of panic, for chrissakes, an urge to cry. But it was gone in a few seconds. Thank God it's

Saturday, and club night for the gang. They scare me a bit, but at least we always have *fun*, we always end up doing *something*.

†

Feynman stared through the viewing panel at the body of Simon Brent, almost lost behind the array of equipment. That crazy old bastard! He should have expected something like this. You don't put yourself in cold storage for two centuries just to *see* a time machine! Yet how could they have barred access to the man who had made all this possible? Who could have suspected he would lock himself in like that?

The early tests had seemed to show that it was, as expected, impossible to create a Paradox, to break the causal loop. The 'travellers' claimed that they were aware of everything they were doing (had done) but were powerless to change anything at all, however much they tried. It was like being observers in a dream, like watching a film of yourself. Indeed, it was not even certain at first that they *had* returned to the past. They might simply have been remembering everything they had already done. Unless they changed something, there was no absolute proof that it wasn't a case of total recall induced by the Transmitter.

Until the Zavinsky case scared the shit out of everybody.

†

At first it was all blackness, nothingness. The centuries in the cryogenic vaults were a journey through emptiness, with just a sudden flash of awareness – the first time he was woken? – before more darkness, and then the images skimmed by like clouds chased by a storm. The lab where they would soon exchange all his bodily fluids, the day the Prime Minister visited the Centre, the opening of the first lab, the day he heard he'd made his first million, cold sex with cold women, the headlines of the local paper stabbing at him . . . and suddenly he is there again, the day of the disco, and reverse time

140

is slowing down like a video tape at the end of the spool, and he sees her walking on the other side of the street . . .

†

Jenny Smith is well and truly pissed off. There are only the usual holiday yobs at the disco, with a small bunch of locals, most of them with no intention of dancing: the pubs have shut, and the only place to get a drink is in the night-clubs. They lounge around, getting more drunk, more self-confident, more obnoxious. "God's fucking gift to the toilet bowl," her friend Mandy declares loudly.

The Sinclair brothers hear that, turn their heads, and think Jenny has said it. Their piggy eyes glower. Their friend Simon looks uncomfortable.

Not long after, they coincide at the bar. Josh does his smooth chat-up line; "Want your twat filled with something to remember?" he asks.

She rounds on him scornfully, ostentatiously staring at his crotch. "What, *that* thing there? That wouldn't fill a barbie doll!"

"Fucking bitch!" is Josh's witty reply.

"You mean 'butch'!" adds his brother. He looks round for admiration.

So when Simon asks her, a few minutes later, for a dance, she tells him to go screw himself. She actually quite likes him, but anyone who hangs around with first-class arseholes like those Sinclairs . . .

"Fucking snotty tart!" growls Josh, and Simon, pretty drunk himself by now, nods in agreement.

Hostility simmers until chucking-out time comes, and they all stagger, half drunk, into the street. The brothers, as they head towards their motorbikes, deliberately jostle the two girls. Simon is already on his bike, and revving up when he sees Jenny with Mandy.

"Going to the club next week?" he calls out hopefully.

141

Mandy answers. "You joking? We can find better pricks than you lot in a bloody gorse bush!" She laughs uproariously.

"And bigger cocks in a farmyard!" adds Jenny, her speech slightly slurred.

Simon revs up angrily, and roars off down the street, skidding dangerously as he takes the corner too fast. The brothers give the girls V-signs, and follow him.

Jenny and Mandy hold on to each other for support as they cackle over their triumph for a few minutes, then Jenny totters off towards home, which is just ten minutes' walk along the almost deserted seafront. She stops to pee in the ornamental gardens, and is just stepping out, still yanking at her tiny skirt, when she hears the roar of motorbikes. Somehow, she knows who it is, but she isn't particularly scared because it's all only been for a giggle and, besides, she knows that Simon fancies her . . .

†

If it had been a nobody, a loner, someone whose life hadn't greatly impinged on the life of others, it might have been all right, any small changes cancelled out by the levelling-out effect of entropy.

But Simon Brent . . .

To change the past was *almost* impossible, but not quite, as Zavinsky had shown. In a routine trial, they put Zavinsky, who had scored extremely high in parapsychic tests, in a locked room for ten minutes, sitting at a table with a pencil precariously balanced on its edge. Zavinsky had to remain absolutely still, in order not to dislodge the pencil. Everything was filmed, and the film put away in a lead safe.

Then they sent him back an hour, a period which included the time spent in the locked room, and told him to try to make his past self dislodge the pencil.

There was the usual flickering, lasting no more than a second,

142

as if a silver sheet had rippled in blue lightning. They undid the straps.

"I did it!" Zavinsky shouted, "I made the pencil drop!"

"What are you talking about?" Feynman asked. "So what?"

"I made the pencil drop!"

"We know, we already filmed it."

Zavinsky stared at them. "But on the film, the pencil didn't drop!"

"Of course it did, I remember quite clearly."

In the end, to show Zavinsky how wrong he was, Feyman took the film from the safe.

The pencil had remained on the table all the time.

Zavinsky's slight movement had distorted *everybody's* past.

Had, in effect, replaced it with a new one, in which the pencil had fallen.

But he, Zavinsky, still remembered the original past.

The implications were so shocking that that night Feynman had even told his wife about it, though this was strictly against the rules. But after twenty years with her, he knew he could trust her.

Now he stood helplessly outside the chamber, waiting for Security to break down the door, wondering why Brent had gone back, trying to console himself with the thought that he couldn't possibly have Zavinsky's extraordinary mental power. And even Zavinsky, after all, had done no more than nudge Schrödinger's Cat.

There was a flickering, as if a silver sheet had rippled . . .

†

They only intended to frighten her, but the drink was in them, and they remembered her mockery, and Josh took out his penis meaning to frighten her even more but it worked too well and she began to scream so they grabbed her and covered her mouth to shut her up and the feel of her body helplessly twisting in their arms changed the nature of the sport and they hurled her to the ground and yanked down her underwear and pushed rough fingers inside her. But in the end it wasn't the brothers who did it, they were too drunk to get erections, so they dared Simon to stuff it in, prove he was a man, and he found he was harder than he had ever been and he thought he might just rub it against her not go right in of course but the moment he felt her heat it was impossible to stop. He came after a few clumsy uncontrollable thrusts, and in an instant what had been thrilling was suddenly sordid and disgusting, and the Sinclair brothers were staring at him almost fearfully. He felt drained and frightened and confused, and pulled her panties back up again, lifted her to a sitting position, and stroked her hair back from her twisted face, almost tenderly: a boy may know the meaning of shame even though he does not, cannot, know the sickness of violation. The brothers threatened her with terrible reprisals if she talked, though it was all bluff, and they all stumbled to their bikes, frantic to get away from the scene, with a blind hope that sheer distance might save them. Only fear, very little guilt, not then.

Jenny Smith, after all, was always flashing it around. Everyone knew that. She was a tall, gangly girl, who worked as a veterinary assistant, and smelled vaguely of animals, and had rough hands, and had asked for it by taking the piss out of them. And anyway, Simon told himself, he probably wasn't even the first boy to shove it in that week.

In the darkness Simon Brent had been unable to see her eyes...

✝

She is staggering along the side of the road, aware only of the pain and the bruised flesh and the need to vomit, and doesn't move away when she sees car lights approaching, or realise that the lights of another car, coming from behind her, are blinding the driver on her side of the road . . .

The everyday dreams of an everyday girl shatter and splash over the windscreen.

†

There was always a suspicion that she'd been raped, of course – they found the semen in her, and no boyfriend came forward – but that suspicion was at first directed towards a middle-aged man who'd been seen on the sea-front just a little time before. By the time he was cleared, no one remembered the three youths, not even Mandy, who had anyway seen them roar away long before Jenny had left her. It was a holiday town, and the holiday season, and few of the people in the night-club had ever seen each other before.

Simon Brent was twenty before he had the first glimmering of what might really have happened that night. He met a girl with flashing eyes and nervous gestures on a train in Belgium, and a month later went to visit her in Verviers, near the German border. He tried to kiss her after her mother had gone to bed, and couldn't understand the trembling, the sweat on her lips, the panic in her eyes. Only when, apologising and beseeching him to give her time, she told him how someone had once molested her in a lift, when she was a teenager, did he at last begin to understand.

He returned from Belgium with memories of cakes and rain and greenness, and fear and longing mixed in a young woman's eyes, and the repressed memories started to claw their way out.

He began to wonder whether it had been an accident, after all.

Guilt was a maggot in his mind that grew fatter day by day.

It was then that he began to dream the impossible.

†

He tried to stop his younger self going to the night club at all. The easiest solution. But that other self was refusing to even admit his existence.

He was near despair. He was only here because a crime had been committed. That crime had led to a timeline of 200 years. Both Simon Brents – the owner of this strong brutal young body, and the would-be intruder in his mind – *had* to converge to become the Simon Brent of the future who entered the Transmitter.

And he now saw something else with horrifying clarity: when he returned to the future, either that future would be very different from the one he knew – in effect, a parallel time line – which meant that in the original time line *the crime had still been committed;* or it would be the future he had just left, and again *the crime would have been committed*, otherwise he would never have had himself frozen in order to reach that future.

There was just one hope: if he didn't return to the future, it was just possible that the future he remembered would never exist, and there would be no cryogenically frozen Simon Brent to return to undo a wrong that had never happened; the Paradox would have wiped itself out.

But he was powerless to influence his younger self. He knew this, even though he repeated to himself like a mantra, "Zavinsky made a change, so I can do it."

The young Simon was getting drunk. Would this weaken his mental hold? Possibly. He skimmed along the timeline between now and the attack on the girl, like a spider racing backwards and forwards across its web searching for its prey.

And found the moment.

He saw himself, just after leaving the disco with the girls' mocking laughter ringing in his head, skidding on something – probably something like fish and chips thrown into the road. He had almost lost control of the bike.

The skid. There was the answer. It had been so close. Only

luck and instinctive reactions had enabled him to keep the bike upright. There was a moment – one, maybe two, seconds – when with the drink and the anger and the unexpected skid the young Simon's mind would be vulnerable. *That* would be the moment to strike.

If he had an accident, his friends wouldn't just leave him there. They would stop and help him. They wouldn't pass the gardens at the exact moment Jenny Smith wandered into view still adjusting her panties.

Perhaps the Paradox of the causal loop would still be there. Perhaps any change he made now – if he did make any – would simply be erased. There was no way of knowing. But he had to try.

He saw the bend coming up, gathered himself. He reminded himself of how he had felt when he had seen those headlines the following day, and as the wheel began to slide hurled himself around the young man's brain to disorientate him . . .

As the bike hurtled across the road into the building on the corner, he had time for a final thought:

Does Time have a moral dimension? Can it make ethical choices?

†

"Yes, I know time travel isn't possible," Feynman declared.

The others looked at him warily; they guessed there was more to come.

"But a hundred years ago I'd also have known you couldn't have a thousand people living on Triton, or photograph dreams, or transplant brains." Tired old arguments, valid enough as they went, but hardly worthy of a top physicist. Because, despite some specious theoretical reasoning, Time itself simply would not allow time travel. He knew this better than anyone, had wasted his whole life on fruitless experimentation. And yet he still had this crazy inner certainty that it really was possible to travel into the past – or the future. An obsession that would have made him a laughing stock in the scientific world but for his undoubted brilliance in other fields.

No, it was more than an obsession. It was a multitude of shadows that came to him when he was half asleep, that whispered forlornly and talked about the undiscovered and untapped power of the neutrino, and said, "Remember, all time is eternally present", and it all made sense until he woke up in his lonely bachelor bed, and dawn chased away the spectres.

†

I dread Peter noticing, how can I explain to him why I wake up crying when I can't even explain it to myself? I'm now even more sure of my love for him than when we got married. So why am I dreaming of Simon? I hardly knew him, just vaguely fancied him a long time ago, that's all.

If you're there, Simon – and I know it's you – then yes, I know you wouldn't have had that awful accident if I hadn't been so rude to you outside the disco. We were just having a bit of fun. Saturday night banter. I did want to get to know you, I really did. But not while you were with those loutish friends of yours.

Everyone tells me it wasn't really my fault you skidded like that. But the fact still remains that if I'd been more friendly, you wouldn't have ridden off in such a temper.

And yet, I don't sense anger coming from you at all. Something quite different.

Ah, if only there were some way to go back and do it all over again.

Change what happened that night.

You might stop haunting me then.

THE BURDEN OF SIN
†

There can be only one. The Immortals must fight and
decapitate each other until only one remains, and that one will
inherit the power and wisdom of all the others.
(Highlander curse)

What egregious nonsense! That idea, almost as ludicrous as the one that Immortals must not fight on holy ground, was cleverly put around by people fearful of our power if we combined, but unfortunately most of the Immortals believed it was true. And there was no escape even for those who didn't, since they were constantly forced to defend themselves against those who did, especially the head-thirsty Scottish Highlands branch. I, however, managed to stay hidden for centuries, because I was the weakest – and therefore the least detectable – of all of us; even my runeblade, Wormclinger, though supposedly forged by an insane hunchback dwarf in Toledo, kept quiet, and would tremble if so much as a dirk or a poniard passed near. But in the end, when there were only two left, and the strong emanations of the other Immortals no longer hid my own scent, Hamish McLoud, who took it all far too seriously, began pursuing me all over the world, seeking to force me into combat.

"I killt yer brother Dmitri!" he yelled once, as I hid at the bottom of a disused mine-shaft, furious at the state my clothes were getting into, "you ha'e tae try tae avenge him! So then I can ha'e ye too!" Yes, it was true that McLoud killed Dimka in Madison Square Gardens in New York in 1986, but I didn't mind. He had been coarse and moronic, had never used a silk handkerchief in his life, and still spoke with the harsh accents of the Steppes. I had always been ashamed of having such an uncouth brute as a blood relative, and it was with a certain relief that I heard that McLoud had lopped off his pustulous head; I had even treated myself to a perfumed pedicure.

But it turned out that Dimka had been the only other Immortal left, so McLoud, who had been occupied the previous five centuries fighting all the others, now turned his full decollatory obsession on me. Keeping on the move to escape him and his equally psychotic sword, Brawnblade, I slept in more beds than Yassir Arafat himself, even in some without clean sheets. For twenty-five years, McLoud tried to shame me into coming out of hiding. An enormous flag appeared on top of the Taipei 101 building in Taiwan (the taller Burj Dubai Tower had been destroyed in 2010, of course, with the rest of the Middle East), telling the world that "Foplamov is yellow-livered and spineless"; once he somehow got access to the Queen's Christmas Message just before airing, and in her usual dead-parrot-like fashion she unblinkingly told her adoring and chomping subjects that "the British people must be brave in the face of terror, which is mare than Foplamov is even when faced wi' a wee sleekit cow'rin' tim'rous beastie o' a mouse" ("Too much bloody time in Balmoral!" muttered the chomping subjects in Berkshire); when the Russian flag was unfurled on Mars, to the surprise of the cosmonauts it warned the world, and any Russian-speaking Martians, that I was a smelly merkin on the retching pubis of the universe. It doesn't matter how stupid you are, if you have bank accounts accumulating interest for five hundred years, you have enough money to pay the right people to do almost anything.

Cowardice? It was a question of good taste and rationality, not cowardice. Fighting was the sort of thing that only lowlife creatures did. Why should I risk my delicate skin battling a brute who not only picked his nose and ate the snot in public, but did it in front of a mosque before sundown in Ramadhan! A mad misogynist who had founded and funded the John Knox Marriage Counselling Bureaus all over Scotland! A vulgar cretin who wore Marks & Sparks

Y-fronts under his kilt – *and* back-to-front! Moreover, I knew I could never beat him in fair combat. While he and the others had spent hundreds of years doing nothing but strain and train and brain each other, I had treated the gift of immortality with more gratitude and respect. I had set out to enjoy life, not risk it. Wine, women, and wassailing; painting, poetry, and philosophy; mathematics, metafiction, and mythology. But especially I appreciated the aesthetic mentality. I reread Huysmans' **Against Nature** every month, whilst reclining on silk sheets, with Nubian princesses fallen on hard times relaxing my limbs, dear Oscar's portrait looking down upon me, and caressing and languid music filling my ears. I had become the most cultured man in the world, while McLoud had remained a mere lout.

So for many years I ignored or avoided his puerile challenges, but with time it became impossible for me to do so. I ran out of safe houses. I began to suffer from travel-sickness. But, more important, I grew irritated. I found it aesthetically unpleasing to suffer such insults.

Late in 2012, I fished out my rusty, rotten, unused sword, Wormclinger.

My first impetuous idea was to silence McLoud forever in his sleep. After all, the fool never tried to hide his whereabouts. I knew he spent most of his time in St Andrews in Scotland, where he had long been addicted to golf.

But I soon realised that it wouldn't be that easy. He would certainly have his defences against surprise attacks. Being immortal doesn't stop you getting killed, it simply means you resurrect each time. But getting killed in the first place is just as painful for an Immortal as it is for anyone else. Despite his brutish skill, even McLoud had been killed a couple of times, but, unfortunately for me, by mortals unaware that they then needed to remove his head within thirty seconds before he returned to life; so *their* heads got removed instead. His whole place would be rigged with alarms, especially those set off by the proximity of cowardly sentient swords belonging to Immortals sneaking in through bedroom windows. I think he was aware that I was too cultured and superior to be slavishly bound by silly old-fashioned laws of chivalry.

No, I would have to lure him into a place of my own choosing, and also ensure that he would be unable to defend himself; the last thing I wanted was a fair fight! I set myself to study his movements, his ideas, his history.

And found his weakness: John Knox had been his childhood hero.

✝

January 2013. Allahabad, northern India. Fog and cold. The Maha Kumbh Mela, Great Pitcher Festival, had come round once again, as it did every twelve years. Here, on the *Sangam*, the confluence of three sacred rivers – the Ganges, the Yamuna, and the mythic Karaswati (yes, one would expect two real rivers plus one mythical one to equal two real rivers, but you try telling a Hindu that!) – a good eighty million people congregated for a few weeks to wash away their sins in *Ganga ma*, Mother Ganga. They believed that this was one of the places where Vishnu's trusty steed Garuda paused when being pursued by demons, and some of the nectar of the gods fell from the Pitcher to the ground. A good dip here, then, might not only bring them whatever they most wanted – money, children, a new sari, a date with a Bollywood superstar, social success – but, more important, free them from having to put up with any more lives. Prevent that dratted reincarnation. Save them from the cycle of death and rebirth. *He who drinks Ganga water that has been heated by the Sun's rays derives merit much greater than that which attaches to the vow of subsisting upon the wheat or grains of*

152

other corn picked up from cow dung. That's the **Mahabharata** itself, really putting cow dung-eating in its place!

As for me, I didn't care whether they got reincarnated or not, or what kind of life they might expect next time round. The important point was that here was the greatest collection of sin anywhere in the world! What interested me was where those sins went when they were washed away.

There could be only one logical answer: downriver.

I spent a couple of days there with the colourful pilgrims, joining them as they crossed on the pontoon bridges to the holy site, admiring the contrast between the dark blue waters of the deeper Yamuna and the grey sandy currents of the Ganges, pining for a decent t-bone steak, shivering a bit, but greatly enjoying the antics of the Naga sadhus. It tickled me that these completely demented characters, naked and covered in ashes, with filthy braided hair down to their bunions, chanting, mumbling, prancing, rocking, blowing conch shells, were respected as holy men, and I greatly admired the Hindus' highly eccentric sense of humour. Mecca and the Vatican would be much more fun places with a few Sadhus to liven things up. I saw one who proved his holiness by publicly wrapping his penis round a stick every day, and another who'd held his right hand up in the air for 20 years. Not hard to guess which hand he used for pleasuring himself! Unless he was as over-endowed in his groin as he was under-endowed in his head. Given the sheer size of the celestial pantheon, I suppose it was just about possible that one or two of the more feeble-minded gods might feel this was an intelligent and respectful way to approach the numinous, and behave benignly in return.

But finally I could put off the unpleasant task no longer. With fifty servants, all confirmed atheists, of course, to carry the equipment, I went a few miles downriver in the direction of Varanasi to a part where we would not be seen by too many people, and where those who did see us could be paid off to keep quiet. In any case, they would never suspect what we were up to.

We cast our nets.

Ganga ma indeed! A slattern, if ever there was one! When we finally hauled the massive nets in after three days (at the point I'd chosen the river was still over a mile wide), I almost despaired. With three or four million people going in the river every day (up to ten million on one of the 'auspicious' days), that was a whole lot of washed-off sins, even if each person had only sinned once, which was unlikely, as so many of the pilgrims were old. I had conservatively multiplied by fifty. But a sin itself is tiny, even to the believer, invisible to the naked eye, although its effects may be enormous. I had, however, underestimated the sheer quantity of extraneous matter. We had to filter out the ashes of dead people (and frequently more than their ashes), burnt charcoal from the cremations, soggy marigolds, chromium drifting down from the leather industries in Kanpur, coins, lost beads, sperm from Shilpa Shetty fanatics, pictures of gods, turbans, regurgitated curries; but the worst was the turds, bobbing turds, bloated turds, blighted and blighting turds. Nearly nine percent of the world's population live in the Indo-Gangetic Plain. That's a lot of turds. Not *all* of them end up in the rivers . . . After five days' stomach-churning labour, we had panned down to a few dozen containers of a thick fluid a bit like runny mucus supposedly painted red by a stubborn daltonic dwarf.

But even this was still not absolutely pure sin. It was contaminated with flecks of remorse, twinges of conscience, fleeting desires of reparation and expiation, wisps of prayer, and other impurities.

Removing that gunge got us down to less than half a pint. But it was half a pint of the most concentrated, heinous, foul and vile sin that had ever existed, the mere thought of which would have given the Devil himself an instant orgasm, if he had existed.

I was ready to face Hamish McLoud.

†

I had initially assumed that he lived in St Andrews in order to play golf every day. (He certainly wasn't there to be near the University!) But that wasn't the only, or perhaps even the main, reason. Hamish McLoud, thug, brute, obsessed decapitator, was a Believer! And a Believer in the worst form of the Christian God! Very early in his life he had come heavily under the influence of the Scottish reformer John Knox, with the paradoxical result that although he was Immortal, he believed in Hell, but wasn't sure whether he was one of the Elect or one of the Damned. Good works, according to Knox, would have no effect: either you were buggered or not buggered. Knox selfishly died before the terrified boy could find out from him which he was. But McLoud never forgot him. My investigations revealed to me that even now every Sunday without fail he would go to Holy Trinity Church in South Street: this had been the town's old kirk, and the reason it attracted him, it seemed, was because it was precisely from here that Knox, in between fulminating against the monstrous regiment of women, in 1559 had incited the congregation to ransack and raze the Cathedral.

It was from these few facts that I had hatched my plan.

Although I naturally didn't believe in the *theological* concept of sin, McLoud obviously did. Things that would make me smile would lay heavily on his conscience. My own 'sins' and those of others weighed as lightly for me as promises to repay borrowed money, as dutiful kisses blown in a hurricane, but those same sins for McLoud were real and measurable and palpable: a burden that if big enough might even send him to Hell. So my plan had been to scoop up and collect the greatest possible amount of sin, and where

155

better than at Allahabad, where tens of millions of people would obligingly leave their sins to float away unprotected in the Ganges? And not just the sins of one lifetime, but possibly those of previous incarnations as well. That is why I had had to work only with unbelievers; belief *in the effects* of those sins would have made their sheer mass and weight unmanageable. By the time I had finished, I had a distillation so potent, so dense, that even for me who didn't even believe in its existence it had physical weight! To McLoud that weight would be a million times greater.

I sent word to him, challenged him to mortal combat at midnight in the grounds of the old castle ruins at St. Andrews, a fitting site, I said, as his gushing blood would be added to that of so many other Scots who had been slain there; and by losing his repulsive head so near to home, his compatriots could admire it the following day spiked to the one remaining castle wall! That, I knew, was the kind of taunting language he would understand, and would be unable to ignore.

He gleefully accepted the challenge, of course.

Although my plan was perfect, I still found I was nervous as I approached the castle, just before the appointed time. At the last moment I hesitated. If my information about McLoud's beliefs were wrong, or my calculations, or if something prevented me from carrying out the plan . . . No, it was now or never! No longer would I put up with his jibes and public assassinations of my character! I repressed my fears, and using a rope ladder I had brought with me, hauled myself over the castle walls.

It was a blustery March night. A cold sea mist hung over the grounds, shrouding off the rest of the town, but still allowing occasional obscure glimpses of a low moon constantly shredded by scudding clouds. Below the promontory, the Atlantic thrashed in anticipation against the rocks as if it were a vast noisy audience of sea monsters trying to scramble up the cliff to see the blood spectacle. Their salty breath poured in over the seaward walls carrying the memories of ghost ships and drowned mariners and depths where no light had ever penetrated.

He was already there waiting. In full regalia, with the stridently exaggerated tartan of his clan. Brawnblade still sheathed, but the burnished dragon hilt alone somehow emanating so much menace that I felt Wormclinger trembling against my thigh. Full red beard, broad chest, proud stance. Right hand already gauntleted.

I checked my jacket pocket for the hundredth time.

"Ach, Vasily Foplamov, so we meet at last! I didnae think ye'd hae the courage. But there can be only yin. I am glad ye hae decided after all tae die like a true warrior! As yer brother did."

I forced what I hoped was a grim smile, and called up one of the clichés I had prepared to make him think I would follow the idiotic rules of these duels.

"My brother was too headstrong, and apt to lose his head in a crisis, but be assured I do not intend to lose mine. I have come to avenge him, and cleanse the family honour!"

McLoud obviously liked that, and almost beamed with satisfaction: this was the tone that all midnight mortal combats ought to have. I wondered how many times he had watched **Rob Roy** or **Braveheart.**

"Bold words," he declaimed, his booming voice making the mist cringe, "but are ye ready tae back them up wi' bold deeds?"

"That, you will soon see, Hamish McLoud," I riposted, with an epideictic curling of my lip and tilting of my chin, "but that will be the last you *will* see! My unforgiving blade Wormclinger, imbued with all the terrible magic of the celebrated insane dwarfs of Toledo, will then cloud your vision for ever!" (I thought I heard a small still voice near my thigh muttering, *Do we have to go through with this?)*

157

McLoud chuckled with delight. God, the man was a *durak!*

"Many a man hae sought tae cross blades wi' Hamish McLoud, and none hae lived tae tell the tale, because Brawnblade, once wielded by the Tricky Cross-eyed Samurai Oda Hideyoshi his self, drinks souls like sassenachs drink weak tea!" He waited expectantly.

I couldn't take any more of this. My cultivated sensibilities were squirming with embarrassment.

"Then," said I, "my strong right arm must avenge them too, as well as my brother. But," casually putting my left hand in my pocket, and drawing out a pewter flask, "fighting is thirsty work. First, allow me to wet my lips in anticipation of a glorious and thrilling combat." I began to unstopper the flask.

"Och aye, ye'd be seeking a wee dram o' courage, and I dinnae blame thee for tha'!"

I moved nearer to him, extending the now open flask towards him, as if in offering.

"Perchance you wish to imbibe your last drink ever?"

"Nay, a McLoud has no need o' . . . "

His voice was cut off as I suddenly hurled the contents of the flask at him. I had meant to throw them full in his face, but the rather narrow neck of the flask caused the liquid to fall short, most of it only landing on his chest, and even a few large splashes on me.

But the effect was immediate. It was as if he had been hit by a pile driver; he gasped and collapsed to the ground. He tried to rise, but it seemed a tremendous weight was holding him down. I moved to stand over him. *Bless you, John Knox!* McLoud stared up at me, agony and disbelief in his eyes.

"What . . . what hae ye done tae me?"

I poured the liquid that still remained in the flask over his legs. I heard the bones breaking with the weight.

"Sin, McLoud, sin. The sins of millions of people, all distilled and concentrated just for you. A weight no true believer could ever bear." I shook the remaining drops out of the flask. "And now I bid you goodbye. Let me give you a head start on your journey to Hell!"

I unsheathed and raised Wormclinger, ready to remove the head of the man who had tormented me for so long. The ancient runeblade began to descend . . .

. . . and stopped, screeching as if in mortal agony, bare inches from McLoud's neck. I felt a recoil force in my arms as if I had struck rock. I dropped the sword in pain. McLoud stirred, trying to rise, striving to reach for his own sword. I picked up Wormclinger again — I had the impression it was trying to wriggle away — once more prepared to strike — and once more some unseen force interposed between the blade and the neck.

McLoud, his face twisted by the weight of the sin pressing on him, forced a rictus that might have been an attempt at a smile.

"Ye fool," he gasped, "this is holy ground. Immortals cannae fight nae kill on holy ground."

His laugh was like a boulder being splashed by an underground waterfall.

"This isn't holy ground! This is a castle! The Cathedral's over there!"

McLoud laughed again, even as I heard more bones cracking.

"Bishops, archbishops lived here. Fer centuries. And martyr's blood . . . Reformation . . . Wishart burnt at stake here. Others. Forest. Hamilton. The ground remembers, och aye, the ground remembers. Relics of St. Andrew his self nearby . . . Not holy?"

What was happening? If the ground itself wasn't allowing Wormclinger to do its work, it meant that holy ground was indeed different from normal ground, had unnatural power. In which case...

Even before I had thought the unthinkable, I felt sharp pains

159

all over my body, as if tiny but potent hammer blows were raining down upon me. I gasped with the pain.

I tried to force away the sudden realisation. If I were stupid enough to even *begin* to believe in holy ground, then I would also have to believe in the same sin that was crushing McLoud *because of* his belief.

The rain of blows increased. Heavier, deeper. I was forced to my knees. It was the sin that had splashed on me when I had thrown the contents of the flask over my enemy. I had barely noticed it at the time, because then I didn't believe in sin . . . but as belief seeped into me like a deadly toxin, so the true weight of the sin on me increased.

At the same time I felt myself being dragged closer to the man writhing on the ground. Dragged by an invisible force. Oh God in Heaven! Not only was the weight of the sin beginning to crush me as it had crushed McLoud, but that same weight was increasing the gravitational force between myself and McLoud. And the more force it exerted, the more I had no choice but to believe in the unbearable weight of the distilled sin of millions of people from another continent, and the more I believed . . .

I felt the ground rise up around us as the laws of Newton and God combined, and my enemy and I, the last two Immortals, began our long inseparable journey to the centre of the earth.

KEEPING IT IN THE FAMILY
†

"I'm bored," said the lover, slouched on the sofa beside the mistress.

The husband turned round from the sink, where he was washing up. "Perhaps if you did a bit more round the house, you wouldn't have so much time to get bored."

"You could at least get a holoscreen," the lover grumbled, zapping morosely through the TV channels, most of which were showing the highlights of the day's Stonings in St. Peter's Square, though one had an old documentary on the Europa landing.

"If we can't afford a bloody cleaning robot, how do you think we could afford a holoscreen?" snapped the husband. "Perhaps if you went out and got a job . . . "

"I've *got* a job! Or have you forgotten how demanding your wife can be?"

On cue, the wife's voice came from the bathroom. "Sweethearts! There's no toilet paper! Someone help a damsel in distress!"

"Damsel!" muttered the lover without moving. The husband scowled at him, wiped his thin arms on a towel, and shuffled towards the bathroom, perfunctorily caressing his mistress' breasts on the way.

The lover and the mistress looked questioningly into each other's eyes.

The eight-year-old daughter, sitting between them, squealed delightedly. "Ooh, did you see that, the first stone got him right on the forehead! Wow! When can *I* do some stoning?"

"You're a little savage!" said the lover, tousling her hair affectionately.

The wife came out of the bathroom, adjusting her false teeth, and caressed the lover's penis.

"Mummy," said the daughter petulantly, "you're blocking the screen!"

"You shouldn't be watching TV all the time. What about your homework?"

"Ain't got no homework today, 'cause the Nuncio came, and they took Mr Jones away this morning."

"Poor dear Mr Jones," said the wife. "But he *would* take his politics into the classroom." She turned to her husband, who was sliding a hand along his mistress' thigh. "Darling, did you know he tried to tell the kids once that the Church has secret shares in Universal Biotech?"

"So?"

"And that's the real reason they pushed for the tough new Adultery Laws, so that they could then make a fortune on Family Indulgences?"

"Well, I suppose they had to get the money somewhere to pay for the garrison in Mecca," said the husband reasonably.

"Oh no," said the daughter brightly, "that's not why. They took him away because he was caught fucking that silly old cow Miss Appleby."

"Nicky! It's not polite to call Miss Appleby a cow! But how could the dear man be so careless? He knows the penalty for extra-familial sex. Poor misguided man!"

"He said what *you* do isn't natural," the daughter informed her maliciously.

"Oh, he did, did he?" The wife's attitude changed abruptly. "Right, I'll be there at his Stoning, and we'll see who's natural or not!" Upset, she let go of the lover's flaccid penis.

"Don't be silly, mummy, you're too old to throw stones.

Anyway, there'll be big queues as usual. Everyone wants to take part in a St. Peter's Stoning, and appear on TV."

"At least it'd give her something to do instead of grabbing my willy all the bloody time," muttered the lover, almost – but not quite – inaudibly.

"Sex-crazed old shrew!" added the mistress, even less inaudibly.

The wife turned and gave her a resounding slap on the face. "You ungrateful little bitch!" she screamed. "I gave you everything!"

"Mummy! You're blocking the screen again!"

The mistress leapt up angrily. "That's what parents always say!" she shouted. "Well, I didn't ask to be born, and I'm fed up with sleeping with your desiccated old husband!"

"Don't you dare talk to your mother like that!" stormed the husband.

"Dad, you keep out of this!" warned the lover.

"Are you telling me what to do, you little brat?" shouted the husband.

Furious, he grabbed a lamp from the table and swung it at the lover's head. The lover, however, nimbly moved aside, and broke the old man's neck with a rabbit punch.

"That's no way to treat your father!" screamed the wife, drizzling feeble blows upon him.

The mistress hesitated, came to a decision, sighed, said "Sorry, mum," and strangled the old lady.

The daughter clapped her hands delightedly. "Oh, this is so *exciting!*"

The young man put his arm gently round the young woman's shoulder. They gazed down sadly at the bodies.

"Makes you feel a bit . . . odd, doesn't it?" remarked the lover: "Seeing yourself lying there dead."

"Why is mummy's tongue sticking out like that?" asked the daughter. She prodded it with her foot.

"When you think about it," said the mistress, "they must have loved each other very much to go to such lengths to please each other."

The lover kissed her tenderly. "Too much. They spent everything on an Indulgence. 'Reinforce the Family Unit while allowing for Human Weakness', was the Papal advertising slogan. But no one allowed for *our* feelings, or people like us."

"Mr Jones said something like this would happen," the daughter said sagaciously. "He said the Oedipus-Electra complex would be even stronger in the case of people like you."

The mistress smiled at her. "You're not angry with us, Nicky?"

"Of course not. But, mummy?"

"Yes, dear?"

"Now that old mummy and daddy are dead," said the daughter, "can I use their bodies for my biology experiments?"

The mistress glanced at the lover, who nodded. "Of course you can, darling. But take them to school, like the other children do. And now come and have your supper like a good little girl."

THE ROSARY

†

The stranger arrived one evening when the rain was lashing down like the whips we used on Obedience Days. He walked into the inn, acknowledged us with tired unsmiling eyes, and drew off his heavy cloak slowly and deliberately, as if each movement caused him pain. Underneath, he was wearing a simple white robe. Round his neck hung a huge chain of shrivelled, ugly, shapeless beads, black and broken and heavy as the thoughts of a man facing execution. They swung slightly from side to side, emitting a cold fuligin power, as he walked to a table in the corner.

Peter the innkeeper asked him if the beads were the ninety-nine names of Allah. The man considered the question for some time, and then nodded, as if to himself. They were, he said, the hearts of women he had met in our country.

We muttered to each other that the stranger was a liar and a braggart: could any one man have won the hearts of so many women? But something about his eyes stopped us from mocking him openly. That night we took it in turns to keep watch outside the inn, and guarded our daughters and our wives and our slave girls, and kept our hands near our knives. But the stranger remained in his room, and also throughout the whole of the next day, which was bleak and glinting and expectant after the rain. Often, when we looked up, we saw him staring out through the window, away towards the ocean which marked the boundaries of our world. It seemed as if he was waiting.

That evening, Yazgül , whose name means summer rose – a flower most of us had plucked, and not only in summer, for she was simple in the head, and her father Moshe was old and infirm – headed towards the inn, her body hunched against the cold and her

165

own madness. Peter was going to refuse her entrance, but the
stranger came down and said something, and the innkeeper nodded
reluctantly and returned to his meaningless centuries-old rituals. We
were angry, and went to Moshe and told him what we had seen, and
offered to drag his daughter out and stone her for him, but he didn't
seem to understand, just picked up one of her old torn abayas,
holding it against his cheek, and weeping.

She did not leave the inn till the morning, tossing her now
uncovered hair in brazen challenge, defying us with eyes that were
no longer downcast and broken, but seemed to read and mock the
longings of our loins, and walking upright as if she were free as a
man.

Honour could not allow this. That afternoon, we dragged her
from her father's house and into the public square, tore her sari from
her insolent body and spread-eagled her so that the whole village
should see her shame, and beat her and spat upon her.

When we let her go, she stumbled, not back to her house, but
to the inn. We followed. She ran upstairs. We waited, daring the
stranger to come down, to interfere, to publicly claim his hundredth
conquest. But the coward did not emerge, so we drank and laughed –
Peter as usual pretending that nothing had happened, and busying
himself with his incenses and his catechisms – and then drew our
knives and went up and burst into the stranger's room.

Yazgül was sitting on the edge of the bed, bare to the waist,
her hands clenched between her breasts, while he was lying on his
back, unmoving, his robe torn open, behind her. She rose and
stepped aside, strangely calm and unhurried, as we rushed forward,
eager to finish our sport . . . but our knives fell uselessly as we saw
only emptiness in his chest where his heart should have been. I
stared at that empty space – cold, pure, infinitely desolate – and
then at the rosary still round his neck, to which had been added one

final bead – a lump that still dripped with blood. In that moment I visualised the final excruciation, as he had gouged out from his own body that last piece and exchanged it for Yazgül's crushed heart.

The heart with which he had finally completed his rosary.

And then, as we stared, frightened and uncomprehending, Yazgül pushed past us and snatched the rosary from the stranger's body. She shook it, and the beads scattered to the ground. She turned to face us – but those eyes were no longer her eyes, nor was it her voice that now spoke.

"He's gone. He had nothing more to sacrifice, you left him nothing to shield you with any more. Now it is our turn."

I knew that it was over, that the final bead had completed the shape of the Forbidden Name, a name, I now realised too late, that we had always known, and always worshipped, in our own heartless way.

Summer Rose began to create her own deadly rosary.

THE CRUCIFIXION CONSPIRACY

†

So here we all are at Nazca (well, all except poor Bertie, of course) and it's bloody freezing up here. But the view's great, if you don't suffer from vertigo; and at least you don't need to worry about rain.

They brought us here to die, cut off from the outside world, so that we can never reveal what we learned.

I should be able to finish my spider in a few days: though I'm pretty sure my fellow Travellers will give first prize to that damn humming bird . . .

†

"So you think you're the first? Haven't you ever asked yourselves," said Jesus, "just why there was no room at the inn?"

He was in the courtyard of the Roman fort and, far from being shackled, was wandering around among the soldiers.

We hadn't. "Filled with paparazzi trying to get an exclusive on the Three Kings?" Bertie suggested. "Brits chasing the winter sun?"

If this strikes you as a not wholly appropriate manner to address the Son of God, bear in mind we'd just had our Time Machine confiscated the moment we materialised, and not only that, but when they'd seen it, the Time Police drafted in for the event had laughed their helmeted heads off, treating the greatest invention of the twenty-first century as a prehistoric relic!

"Dr Flintstone, I presume!" one of them had quipped.

Sassy little bastards! OK, so they had foldaway models they could slip into their shirt pockets, but where would they have been without our prototype? "You're just pygmies standing on the shoulders of giants!" I yelled (Jesus frowned), but they didn't understand: ah well, culture was already well on the way out when we left: *Hello Magazine* had become required tertiary education reading.

Jesus, bearing an uncanny resemblance to Engelbrecht the Surrealist Sportsman immortalised by Richardson and Hughes, almost came up to my armpit. You can see why we were initially a bit doubtful about his claims. I personally believe that his small stature may well explain the mystery of Why the Stone was Moved (I now know *Who* Moved it, of course) but we'll get back to that. Or forward. One result of my journey is that I tend to remember things backwards too, but I'm doing my best.

Jesus didn't seem to notice Bertie's tone, anyway. "Time Travellers, that's why! Hundreds of 'em! Supposed to have come to honour *me*, and then hog all the accommodation, leaving me and the Womb in a stinking manger!"

Referring to one's mother as 'the Womb' struck me as a bit odd, but then I didn't have much experience with gods. I guess he must have picked up this way of thinking from the Holy Ghost; some wasps, so I've read, have a similar habit of laying eggs in other creatures; no one says how wonderful *that* is, or starts a cult to the Virgin Caterpillar!

You think you got a big audience for your birth? I thought to myself. *Just wait and see the full house when you snuff it!* OK, as it happened, that's exactly what he was doing, but I wasn't to know that then.

I must admit that I felt no more friendly towards the other Travellers than he did. Trillions of research dollars, decades of the most intense and painful training, presidents and kings turning out to wave goodbye to Bertie and myself, the world's first Time Travellers – and when we get here, the place is already packed with them! All from our own future, of course. The ungrateful bastards could at least have stopped off en route and said thank you!

Crucifixions were the in-thing in those days. Six thousand followers of Spartacus had been crucified along the Appian way seventy years before as proof of Roman enlightenment. So being crucified was nothing to write home about, even if your hands had been free to do so. Rising from the dead, though, was, even then, considered a pretty nifty thing to do. So Chronocorp had sent us back (despite my most energetic protests: I'd wanted to go to the court of Cleopatra) to see if Jesus really did pull off that little trick.

I asked the other Travellers why they'd all bothered to come here: hadn't they seen the documentary we intended to produce? What documentary, they asked? And why did you never come back?

That's the sort of question you pretend you haven't heard.

At that moment, a Roman soldier passed by, and for no reason at all, gave Jesus an almighty shove. Incensed, Bertie sprang forward, and knocked him to the ground. I expected him be beaten to death by the other soldiers lounging by, and stepped out of the way just in case, but they just laughed, and one of them even offered him a cigarette.

A cigarette?

"You're coming on well," said Jesus, as he got up and dusted off some dried sheep dung and nodded approvingly at the man who'd just pushed him, "but you forgot to sneer and spit in my face." He turned to us. "A few have got into the spirit of the thing, as you see, but some of them are such poor actors, it'll look more like a medieval miracle play than a crucifixion! And there still aren't anywhere near enough soldiers. I don't suppose you'd mind slipping on skirts and helmets, and looking pitiless and aquiline for a bit?"

"You mean, these soldiers aren't real? I mean, real soldiers?"

"Good Lord no, all the original soldiers got murdered by a Christian fundamentalist Traveller who came into the past to Save

170

me. Before I could explain that I didn't want Saving, she'd zapped the lot with some sort of Death Ray. Typical female emotional overreaction! Nearly ruined everything. The Time Police frisk the lot the second they arrive now, of course."

As we knew to our embarrassment. When we'd stepped out of our Machine in the early Friday dawn, two black-suited figures (why do these types never wear pink or turquoise?) had stopped us.

"Spoilsport or Pervert?" they asked.

"I don't understand," I said with as much dignity as is possible when one is being lifted, turned upside down, shaken, and frisked. They confiscated my pork scratchings.

"Most people who Travel here either want to stop the Crucifixion – without much success, as you must already know – or else indulge in a bit of the old *schadenfreude*."

The frisking suddenly became extremely – one could say *too* – thorough. "What's this?" one of them sniffed suspiciously. "Why's it hidden there?"

"It wasn't hidden," I said, squirming, "it's for my haemorrhoids."

I thrust away the bowel-wrenching memory. Jesus went on:

"Trouble is, though we hushed things up as much as we could, word got round that I spelt trouble, and even the locals are keeping low-key now. Haven't seen a Scribe or Pharisee for days! Pilate's also been giving me a bit of a headache, tried to resign twice yesterday. Worried about his reputation. I've had to promise him a place on God's right hand side in Heaven (luckily, he never thought to ask me just *how far* from his right hand side!). Why, even the unclean spirits have made themselves scarce!"

I was beginning to think that this chap wanted to get himself crucified.

"I'm beginning to think you want to get yourself crucified," I said. I usually liked to say what I thought, though I frequently had to make an exception with Bertie's father, of course. After all, he was the President of Chronocorp.

"I have to do *something*. Father's obviously never going to shuffle off his immortal coil. Still fit as a bloody fiddle. A million press-ups – at his age! – and he doesn't even break sweat! I'm heir to a throne I can never inherit. Unless I seize it by force."

This I could understand. The same thing had recently happened in England, when Prince Charles, soon after his hundredth birthday, had finally lost patience and, after confiscating all her dogs and hats, had the Queen locked up in the Tower. Her presence there greatly increased the revenues from tourism.

However, I couldn't see how being crucified would help Jesus, unless he intended to take the nails with him and hammer them through God's unsuspecting head.

"My crucifixion will be a great PR job. Future ages will worship me, not Father."

I'm a real softie, and I didn't want him crucifying himself for nothing, so I pointed out that God, in fact, *was* still worshipped – in my time at least – despite nagging doubts as to why he'd had to use the Holy Ghost instead of pleasuring Mary himself.

Jesus smiled. "Ah, but that's just the first couple of millennia. Later, people will finally realise that sending me down to be crucified to save the world, instead of having the guts to do it himself, was morally reprehensible. Only slightly less savage than Saturn eating his children, really. Hardly paternal. There'll be a hate campaign on something called the Internet. By the third millennium, so the Time Police have told me, Christians will worship me alone, with Father seen as a servant of the Devil."

I was a bit suspicious about what the Teepees might have told Jesus about the future state of Christianity. They must have realised that, just in order for them to exist, the Crucifixion, and everything that followed from the spread of Christianity, had to go ahead. In such a situation, they would not hesitate to tell little white lies to make sure the Crucifixion did go ahead. Indeed, I was later to find out that their pressure went beyond this. As for what they had done to the woman who had killed the original Roman soldiers, I dreaded to think.

And look what the bastards did to us!

"But how will this help you get the throne?" I asked.

"When the angels find out that Father has let me die, without lifting a blessed Finger to save me, I'm pretty sure they'll back me in a coup."

"Will you win?"

"I'm a god, not a fortune-teller! But whatever happens, I'll be treated with a bit more respect, that's for sure!"

At this point he was felled by another ersatz Roman soldier hoping to make a good impression on him. This one remembered to sneer and spit. Wiping the spittle from his face, Jesus thanked him, and said with a rather cocky expression:

"Oh, by the way, I intend to rise from the dead, and wander around a bit before Ascending. Might take a stroll to Emmaus, always wanted to go there. Don't you think that's a rather super idea?"

I forbore to answer. I was pretty sure the Time Police had given him that idea, too.

(Judas later told us that Jesus was already dying from some horrible disease, picked up from all that laying on of hands and raising dead bodies without washing the divine digits after, and so he was simply trying to make the best of a bad job: better to go out with the glory of a Crucifixion than an ignoble wasting away. Maybe so. But Judas didn't strike me as a particularly honest fellow. Come on, thirty pieces of silver just for pointing out the shortest chap in Jerusalem! Daylight robbery! But I'm getting ahead of myself again.)

I still wonder which came first in this ridiculous loop. Jesus had decided to get himself crucified because the Teepees (and other Time Travellers, no doubt) had told him that in the future he would be worshipped because of this act. But presumably they (like me) only got the story from the Gospels because it had already happened. But it only happened because Jesus had been told it was going to happen. Unless, of course, the Gospel writers had made the whole thing up, which meant that Jesus was about to do something which had never happened in the first place. In which case, he would be altering history, after all. But then the Teepees wouldn't have allowed that to happen. But then they themselves would be the product of an alternate history.

I scratched my head and dragged Bertie off to the nearest tavern. Nothing but bloody unleavened bread: I'd forgotten it was still the Passover period. Luckily, in these relatively primitive times, Bertie's rather pungent body odour wasn't particularly noticeable.

I knew Jesus wasn't due to be crucified until the third hour, which for some reason I never understood actually meant nine in the morning, so we struck up a conversation with another Traveller from the twenty-second century who was also being roped in as a substitute Roman, and who had arrived a few weeks before us. An ornithologist, apparently, who'd spent his whole life studying humming birds. He revealed that the gospel writers had indeed been a bit creative with the truth. The five loaves and two fishes, for example: in actual fact, that's what had been *left* after the Sermon, since the listeners, knowing that Jesus was prone to going on a bit, had wisely brought their own picnic baskets. It also transpired that the unclean spirits who drowned with the Gadarene swine were really a largish group of smallish Ayon pygmies, Travellers from

Papua New Guinea, who had roused Jesus' ire by a spirited defence of animism and an equally gutsy apologia for cannibalism. He chased them through the streets. A moneylender, smarting from an earlier outburst of the prophetic wrath, told them how Ulysses had escaped the Cyclops Polythemus by clinging to the underside of the giant's sheep, and persuaded the Papuan pygmies to do the same with the crazed pigs. No one, however, had mentioned the cliffs. It also seemed that Lazarus, although he *had* been raised from the dead, had tottered around in circles for a few seconds, said "Christ, I feel like death warmed up!" and then keeled over again, as dead as a Monty Python parrot. Elisha had done a much better job.

Now, of course, all this isn't to say that Jesus wasn't really the Son of God, simply that things weren't as cut and dried as some would have us believe.

Anyway, we agreed to go along with his plans, and got our Roman uniforms. Bertie looked rather sweet; his legs were surprisingly shapely. There were about a hundred of us in on the act. The other Travellers knew nothing – their function was to return to their own times, and confirm the historical reality of the Crucifixion. I must admit we felt a bit superior with our nice uniforms and our little secret. If only we'd known!

Well, I guess you all know the story, so I won't repeat it, just clear up a couple of errors. Judas, for example. We'd grown kind of fond of Jeez, eccentric or not, so we strung Judas up, made it look like a suicide, and used the pieces of silver to pay for snacks during the Crucifixion. That was the technicality the Teepees used against us. (Yes, I know all about that story in Acts that, 'falling headlong, he burst asunder in the midst and all his bowels gushed out', but that was just a bit of exaggeration by St Peter, hoping to distract historians from the three cock crows.)

The thunder and earthquake, of course, was just future

technology, as was the Star of Bethlehem, which I was told normally crowned the Dome of the future World Stock Exchange.

But I do want to tell you about Bertie. I owe it to him. I know I may sometimes have spoken of him with a certain asperity, but when it really mattered, he came up trumps. British pluck at its best.

It will also help to clear up some apparent contradictions in the Gospels.

First, though, I have to refute those who accuse Jesus of being a cry-baby for shouting out on the Cross, "My God, my God, why hast thou forsaken me?". Let me tell you that he displayed amazing fortitude throughout the whole proceedings, and that when he uttered those words, he winked at Bertie and whispered, *"That'll turn 'em against him!"* He was a credit to all people of unostentatious stature.

Ah, you say, and how come Bertie was so close, how come no one else saw the wink? Yes, well, those contradictions I mentioned . . .

St Luke says that one of the thieves crucified with Jesus believed in him, saying, 'Lord, remember me when thou comest into thy kingdom.' And that Jesus answered: 'Today shalt thou be with me in Paradise'. Very heart-warming, and the kind of uplifting conversation that ought to grace all worthwhile crucifixions. But both Mark and Matthew tell us 'they that were crucified with him reviled him.' Not nearly so nice: quite downdropping, in fact.

What, of course, you can't know is that one of the thieves, cottoning on to the fact that the Roman soldiers weren't soldiers at all, and feeling insulted at the prospect of being crucified by blackleg civilians, did a bunk half an hour before the Crucifixion was scheduled! No sense of history, of occasion.

"I've got to have two thieves!" yelled Jesus, who by this time was, not unnaturally, showing signs of tension. "Symmetry!"

Symmetry my foot! It was those Teepees putting pressure on him again.

Well, they stepped in, made us draw lots, and poor Bertie drew the short straw. I'd like to think that this was an entirely aleatory event. And yet Bertie had certain . . . qualities which almost made his choice inevitable, his body odour being the chief of them.

I could, I suppose, have tried to summon the Spatial Mobility Module to get us out of there fast, but I realized that if I succeeded (unlikely, with the Teepees guarding the Time Machine), I would in fact be changing the past. Jesus had died with thieves on either side of him. The Travelling zapper had created a hole in the past, and it was Bertie's destiny to fill it in.

Bertie himself seemed a bit dubious about the honour.

"Fuckit, fuckit, fuckit!" said he.

For a moment, I thought he was conjugating a long-forgotten Latin verb, but then realized it was a heart-felt, if rather selfish, complaint against his destiny.

But Jesus whispered, "Don't worry, I'll see you're all right!"

After that, I didn't feel so bad, and indeed was rather hurt by the mute reproach in Bertie's eye.

We bade tearful goodbyes, and up went Bertie with a martyred expression.

"Lord, remember me when thou comest into thy kingdom," he said, remembering to keep to their funny way of speaking, and Jesus swore he would, just as Luke records, and that they'd share a bottle or two that very night in Paradise. But then he realized they could be heard, and he whispered to Bertie, "You'd better start reviling me, quick, or they'll get suspicious", so Bertie dutifully weighed in with some really vile insults, to which the other thief added gratuitous refrains.

But I noticed one Jew, who gave me the impression of being a doctor, scratching his head in surprise. He must have overheard the earlier part of the conversation. I guess the other gospel writers dismissed his astonishing testimony, but St Luke chose to believe a fellow physician, and included a (doctored) version in his Gospel.

Jesus got a bit more than he bargained for, poor chap. He was all hyped up to take his Crucifixion like a Man, and even used his knowledge of carpentry to coolly criticize the shoddy construction of his cross and the poor quality of the nails, but he hadn't counted on the three crosses being so near to each other. That, I'm sure, is why he, supposedly a god – or, at this stage, a demi-god – died before the other two, who were mere mortals. Poor Bertie is . . . olfactorily assertive, and divine nostrils are known to be delicate.

It also explained why the group of mourning women were keeping their distance and 'beholding afar off', as the Gospels so tactfully put it. I asked someone which one was Mary Magdalene, wondering whether she'd be up for a quick drink afterwards.

Still, despite Bertie, Jesus managed to hang on for six hours up there, including three hours in almost complete darkness (something arranged by the Teepees for effect) and it wasn't till the middle of the afternoon that he finally died.

The Teepees were ready, and the veil of the temple was rent in twain, the earth did quake, and the ersatz soldiers went off to their Chronocamp outside the town for a celebratory drink and, as they believed, to receive their Crucifixion Medals, before returning to their own epochs. My humming bird enthusiast invited me to join them. I gratefully accepted the offer, and had started to follow him when he said:

"I meant . . . well, of course you'll want to stay with your friend until . . . well, you know. We'll keep some drink back for you."

"Thank you," I said, my thirsty leg caught embarrassingly

mid-air, "of course I couldn't possibly leave him while . . . see you later."

To pass the time – why did Bertie have to do everything so slowly! – I secretly filmed Jesus being taken from the cross. Mary Magdalene had now approached. Was this a sign of interest in me? I do have a rather imposing figure, a noticeable air of rugged nobility, I can't deny it.

"Hssstt!" said Bertie.

"What?" I whispered.

"Jesus is dead now, isn't he? Can't you get me down now? This is bloody painful!"

I thought rather resentfully that it hadn't been that comfortable for me either, six hours on my feet like that! But before I could do anything, Mary Magdalene stopped her silent weeping, looked across at me, and hissed:

"Oh no you don't! You two have caused enough trouble. We're not having any more hitches. Shove off!"

Mary Magdalene was a Teepee!

I mouthed "Sorry, old chap" to Bertie, and went off to think about things. Cross or no Cross, you don't cross Teepees if you can help it!

After pondering deeply, I decided I would, after all, join the other 'soldiers'.

Even if we could Travel back to our own time now, it would leave our job half done. We had to be here for the Moving of the Stone. After all, Jesus' dying on the Cross was no proof that he was really a god. A lot of quite ordinary people tended to die on crosses. The local Jews, in fact, perversely took it as an obvious proof that Jesus wasn't a god. The real test would be whether he would Rise in three days or not.

Though the Teepees had assured him that this would indeed

be the case, even Jesus himself wasn't a hundred per cent sure that he could manage that nifty little number. Towards the end, it had finally clicked as to why the Teepees were so desperate to help him. "If my body doesn't Rise from the dead, history will be changed, and you lot will be well and verily buggered," he said bluntly, "so you'd better make sure that if I don't manage it by myself, my body isn't there when they move the Stone."

I don't wish to sound unchristian, but perhaps Jesus was so insistent on this point because he didn't want future ages to find his bones, and learn how short he really was. People have certain minimum requirements of their gods. Religious discrimination of the lowest sort, but there you are.

Occupied with these thoughts, I didn't become aware of the unusual silence in the Chronocamp until I arrived there. The trestle tables were overturned, and plastic mugs and empty crisp packets were scattered around. But the camp was deserted.

Almost.

A lone Teepee was awaiting me.

"Ah, there you are," he said.

Funny how a far-future weapon looks so similar to our own. Though the one now pointing at me was probably capable of sprinkling bits of me in the asteroid belt.

I tried to hide my trembling.

"Why are you pointing that thing at me?" I blustered.

"Because it makes people tremble and bluster, and that's one of the perks that make up for my low salary and this ridiculously tight and cod-sinister-looking uniform."

"Oh."

"Besides which, we can't leave witnesses."

My mind did a triple take.

Jesus had said that some well-intentioned Time Traveller had

180

massacred a lot of the original Roman soldiers. So the Teepees had 'bussed' in a hundred new 'soldiers' so that Jesus could go ahead with his highly eccentric plan to seize Ultimate Power. They hadn't been expecting Bertie and myself, but a couple more soldiers made no difference.

But a hundred people who knew that had really happened *couldn't be allowed to return to their own time to reveal that knowledge*. Because then Christianity, at least in its traditional form, would be recognized as a put-up job, and that too would inevitably alter history.

"You can't kill me!" I said. "We're the world's first Time Travellers. Our Machine is the prototype. If it gets stuck here, they may never build another one, and then you won't exist."

"Excellent point. We fully intend to return your *Time Machine* to where it belongs – just without you and Bertie."

Trembling and blustering hadn't achieved much. Stronger measures were called for. I threw myself at his feet, and blubbered piteously.

"Oh, stop blubbering piteously! We're not going to kill you, anyway. Perhaps I phrased it badly. In fact, we *are* going to leave the witnesses – here, in the past, in order not to have them anytime else. Well, not exactly *here*, of course, but somewhere else, where they'll never be found. Come on, the others are waiting for you."

†

So here we are in Peru, watching sunsets over Nazca. Those Teepees are making damn sure we don't return to our own times to reveal what really happened in Jerusalem. No doubt they'll destroy everything we build, any messages we try to leave. But who knows, even they can make mistakes . . .

Their landing strips stretch into the distance, a constant reminder of their treachery.

Last night Jesus appeared in a vision and said, "Thanks a million, you lot. It did the trick." Behind him, an enormous caged and fettered figure with a *very* loud voice – I'd say a voice of thunder if I didn't think you'd accuse me of exaggerating – was threatening all kinds of things, from plagues and boils to floods and meteor impacts.

Well, that answers one question, at least. Jesus will be able to keep that promise he made to Bertie on the cross.

After the spider, I think I'll try a monkey. There's nothing to do here except draw.

BAIT

†

It is still hardly light when I become aware of his presence. I do not need to see him or to hear him to know that he has found us. We are in Madrid, hiding in a tiny pensión, because Rosana insisted on being close to her mother and her child. I hadn't argued. It would have made no difference if we'd run to New York or Tokyo, to Easter Island or the Arabian Empty Quarter. I think I'd known that, but we had to try.

Rosana is still sleeping. Her midnight-black hair, sparse and tufted just a few days ago, now spreads lustrous over the pillow, and even in the pale light of dawn her cheeks still have that impossible healthy glow.

I force myself on to the balcony overlooking the small plaza, and stare down at him, at the Emissary, waiting there five storeys below. He looks up, and even from that distance I believe I can see the early daylight being sucked into his eyes. I plead silently, give me more time with her, just a little more time.

And the answer comes that I have a bargain to fulfil, and payment has already been made. Or do I wish to return the gift? It can be done.

I step back inside, and fear crawls in with me, coating my tongue, sliding down my throat, and coiling round my lungs with every jagged breath.

But there is relief, too. Relief that I can stop running because now there is nowhere to run to. Relief that there are no more choices to be made. Relief, above all, that the gift has not been taken away.

Ave María!

But the devil giveth and the devil taketh away. I have seen Rosana's illness lifted from her, peeling off as quickly and cleanly as a lizard's skin. I have seen love in her eyes once again, in her voice, in her touch. The loss will now be all the greater.

Is this why I was allowed to escape? To improve the flavour?

I gaze down at her, and marvel that she can sleep on with the weight of so much love crushing her, but I dare not kiss her goodbye in case she should awake and destroy my resolve with a single tear, with a clutching hand. She wouldn't believe me, anyway: the icons and rosary lying on the bedside table are proof of that.

A few minutes later I step out into the street. First stop on the way back to Hell.

✝

The year 2015 was the Year of the Miracle, when the Virgin Mary returned to Earth in truly lactifluous mood.

For a time, in the early Middle Ages, if religion was the opium of the masses, the Virgin's Milk was their Coca Cola. Phials containing her milk were venerated in shrines from Walsingham to Chartres, from Padua to Naples. Almost every village in Europe managed to churn out a bit. So much so that Calvin, ever a merry fellow, commented: "There is no town so small, so mean, that it does not display some of the Virgin's milk. There is so much that if the holy Virgin had been a cow, or a wet nurse all her life, she would have been hard put to it to yield such a great quantity." But the milk began to dry up when it became not quite respectable for the Lady in Blue to reveal her breasts. The faithful soon had to make do with weeping or bleeding virgins, not lactating ones.

The centuries might have passed, but the Lady kept to her tried and tested formula. She appeared – still radiantly beautiful, of course, despite her great age – to the two daughters of a sheep farmer in the middle of the Patagonian desert in Argentina, and told them – a touch of vanity? – to build a shrine to her. Their father complied and, not long after, a small stone statue of the Virgin produced milk, which – lo and behold! – cured him of cancer. Word got around, and within a very short time there were enough "cures" to interest the Church officially.

So it was decided to milk pilgrims as well as the Virgin. Despite the logistics of the operation – the nearest settlements of any size were hundreds of kilometres away – a church was built around the Shrine, and a makeshift dormitory city grew up on the arid plain to house pilgrims. While Our Ladies of Guadalupe and Lourdes and Fatima and all the rest looked on enviously, *Nuestra Señora de la Leche* attracted half a million visitors in the first few months alone.

More sheep, I thought, to be fleeced along with the four-legged kind who had long ruled the vast *estancias,* yet another example of superstition and its sinister old camp-follower, the exploitation of despair. I was convinced the whole thing was simply a mass hallucination, and laughed at the absurd stories about the magic Milk.

Rosana, despite her own early Catholic upbringing in Spain, tried to laugh with me. We needed to laugh. Things weren't good between us. Not just because of the baby, which I'd thought I could love simply because it was hers. I tried, I really tried. Thank God she believed those bruises had come from an accidental fall. But she still wanted me to 'lighten up', I was too 'intense', why didn't I have friends, interests, a life apart from her? Why wouldn't I see a doctor about those nightmares? How long was I going to use the accidental killing of the Moroccan boy as an excuse for self-pity?

I knew that the pressure of my need was driving her away, that my obsessive love was a burden too great for her. Once she yelled, "Give me some air, I can't take it any more, go find yourself someone else to worship!"

Ah Rosana, my love, I did that all right!

So we grew apart, and she looked at the baby to keep from

looking at me, and accepted my furious diatribes against this new superstition with a tight smile.

Until she was diagnosed with leukaemia. Nothing like a rampaging mob of leucocytes to lead you to religion. I watched Rosana, my lovely sparkling Rosana, lose her glow, like a fish yanked out of water. I scraped her hairs out of the sink with fingers rigid with fury and helplessness, saw how the toothbrush remained dry because her gums were too inflamed to use it, watched her wither and decay before me.

The Catholic lies of her infancy roiled to the surface. She began to speak of making the pilgrimage to Argentina. I resisted, of course I resisted. But the drugs weren't working, not even the new genetic therapies, and we both knew they weren't going to work; and it was proving impossible to find a suitable donor for a bone marrow transplant.

So we went. Better a false hope than no hope at all.

†

Patagonia. The Argentines' very own Siberia. "A backdrop for a dinosaur skeleton in a museum', as a travel writer once put it. But the bones of that skeleton would soon have been scattered by the brutal unceasing winds that thrashed and flattened any vegetation hardy enough to grow. A vast flat emptiness with just a few sheep, and the occasional guanaco and rhea.

And a brand new Virgin.

The Shrine was in Santa María, just north of Paso de Indios, half way between Trelew on the Atlantic coast and Esquel at the foot of the Andes. We flew south from Buenos Aires to Trelew, but then, because the airport at Santa María was still under construction, had to travel three hundred kilometres along the old road that crossed the arid plains. We had exchanged an English summer for an Argentine winter, and the dismal fleets of pilgrim-bearing buses, after leaving the relative lushness of the Chubut Valley, passed through utter emptinesss, only relieved by the occasional luxury of scrubby grassland, and phantasmal sheep obscured by wind-whipped clouds of dust.

Santa María was a depressing sprawl of hastily constructed hotels and *pensiones.* We booked in at one of these, and were given a cold, almost bare room, with tawdry pictures of gauchos and Madonnas competing with each other on the dank walls. Even Rosana's rekindled faith could not resist such cheap commercialisation. She collapsed on the bed without a word. I left her to rest, had a soggy *empanada* in the hotel bar, tried my first *mate amargo*, and stepped out into the freezing wind of late evening.

The Emissary was waiting.

I thought afterwards, of course, it was *Rosana*'s need which drew him to us, the smell of *her* fear and helplessness.

When the despair is too great, we all fall into the same ritualistic patterns. I found I was stupidly repeating to myself the ages-old pathetic mantra: *why her, why not me, why her, for Christ's sake, why can't it be me!*

"Nothing is that straightforward," said a harsh voice beside me, a voice gutted with pain and bleakness, "though it is true that if you take something away – even suffering – you have to put it somewhere else." Afterwards I realised it should have been impossible to hear him through the constant roar of the wind.

I was only aware of lips so thin they seemed to have been eaten away by the cold. And the eyes – I glanced into them, then had to look away again immediately, because it was as if I'd glimpsed utter desolation, the bareness of death itself.

"You think you are too intelligent to believe in those stories about the Virgin's Statue producing Milk," he said, "but in a way the Milk did – and still does – exist, and your Rosana really can be cured."

I stared at his mouth and his chin and his neck – anything but his eyes – as he went on:

"But there is a price. Think of the Milk as a pearl, and remember how a pearl is created from the suffering of the oyster. Like this . . . "

The insistent clamour of disjointed, desperate minds, a screeching inside my head as if countless stridulating insects are boring into me, the stench of illness and decay gagging me, choking me, and a terrible knowledge that I must go on and on . . .

The world reappeared, a child shouting, a buzzard winging overhead, but the echoes of that agony hurtled round my skull.

"This is what it costs my Mistress to be here, to bear the pleas of thousands upon thousands of diseased minds, all beseeching, imploring, grasping, all thrusting their pain upon her . . . Are you willing to serve her for a time, to ease her burden, to share some of that pain? That is the price for curing Rosana."

This was all unreal, impossible, but I *knew* he was telling the truth. And yet he terrified me.

Marlowe's Faustus conjured up Helen of Troy in *his* pact with the devil: a woman whose beauty 'burnt the topless towers of Ilium'. I pictured Rosana slumped on the edge of the bed that morning, menstrual blood trickling unnoticed down the inside of her thighs. I remembered the veins in her hands as she held her head, with her hair, once so rich and wild, straggling over them like the splayed feathers of a sparrow's corpse. I recalled her breasts and calves starting to cave in like deflating balloons, her skin the dead colour of used condoms.

What the fuck did Faustus know about love?

"I accept," I said, "give me the Milk".

"You think I'm some kind of quack, with little phials of elixir

188

in my pocket? Your Rosana has to pass the Shrine, like everyone else. But my Mistress will honour this agreement."

And then he just walked away and disappeared in the sudden darkness.

†

The Statue was unimpressive, only unusual in that it was of Mary suckling Jesus, rather than just holding him, although something hovered just beyond the reach of my memory when I saw it. A silver chalice placed optimistically between its feet to catch the miraculous Milk remained stubbornly dry. Steel bars kept us from getting too close: apparently, in the early days, the *really* credulous had tried to squeeze Milk out of the stone breast.

I was just convincing myself that I must have been taken in by some madman with hypnotic powers when I felt Rosana's hand clutch mine with a force that almost hurt, while for a few seconds her whole body went rigid. Then she relaxed and looked up at me with an expression of incredulous joy before sinking to her knees before the Statue, mumbling incoherently in her native Spanish.

†

Difficult to believe that first contact was less than three weeks ago. Now I'm back from Madrid, back in the bunker, back in my old Sharing Room again. Everything as I left it. Even my notebook, thrust carelessly under the mattress.

I glance through the pages, revisiting my lost innocence, remembering what led me to flee. Trying not to think about what comes next . . .

†

August 15

Rosana's just left, to get back to the baby being looked after

189

by her mother.

It's only been three days, and yet already she's almost back to her old self. It's as if she's exhaling huge chunks of her disease with each breath, the leukaemia just an old scab which, picked off, exposes glistening new flesh lying underneath. And the warmth has returned to her eyes, each smile helping to loosen the clamps around my heart.

We lay curled up together most of this morning, listening to the wind shaking the shutters, obliterating both our laughter and our tears.

She could hardly take it in when I said I wanted to stay for a time, to try to help some of the other pilgrims here. But she accepted it, pleased that I've 'found something to believe in at last'. She knows nothing about my pact with the Emissary. I was going to tell her, but something prevented me. No, that's wrong. The *Emissary* prevented me.

But that's just fine with me. I'm not just simply *prepared* to keep my part of the bargain, I'm *looking forward* to it, looking forward to the pain. I *want* to repay. To atone. To earn the right to go back to my Rosana.

August 18

It's been worse than I ever imagined it would be, and yet . . .

The first day the Emissary took me to the cellar of an insignificant-looking building behind the church, and then through dank badly-lit passages sloping downwards to a kind of underground barracks that vaguely reminded me of the wartime bunkers on the Channel Islands. At the far end of the barracks were the 'Sharing Rooms', little more than cubicles each containing a bunk bed. The Emissary strapped me down on one of them – to prevent me harming myself, he said – and I did my first *sharing*.

They needed the straps.

The Shrine attracts minds turned in upon themselves, bitter, rancid, despairing. Our Lady, despite her power to cure, seems to have no defences, no way to control the psychic babble. Her cup is full. Overflowing. She needs to siphon off the excess, offload some of the agony. I caught snatches of hundreds of languages, and I seemed to know that she was only siphoning off the tiniest fraction of what was assailing her. Those minds were so voracious, destructive, the universe twisted up into the searing ball of their needs. Their sickness poured in like burning lava, settled and festered, oozing into my darkest places.

If you take something away, even suffering, you have to put it somewhere else, the Emissary had said.

But where do *I* put it?

Three days, alternately 'sharing' and recovering from the pounding! My mind is so battered, so bruised! But the Emissary tells me that I've made his mistress' burden that much lighter, and that tomorrow I can rest.

August 19

They've dropped the fiction of the Madonna!

Now that I've passed the test, I have the right to know the truth. The truth is both terrifying and wonderful, yet not without a touch of the absurd.

The 'Virgin' is really some unknown creature living deep beneath the church!

None of the 'Sharers' have ever seen it. But they're all willing to worship it.

John Ransome is the only one I've really talked to. The others don't speak English. He used to be a priest. His health is poor, his clothes and body unwashed, but he glistens with fanatical conviction.

"I don't know what this . . . *thing* is, any more than you do. The Emissary says it's alien. Maybe it's just a great unthinking osmotic bladder – physical pain in, psychic pain out." A cough knifes its way through him. "I think I always knew deep down that Holy Writ was a human construct, but I trusted there was some truth behind the myth. But no. No God, no Son, no Sacrifice, no Salvation. Then suddenly . . . *this*!" His words are coated with phlegm. "For the first time ever, real miracles! A real hope! *This thing cures*! So I don't care what it is. Could be the King of Hades for all I care! Or one of those underground monsters the Ona Indians believed in down in Tierra del Fuego. But it *does* something, it's the first god we've ever had which gets down to business without requiring praise, or worship, or rituals. It *acts*!"

"Oh yes, it acts all right, and our minds are torn apart to enable it to do so!"

"Would you prefer your old loving Christian God who looks on benignly as one soldier forces another to hack off his friend's testicles, and then stuff them down his throat with his own shit for garnish, and if we find this rather odd, it's simply because we're too fucking thick to understand God's wondrous ways!"

He knows I'm an atheist. Or was until a week ago. I think he's only lashing out at me because he's been pushed to the limits of his endurance. He's been here for two weeks.

August 21

. . . so many questions. *If* it's alien, did it *choose* to come here? Was it sent? If so, by whom?

Ransome is convinced that there really was Milk at the

192

beginning, that it was an offering, a gesture of peace. But after the initial cures, the greed of those who then came drove the creature underground, scrabbling to escape the psychic violation.

He believes it could have saved itself by ceasing to heal. But finding itself assailed by the terrible sickness of the collective human mind, it decided to cleanse that sickness, but found the task was too great for it, and thus sought out other minds – the Sharers – to share the burden.

Wouldn't that be an even greater miracle than a Virgin Mary? An *alien* suffering voluntarily to aid human beings?

August 22

I think I've had direct contact with the creature's mind! This morning, in a temporary respite from the constant psychic battering, I caught glimpses of a vast ochre plain, covered with soaring geometric structures, and three moons in the sky. Its home world?

. . . but why ask for a shrine to the Virgin Mary? Why the Milk? Why choose such an outmoded way of presenting a gift of healing?

Could it be that it already had memories of a Virgin Mother? In which case . . .

August 25

Ten days now. I don't know how long I can go on. But I dare to hope that when this is over, when I'm released, I will at last have earned the right to look into Rosana's eyes without shame.

But my mind! I feel as though it's being wrenched from the moorings of reality, cast off to bob helplessly on an ocean of pain, or be sucked under by boiling currents.

Or like a kite straining to snap away, and the string is so frayed . . .

August 26

I asked Ransome about the Emissary, whom I've seen only a few times since the first day. He says that 'ours' isn't the only one, that there are perhaps a dozen, ex-Sharers who've chosen to stay on to help the creature communicate. For this, they've been given a limited telepathic ability.

But I sensed nervousness in him when he spoke – perhaps the same fear that I feel in the Emissary's presence.

But one small mystery at least may have been solved. I mentioned that I'd seemed almost to recognise the Virgin's statue in the Shrine, and he told me the two girls who first saw the 'Virgin' came from a family of Italian immigrants. Their grandparents had brought a few prized possessions with them, including a reproduction of Rogier van der Weyden's *St Luke Painting the Virgin*, a Madonna and Child scene in which Mary is seen suckling the baby Jesus. The girls had grown up with this painting, seeing it every day: Mary, the Giver of Milk, formed part of their deepest memories.

Was this what had led the alien to make its unusual peace offering?

August 28

This morning Ransome went crazy.

He began running round the bunker screaming, "It's not possible, it's not possible!" Then, seeing me, he shouted, "Craig, it's bait, it was bait all the time!"

The Emissary appeared at once, and Ransome cowered like a dog that knows it's done wrong.

"You have earned your freedom," the Emissary said, staring at him, "and your reward. My mistress will heal you."

Ransome stumbled, whimpering, out of the room with him, but he held a hand out to me imploringly, the fingers twitching.

What does he mean, '*bait*'?

August 29

He's recovered amazingly well. He's standing tall, exuding power. The cough has gone. I think he meant to go without telling me, since it was only by chance I spotted him about to leave the bunker. When I asked him about what he said yesterday, he said he couldn't remember, it had just been a moment of madness. He promised to phone me from Buenos Aires.

For just a moment, as I looked into his eyes, I was reminded of the Emissary.

But at least it shows that there will be a limit to how long I have to stay here myself. Ransome came only a couple of weeks before me.

August 30

Oh God, now I know what he meant!

Far from being weakened by the presence of all the pilgrims, the alien is being strengthened. It is deliberately luring them here.

Patagonia, one of the most arid places on earth, thousands of square kilometres with almost no people.

And therefore, for a being of its nature, almost no sustenance.

But it had probed the only minds within reach — two little

girls searching for a missing sheep – and there found the cult and image of the Virgin Mary.

And the pilgrims flocked in their thousands to Santa María. All with a desperate need, all weakened already because they put their faith, not in themselves, but in an enslaving fiction, all leaving a gaping hole for it to enter.

Such a feast!

And they would return home, to every country in the world, and if dementia set in, if they died just that little bit early, nothing unusual would be noticed. No need to drain each cup, just a thousand, a hundred thousand, sips, like the bee buzzing ceaselessly from flower to flower. Always new victims. Always new delicacies.

Does each fear, each dread, each crippled hope, have its own flavour?

And every now and then, to ensure the supply would never end, the occasional cure.

The Milk was never anything other than an illusion, even before the building of the Shrine; an image from a still potent religion implanted to attract the victims.

How do I know all this?

Because it has 'told' me itself, simply placed the knowledge in my mind.

Why?

August 31

Why were we really chosen, the Sharers?

Ransome mentioned once, refusing to look at me, that a child in his congregation had tried to commit suicide after being sexually molested. He never said directly who had done the molesting. I also know that the quiet Negro who always smiles politely was deeply involved in one of his country's worst massacres.

The creature needs minds already toughened from earlier scarring, like the karate fighter's hand, where the bones have been deliberately broken and allowed to reset. It need minds cauterised by guilt, so that unconsciously they will recognise, and *accept*, the underlying justice of it all.

I meant to kill the Arab kid. I can admit it to myself now. There we were, the shiny new European Arm of a reformed NATO, struggling to atone for Yugoslavia, and the bloodletting in the Aegean a couple of decades later, by stopping the Moroccans from massacring the Saharaui people in what had been the Spanish Sahara. But the Moroccans didn't see it that way, to them we were outsiders, intruders, the enemy, and they started their own little *intifada*, and after you've had a certain number of close shaves, insults, stones, with the sun beating down so that you feel like a giant's anvil, something gives. I told myself the kid was armed, that I was only defending myself . . .

Oh, but it felt good! To be able to retaliate for just a few seconds, to smash down another creature! Like a mosquito that has kept you awake all night, and finally the rolled-up newspaper does the trick, and you look at the red stain on it, and feel a vicious elation.

Like Rosana's baby. The father had died in an accident, but had left behind something I could never give her. I couldn't have Rosana without having another man's . . . *droppings*. But I couldn't live without her, either.

The alien must have detected me before I even stepped off the coach.

We have fallen for two of the oldest tricks in the book: the insidious idea that suffering is a good in itself, that it is noble, that it can somehow atone for cruelty and injustice; and the human yearning for divine intervention in the world, the chance to start again, to undo that which has been done.

Redemption. The innate belief that there *is* salvation, you simply need to know how to attain it. I, like so many others, had always been a believer, simply waiting for something to believe in.

What had Rosana said? Go find yourself someone else to worship.

But why was I warned beforehand of the suffering that would follow her cure?

Because a vampire can't cross the threshold unless you invite it in? And I had invited it in because of my own guilt. But also because of my love for Rosana . . .

But does that really explain why the creature wants *us*, the Sharers, here?

September 1

I think I may have an answer.

In China, they eat dogs. Why not? We eat pigs. But there's dog and there's dog. So in the best places they stuff Rover in a sack, and beat him with iron bars for fifteen minutes or so before finishing him off. Because the pain and fear of the dog sends adrenaline into the mashed-up body, giving it that extra piquant flavour to delight the palate of that creature 'made in the image of God'.

We, the Sharers, are the Sunday lunch, the strong spiced meat. The creature can only sip at the pilgrims, it can't afford to frighten them away. It can only glance off their minds, brush against them. But with us . . . we have given it *carte blanche* to invade us, to masticate our every dream, to savour our guilt, to gulp down our pain.

Do I hear an echo of laughter as I think these thoughts?

And why has it revealed so much to me?

I fear I'm finally losing control, like Ransome, as if the kite has finally broken free, and is being buffeted by the wind that is always howling outside on the surface.

September 2

I have a chance to escape!

Two of the Emissaries were involved in a heated argument, and they left *without locking the door!* I don't really think I can get away. Isn't it too obvious? But such things do happen, mistakes *are* sometimes made. Even if I can spend only a little time with Rosana . . .

†

*Pathetic last words on a pathetic scrap of paper! I see now that my 'escape' was the final spice, the delicious taste of torture by hope. I sense that my death is very near. But I **was** able to spend that time with my Rosana before the Emissary came for me, to feel her love again, and to feel I had **earned** that love. This hasn't all been in vain. She's cured, that's the important thing. With that knowledge I really do believe I am now strong enough to face whatever is coming. Because of me, she's cured.*

†

The alien intelligence that lay trapped and dying beneath the Shrine prepared to give birth again.

The pilgrims had given her sustenance, but not mobility.

So difficult to find suitable minds, so difficult to delicately unravel the billions of neurons without damaging them, to loosen them to the point where one sudden overwhelming shock would be enough to snap them entirely from their host's control without destroying the memories and conceptions necessary to understand and move about the planet. The unit that called itself Ransome had almost been lost.

The Craig Unit had been more carefully primed. Tonight, the new Emissary Ransome would make it believe that the human called Rosana had been destroyed, make it believe that its attempt to escape was responsible for that death; and in that moment of utter despair, shock, and dislocation, every already weakened link to its humanity could be finally snapped, and all the freed neurons brought under her own absolute control, ready to Receive.

The stranded alien took no joy at all in the pain of other species.

But her children had to live somewhere.

NASTASSJA'S HONOUR
A Cautionary Tale
†

Ronnie Hughes had never heard of the goddess Diana and the hunter Actaeon, who was turned into a stag, and torn apart by his own hounds, as punishment for having seen her naked. If he *had* known the story, however, he would have been interested only in the part where the goddess came to 'lave her virgin limbs in the sparkling water of the fountain', as Thomas Bulfinch delicately put it.

Ronnie's goddess was Nastassja Kinski. Especially when she was naked.

Luckily for him, she was just that in most of her early films. His own favourite was *Cat People*. The actress plays Irena, a woman who turns into a panther when sexually aroused, and who can only revert to human form by slaying someone. Her brother has equally disconcerting habits. Ronnie had once, long ago, seen the whole film, but since then had only watched certain parts of it. Those parts, however, he had watched twenty or thirty times. With well-trained fingers on the 'pause', 'slow', and 'rewind' buttons of the remote control.

Yes, gentle reader, our obviously doomed hero was of that sad lost generation of British men forever corrupted in puberty by the final issues of *Health & Efficiency*.

Now, lights low, whiskey and tissues to hand, he was watching those scenes once again.

He had started the video, as usual, on video tape counter 61 – he knew the blissful numbers by heart – the scene where Irena stalks naked through the forest at night, and hunts down a rabbit. The screen seemed to fizzle for a moment, and then he noticed a bit of fluff on the back of his left hand. Must have brought it in on the sleeve of his coat, he thought.

He didn't waste time wondering about it, but, obeying the penile imperative, fast forwarded to minute 92, where Irena loses her virginity to Oliver Yates, the zoo keeper, played by John Heard. That was odd! He didn't remember that! She had just lifted up her white sweater, and at this point, Ronnie was sure, Oliver follows her into the bedroom. But this time, he turned round first, stared straight out of the screen, and mouthed something: something that looked suspiciously like "bugger off!"

Despite its owner's considerable surprise, Ronnie's peremptory and spoiled penis would brook no delay. It instructed Ronnie to keep on watching. After coition, Irena's panther senses are awakened, and she instinctively lashes out at a fly buzzing in the room, easily striking and killing it. This time, Ronnie distinctly saw something land on the dirty coffee table beside him. A dead fly, although it didn't look very real. What an amazing coincidence!

This was not the moment to ponder coincidences, however. These two scenes had as usual brought him to the point of orgasm, and now all he needed was to watch the third, his favourite, minute 103, when the naked Irena lies spread-eagled on the bed, while her hands and feet are slowly (deliciously slowly!) tied to the bed frame by an Oliver who doesn't want to be killed when she turns into a panther again. The culminating moment of this scene is filmed from behind Oliver, so that his body conceals hers as he lowers himself on to her. Ronnie always imagined himself as the lover. He had sometimes wondered how many other thousands of middle-aged men had the same fantasy. As many as sweatily clutched their remote controls for Kim Basinger on the steps in the rain in *9½ Weeks*? Well, the big-tit fanatics were entitled to their preferences . . .

Once again, the actor seemed to turn round and stare out of

the screen with a look of fury. Ronnie nearly lost his erection, but this was his favourite moment. As usual, he imagined himself pressing down on the girl, felt her moist warmth enveloping him . . .

When a hole suddenly appeared in the television screen, and two tiny naked men tumbled out.

Ronnie tried to hide his annoyance. As the men got to their feet – in the process, their height increased to about a metre – he calmed his breathing, wiped his penis, flicked the tissue towards the waste paper bin, missed, zipped up his trousers, and then politely asked the men – who he now saw were both identical to the lover in the film, except that one penis was more erect than the other – if they had any particular reason for stepping out of his TV.

Geotropic Penis was foaming with rage.

"You and your dirty bloody mind!" he snarled. "Watching those scenes hundreds of times. I could always feel your eyes just behind mine, feel you watching Nastassja through me, trying to press down on her through *my* body even after the director had called 'cut'".

Church Steeple Penis said nothing, just stood there panting and twitching.

"I don't know why you're so upset," said Ronnie, addressing Geotropic, "after all, the film crew were watching you as well."

"They didn't have their hands on their peckers!"

"Are you sure?"

"And they weren't inside my mind, urging me on – 'go on go on, deeper deeper!' – so I couldn't concentrate on my acting at all. "Get that bloody thing out of me!" Nastassja hissed. She's not prudish, as you know, but there are limits . . . "

At this point, he seemed to notice his twin. "And what the fuck do you think *you're* doing here?"

Church Steeple looked up. His eyes were glazed. He shook his head. His whole body seemed to be wavering slightly, except his erection.

"You think I *want* to be here? Just when I was finally making it with my sweetheart? But since, unfortunately, I can't exist without you, here I bloody well am!"

Diurnal masturbation doesn't make you blind, and neither does it too obviously damage the intellect. Ronnie had no difficulty deducing that Geotropic was John Heard, the actor who had played the lover, Oliver Yates, and Church Steeple was Oliver Yates himself.

Their height, it seemed, was a compromise between the two realities.

"Well, this is all very interesting," he said, "but I have things to do, so I'll say goodbye to you . . . and I'd appreciate it if you'd take that bit of rabbit fur and that dead fly with you when you go."

"And just how do you expect us to leave?"

"The way you came, perhaps?"

"We don't *know* how we came! Except it had something to do with your disgusting mind!"

"That's the second time you've made personal comments about my mind. Might I remind you that *you're* the one, or ones, who spend all their time indulging in zoophilia!"

"I *am* a zoo keeper," said Church Steeple. His erection was at last beginning to come to earth.

"So since it's because of you we're here," continued Geotropic, "would you kindly send us back where we came from?"

"I don't know how to."

"What?"

"I don't know how to send you back. And if you don't know how to put yourselves back . . . "

They stared at each other.

The cassette tape came to an end, clicked, and began to rewind.

Realising that it was no good quarrelling, Ronnie gave his visitors some blankets to throw round themselves, and offered them some whiskey.

✝

Half an hour later, however, they were all slightly drunk and still quarrelling. The twins were each sitting on an arm of the only other available armchair. At first they had been distinguishable only by the colour of their blankets and the sadness in Oliver's eyes, but now John Heard already looked much older than when he had arrived.

"What I still don't get," said Ronnie, "is why the force of my desires brought you two into existence, and not Nastassja."

"Irena," corrected Oliver for the hundredth time.

"You didn't bring *me* into existence," John growled. "I happen to exist already – in, I might add, somewhat more luxurious surroundings than you have here. Pink wallpaper, I ask you, with dandelions! *He's* the one" (pointing to Oliver) "who doesn't exist."

"Without me," Oliver muttered, "you wouldn't even have had a job! And you certainly wouldn't have got anywhere near the gorgeous Irena."

Ronnie said: "I tear a hole in Reality itself to reach Nastassja, and what bloody well happens? You two slip through! And anyway, I only rent this place, I didn't choose the wallpaper."

"It's obvious to any cretin," said Oliver, " that the force of the love that Irena has for me – and I for her – is what burst the fabric of reality, and not your pitiful little fantasies. Our passion was too great for a mere TV screen."

"Don't kid yourself," said John. "Nastassja was only acting."

"I'm not talking about Nastassja, I'm talking about Irena!

205

Anyway," he added, "the two of you are pathetic! One of you wanks over twelve-inch-high images, and the other can't even get an erection. *I'm* the only real man out of us three!"

"*You!*" sneered John. "You don't even exist. I'm the one who brought you to life! And how long do you think I'd have kept my job if I'd allowed myself to get an erection? The director was Nastassja's bloody *boyfriend*, for God's sake!"

"Wanking," said a highly aggrieved Ronnie, "is, I'll have you know, a respectable worldwide activity. Why, in some countries it's even a mathematical science. In Turkey, for example, it's called '*kirk numara*', which means 'forty times', which is, apparently, the optimum number of strokes to reach orgasm. In ancient Greece . . . "

"Oh shut up!" said the twins.

And he did. Because he wanted to think. In the three main nude scenes, only minor characters had come into his sitting room: to wit, a bit of rabbit, a dead fly, and two Olivers. He supposed that the rabbit and the fly had done their own stunts, which would explain why only one of each had arrived.

But why these? Perhaps because he'd been intent on Nastassja alone, hardly aware of anything or anyone else. So, in *that* reality, the reality of the film, to all intents and purposes only the actress existed. So the arrival of the others in his room was clearly a subconscious plea to be accepted, to be considered real.

Which implied that flies were not as nonchalant and independent as they pretended.

So what if he did the reverse? Watched the nude scenes again, but gave all his attention to the rabbit, the fly, and the lover? Pretended the actress wasn't there? This wouldn't be easy. But if he could do it, if he could deny Nastassja reality *within the film*, she might arrive in his room as the two men had . . .

Maybe only three feet tall, but he'd always liked small

women. And this would be concentrated Nastassja Kinski!

But at this point, Oliver leapt to his feet and stared horrified into his twin's eyes.

"Oh my God! If I'm here now, and you are, too . . . who's covering my darling's . . . my darling's . . . ?"

Ronnie realised what he meant. Like a child who thinks he hears Father Christmas coming down the chimney, he grabbed the remote control, started the video again, and fast forwarded it to the final erotic scene.

Nastassja Kinski's knots slowly and surrealistically tied themselves, and then the camera panned round to show, not John Heard's broad spoilsport back, but . . .

Ronnie's hand automatically headed for his zip, but Oliver spotted his intention, and shouting, "That's my sweetheart's pussy you're gawking at, you bastard!" he tried to block Ronnie's view. Ronnie pushed him to one side easily. It was odd, but he didn't seem as *solid* as before.

"Wow!" said John, "even I never actually got to *see* that because I was on top of her."

"What about when you tied her feet?" snarled Oliver, twisting under Ronnie's restraining hand. "You were at the foot of the bed looking right up at her."

"*You* were the only one with sex on their mind! With the director yelling at me, and all those other people, do you think I had time to pussygaze?"

The scene came to an end. Ronnie guessed what had happened. The actor couldn't be in two places at once, and as he was now in this sitting room, then he was no longer in the film. Clever camera shots to allow Nastassja a vestige of privacy were in vain.

Then he had another thought: was it just *this* video, or had the same thing happened on all the tapes?

It was easy to find out. He rang up his old school friend, trapped in the same time warp as himself. There were minor differences – Charlie vacillated between Jenny Agutter in *Walkabout* and Susan George in *Straw Dogs* – but he knew that they shared the same glorious cultural heritage. Their friendship went right back to Jane Fonda's floating striptease in *Barbarella,* and their schooldays when they had been nicknamed Smegma One and Smegma Two.

"Watch *Cat People*, tied-up scene," he said, "but keep the phone off the hook!"

"But Mary'll be back in a minute . . . "

"Do it! Now!"

Charlie must have caught the urgency in his voice, for he heard the sound of a cassette being ejected (a give-away whirr that had brought about Charlie's first divorce), another one being slotted in, an indrawn breath, an astonished and delighted "WOW!", the sound of a zipper, and a sound peculiarly reminiscent of blankets being shaken out of a tenement window. Then came a woman's voice, and the phone went dead.

It was enough. So *all* copies of the film had changed.

Which meant that now *anybody* could see the luxuriant paradise previously hidden by the actor's broad back.

"God damn it!" he cried, "it's *my* fantasy, and now every connoisseur in the country can get in for free!"

"Arrgghh!" cried Oliver, "it's *my* girlfriend, and now every dirty swine in the country can see her cloistered jewel!"

Judging from Charlie's reaction, the film had only changed in the last few minutes. The change hadn't been retrospective, so at least he hadn't created a time paradox by taking John Heard out of the film. Of course, he wasn't an expert on time paradoxes. Perhaps they took some time to kick in, like marital erections, or the realisation that people don't find your jokes funny. In any case, the mortality statistics for heart attacks suffered by the world's grey army of armchair wankers would soon greatly increase.

Before guilt could set in, he saw that the changes he had earlier noticed in his guests were speeding up.

John Heard had visibly aged. Two teeth had already fallen out. Well, that made a kind of sense: maybe this version was catching up with his real self.

Oliver wasn't *ageing* so much as *disappearing*, buckling at the edges. That, too, made sense. He was a fiction, and a fiction is ageless. But a fiction also has to be believed in. The presence of the actor made this difficult. Ronnie thought he now understood the friction between the two.

"I feel a bit weak," Oliver groaned, collapsing back on the chair. For the first time, Ronnie found his jealousy tempered by sympathy.

"There, you see!" croaked John. "That's because you aren't real, like I told you. *I'm* all right here because I'm real, and all I've done is move around in the same reality." Clearly, he was unaware of the wrinkles that were starting to huddle together on his face like sheep in a storm.

"You have to help me!"

"After what you said about my manhood! Why should I?"

Oliver gave a crooked smile. "Because if I get ill, you won't have a role, and you'll never get near that divine creature that you insist on calling Nastassja Kinski."

That did the trick. John swung round on Ronnie.

"We have to get back in the video, or at least Oliver does! Or do you want to be responsible for his sickness? Perhaps even for his death? You got us out, now get us back in again!"

Ronnie felt despondent. So much for his half-formed plan to

bring Nastassja out! Presumably the same thing would happen to Nastassja and Irena as was happening to John and Oliver. Moreover, Nastassja's status as goddess depended on her living on her celluloid Olympus. Why, if she came down, she might even insist on getting dressed! Or burp, or scratch her ears.

Still, he told himself, things had definitely improved. With the film as it now was, he was guaranteed satisfactory orgasms until arthritis set in or he was caught stealing in Saudi Arabia.

"Perhaps," John was saying, "if we all concentrate our thoughts together – a kind of *gestalt* – we can summon up the strength to reverse the flow, to make *this* reality seep into *our* reality."

"Yes. With Ronnie's help, we should be able to reopen the crack."

They clearly hadn't understood how important his hobby was to him.

"Surely you don't expect *me* to help you!"

They looked at him in surprise.

"Sorry, boys. But, come on, if you go back in the film, you'll cover up Nastassja again."

"But our *lives* may be in danger!" Another wrinkle crawled wearily into place.

"Not really. Oliver doesn't really exist, anyway, and never did exist, and *you* just need to spend some time with the Avon lady. Anyway, get to see a good doctor, and you could both have a fine career ahead as identical dwarves. Or as hobbits in the prequel to *Lord of the Rings*."

"I can't believe this! *You* dragged us out into this disgusting room."

"Why did Nastassja keep taking her clothes off? Because the director told her to. Why did he tell her to? So that cognoscenti like me could enter a state of bliss seeing her naked. I was simply doing what was expected of me. If you want to blame anyone, blame Schrader!"

"Are you saying you're risking our very lives just because you want to see Nastassja's pussy all the time?"

Ronnie considered the question carefully. Put like that, he had to admit . . .

"Yes!" he said.

"That's my Irena you're talking about!" said Oliver weakly. "Only *I* get to see those parts."

"Sorry, lads, you've had your fun for twenty years. My turn."

Ronnie was a little surprised at his own firmness. But they had accused him of having a dirty mind, their comments about the dandelion wallpaper had hurt him deeply (he'd lied: he had in fact chosen the paper himself), and if they returned to the video, it would be like having a free ticket to Heaven whisked away again. Also, they were only three feet tall, which made him feel braver.

Yet, deep down, he knew that he would probably relent, given time. He wasn't a bad wanker, just a sad one.

He wasn't given time.

There was a *slurping* sound, the sound a Sumo wrestler makes when he lifts himself off the toilet seat in a particularly humid summer, and another hole appeared in the television screen. More a funnel than a hole. At the rim of this funnel stood a figure cloaked in black – the director Paul Schrader? The Censor? – who threw a rope which instantaneously increased in size and landed next to Ronnie's two guests.

Diurnal masturbation *does* damage the sixth sense. Ronnie was taken completely by surprise when Oliver seized the rope, fed the end of it to John Heard, and then each of them grabbed one of Ronnie's legs.

"Now!" shouted Oliver.

The rope tightened and was jerked towards the funnel. Ronnie just had time to see the face of the person who had thrown the rope – no, it couldn't be, she wouldn't! – before, as is traditional, indeed almost sacrosanct, in these cases, everything went black.

✝

Most people who watched *Cat People* after this didn't notice any difference from the first time they'd seen it, although they were a bit surprised at how bad John Heard's acting was in one part. There is a minor character called Yeatman Brewer who is killed by Irena in panther form as she returns to her house, before the 'tied-up' scene where she makes love to Oliver a second and final time. Oliver discovers his mangled body hanging from a tree. And this time he smiles! It is only a fleeting smile, to be replaced immediately by a look of appropriate shock. But, somehow, the smile seems more real than the shock.

One person, however, noticed something more. The night before, Charlie had only had time to watch a few seconds before he had almost been caught out by his wife. Now, with this poor substitute for the real thing safely at Bingo, Charlie was looking forward to a real treat. In his excitement, he wound back a few seconds too far – and immediately recognised the face of the man who had acted the part of Yeatman Brewer. The man whose body was dangling from the tree. With dandelions in his mouth. A body torn to pieces like that of a deer by hounds.

Charlie was a sentimental fellow, with a strong sense of what was right and proper. He stopped the tape, put it under the floorboards for another day, when emotion could be recollected in tranquillity, then, a tear in his eye, honoured the memory of his friend the best way he knew how. He took out *Barbarella*.

212

SACRIFICE

†

John Caine watched the two nurses help Cathy Stevens shuffle to a seat in the shade of the old cherry tree. In her condition, she would be dead within a month.

In the normal course of events.

Michael Stevens turned to him. In his expression there was grief but also fanatic determination.

"Do it," he said, "get the girl to come to England. I'll arrange the rest. And do it *soon*."

Shouldn't you be donning a black cap for this, you bastard? But Caine knew he was pushing the guilt away from himself. Until this moment, he had almost believed that in the end there would be some other way. But there wasn't, not now, not since that last unexpected, almost fatal, heart attack.

He looked bitterly at the woman in the garden.

"You've had your life," he thought. "Alice . . ."

But Stevens was calling in his IOU.

†

He knew he wasn't really needed, not any longer. It simply made it easier to lure her to England if he invited her. Well, he thought, Judas hadn't really been necessary, either.

And if Judas had warned Jesus instead of betraying him, would it really have made any difference?

He lay on the bed, whisky bottle beside him, eyes closed, imagining the scene unfolding before him.

She'd have to be brain dead, of course. Easiest would be a traffic accident. A simple phone call to Spain: something odd about the last test results, he'd say, just needed to check a few things. And his part would be done. He'd never have to look at her face. Never

213

have to say, like Webster's Cardinal: "Cover her face, mine eyes dazzle: she died young."

She'd be met at the airport. Probably by a man and a woman: a couple always seemed less suspicious. Somewhere – but not too far away, six hours was still the maximum time lapse possible, the 'cold ischaemic time', in the dehumanizing jargon of the profession – they'd turn off the new eight-lane superway. A single blow to the front of the head, to simulate hitting the windscreen? Or would they stage a 'real' accident, a hit-and-run incident, perhaps? Whatever. The girl would be found dead, or as good as dead, with her donor card on her. Stevens would hire the best. There'd be no mistakes.

Then the call would go to the private hospital. "Dr. Williams? I think we have something for you . . . "

James Williams. Pontius Pilate? As outstanding in his field as Caine had been in his. Both in Stevens' pay: one to give life, one to take it away.

His mind drifted . . .

†

The Spencers lived in a luxury villa high up on the hills overlooking the sea in Almoraira in the Spanish province of Alicante. They had gardens, a full-size swimming pool, servants. Not bad for people who had been unemployed when they had been approached that day.

Alice, the daughter, was now eighteen, blonde, tanned, bilingual, studying medicine – *his* influence – at the ancient University of Salamanca. Pocket money had never been scarce. She had already travelled to a dozen different countries. Yes, apart from some unusual genetic defect that necessitated frequent check-ups in Caine's Fertility Clinic in England, she had a good life.

A scene from an old film often haunted his dreams. *Blade Runner.* The android Roy Batty learns that he has been programmed to die after four years. His creator tells him, "The light that's burning twice as bright burns half as long – and you have burned so very, very brightly, Roy!" And the android, aware of the betrayal in the very moment of his creation, destroys his creator.

That was just fiction.

But Alice Spencer, too, had burned so very very brightly . . .

Unlike his son Mark. Vivacious, sharp, warm, sensitive. Crippled. At the age of two, it was certain that he would never be able to walk on his own two legs. Indeed, would probably not even survive into his teens. That was when his father sold his soul to Michael Stevens.

He didn't sell it cheap. Over the years, he couldn't calculate how many thousands of pounds he'd been given to allow his son the benefit of every advance in the field. Mark's legs were little more than bones, but he *could* walk, hesitatingly, laboriously, but nonetheless triumphantly. Because Stevens always kept his word. For good or ill.

Indeed, it had seemed a bargain. Even then, at the turn of the century, artificial bladders for beagles had already been grown using tissue taken from normal dog bladders. Pluripotent stem cell research not only allowed the injection of healthy cells into a damaged brain or a weak heart, but also seemed to promise that within two or three decades whole organs could be cloned – livers, kidneys, hearts, even limbs.

And the promise had been fulfilled. At this very moment there were three hearts growing, quite legally, in the Clinic. Just hearts. Organs without sentience. One hundred per cent compatible with Cathy Stevens, since they had come from her own cells. He had felt safe.

But then she'd had another sudden, massive heart attack.

And the hearts pulsating rhythmically in the lab were still far

215

too small for transplant.

That left just the one inside Alice Spencer.

✝

He should never have formed any personal bond with her, of course. Limited the relationship to the clinical tests. But as medicine advanced, and especially when his Three Poes, as he called them, kept on beating steadily, he'd allowed himself to relax. He needed to know his creation.

He bought a villa very near the Spencers' in Almoraira, stayed there often, became 'friends' with the family. They were hardly in a position to refuse. And for her it was exciting to spend time with such a famous man. His Clinic had been the first, after legalisation in 2010, to create a clone for an infertile couple, and though there had been a furore at the time, it was now an acceptable last-resort procedure in such cases. Not only that, but he was also at the forefront of therapeutic cloning, with the first solid human organs already growing in his labs.

Perhaps if his wife had still been alive, it would never have happened. But, when she was fifteen or sixteen, Alice excitedly introduced him to a handsome young Spaniard with whom she was obviously smitten. Francisco, Paco for short, he still remembered the name.

And how intensely, ridiculously, pathetically jealous he had felt.

✝

Once, Alice had confided a secret fear to him. A fairly common fear in those days.

The hysteria had died down, but, even so, everyone with an identity crisis, everyone who felt estranged from their parents, at some time or other asked themselves the same question. It was the current insult in the playgrounds: "You're just a dirty little clone!"

216

"Easter egg, Easter egg!" "Yuk, you came from a bit of your mum's bum!" The variations were endless.

Alice had asked, coquettishly: "Would you still treat me so nicely if I were one of your clones?"

They were lying on poolside loungers. He now spent a few days in Spain every month. The late afternoon sun was glinting off the bougainvillaea, and giving the down on her thighs a golden sheen, creating tantalising shadows between her breasts.

"I'm sure I would, but it's impossible, anyway. We've only had clones for a few years. Isabel Iglesias herself is only eleven years old."

He was aware how stilted he sounded. Trying to repress the desire.

"But what if I was cloned before her?"

"She was the first."

"The first *registered* clone. Everyone knows there'd been secret cloning before then."

" Oh, do they, indeed! And no one told me! Alice, my dear, I told you not to have so much sangría with your lunch!"

She flushed slightly. "It's possible. The people who did it wouldn't come out and say 'Come and burn down my lab, and hang me from a lamppost', just so they could show off, would they?"

He had to deflect this line of thought. "Well, I can prove you're not a clone, anyway."

"Ah, sí?"

"If you were a clone, that would mean that someone somewhere is as beautiful as you. This is a clear scientific impossibility. Ergo, you can't be a clone."

She smiled, innocently pleased. It was clear she had no idea how he really felt. He was three times her age.

"Convinced?" he asked.

"Not at all." She became serious again. "What about those bodies in France with half their innards gone? No one ever found out who they were. No one was reported missing. How do you know they weren't clones, grown just for the organs?"

"Alice, what *have* you been reading! *The Sun*? That's nonsense, young lady, and you know it. We've had perfectly acceptable animal organs for transplant for years now."

"I know all about that. But they say lots of people – and not just religious nutters – can't stand the thought of animals' organs in their bodies."

Yes, Caine thought, some sources put the percentage of psychological rejection as high as five percent.

"So some mad scientist had you cloned because they wanted, what? That squidgy little nose of yours! All right. But you can't just disappear, you know. If someone had cloned you, they'd have kept you hidden away. Alice, this is the real world, not a television show. Besides, all organs are checked, double-checked, and then checked again!"

But then it depends who's doing the checking.

He tousled her hair, and turned the conversation to the recent discoveries on Titan.

†

Lying there on his bed, the whisky finished, his befuddled brain envisioned how he would warn her. Though the warning would be in vain, of course. No one escaped a man like Stevens.

He'd take the next flight to Alicante, tell her everything. The 'confession' scene played itself out before him. The two facing each other across the enormous wooden kitchen table, splattered with wine stains and always exuding the odour of garlic, her 'parents' banished for the day. Her hair would be sweeping down her face, masking the shock in her pale green eyes. His voice at first would be

218

cold, clinical, detached.

"It was only just in case. Cathy Stevens' heart wasn't particularly weak then. A kind of insurance. Maybe a bit of bone marrow, maybe simply blood transfusions, things like that. Jane Spencer brought you to term. She and her boyfriend were both on the dole. We said we needed a surrogate mother for an IVF baby, a rich client would pay them well. Seven months into the pregnancy, we told them the egg donor had died in an accident, and that the father felt incapable of bringing up the child by himself, but would instead pay extremely well if the Spencers would bring up the child as their own. We arranged for them to move to Spain, whose genetic data bases at that time weren't shared with Britain. Everything paid for. Conscience clear, you'd have a wonderful life. To explain the frequent tests, we hinted that the father was very rich, and that we'd altered a couple of genes to give you an advantage in life – I won't use the loaded word 'eugenics'. Whether the Spencers ever suspected anything else, I don't know. Probably not, why should they?"

Her voice low and bitter, but controlled.

"So all those tests were to see if I was going to turn out a monster." *Twilight Zone* dialogue.

"That could never have happened. But . . . something might have gone wrong . . . "

"Such as . . . ?"

"The most obvious was whether the DNA clock would reset back to zero, or whether you began life with cells already thirty years old. We now know there was nothing to worry about. But at the time, experimental results were contradictory."

"So I'm just an experiment! With 'parents' paid to love me!"

"Paid to *have* you. I've come to know them. Their love for you has nothing to do with the money. Don't blame them for our crime."

"But nevertheless, just an experiment."

"We gave you life," he murmurs, "a life you would never have had otherwise."

"I've heard that shit argument used here to defend the breeding of bulls for the *plaza de toros*."

"So have I. It doesn't convince me, either." Making no attempt to justify anything.

"So why didn't you keep me penned up like an animal, since that's all you intended to use me for?" Her responses automatic, like those of a second-rate actress going through a bad script. Deep down, she is still in denial.

He stands up, moves to the window, stares out.

"That might have been the best way. It would have avoided... this. But . . . you at least deserved to have a good life. Just in case..." He is beyond pretence, stating the underlying meanings of things.

"Yes, I've had a good life." Now she would sweep her hair back, gaze at him with those disquieting eyes of hers. "You know what one of the nicest parts was? Thinking that I was special enough to attract the friendship of the great man himself. That you really cared for me."

He sees himself turning to face her. No longer the celebrated pioneer, with a name to rank alongside Crick and Watson, Zavos and Antinori. Just a weak old man with eyes that glisten.

"That was the only true part."

The slap catches him fairly across his left cheek, sends him staggering back. He leans with both veined hands on the back of a chair.

"It was you or Mark," he says. "No, that's not right. Not you. A scrap of tissue, a cell that I couldn't even see without a microscope, not even a thing, let alone a person. Mark was a two-year-old boy, who was going to die unless he could get the most expensive, advanced care in the world. No contest. Mark was my son. You were nothing. Then."

She gazes at him. Then the tragedy of it all breaks over him, like a wave crashing over a dried-out sand castle, and he finds himself whimpering on the floor, with tears like so much spittle dribbling down his face.

†

There *was* a way to save her. He tried to sit on the side of the bed. Another scene . . .

The package arrives by special delivery. It contains photos, hundreds of them. No words. That wasn't necessary. The photos scream their own message, enter their own plea. As soon as he sees the first one, Michael Stevens knows he should look no further. But his heart will not obey his mind.

"You bastard!" he whispers, as his hands, as if of their own volition, uncover each photo, resurrect memories that the girl in the photos has in fact never experienced. "You evil old bastard! You're a dead man, John, do you hear, you're dead!"

For he knows, in that very first moment, that the photos mean the death of the only person he has ever loved. The one thing he has never allowed himself to do is to *see* the girl. He is not a monster.

†

Things would move quickly then, rushing to an inevitable conclusion, the meaning and futility of his life squeezed into this moment, like a river rushing through a gorge before bursting out, in a last suicidal plunge, into the vast stomach of the sea.

"A life for a life, John, you know that."

He doesn't answer.

"Why did you do it?"

He shrugs, then almost smiles.

"You could say we both love the same woman."

Stevens nods slowly.

"So that's it. You could have tried to run, to hide."

"From you? Impossible. I'm too old, Michael, too tired. Besides, remember when we were younger, we always said that, whatever else might happen, we'd always pay our debts to each other."

Stevens raises the gun. "Nothing can repay this debt, John. You've destroyed me, too."

"Only because you let me, Michael. You didn't *really* need me to get Alice into the country. You didn't have to tell me your plans. You *expected* me to warn her, didn't you? To stop you?"

Stevens looks at him, neither confirming nor denying. Then he says:

"You know I have no choice. Goodbye, John."

"Goodbye, Michael. I'm sorry."

"I know."

He pulls the trigger.

†

Michael Stevens is very old now. Flayed, broken. His skin the colour of the ashes of the fire that once raged there. Sometimes he remembers, sometimes he doesn't. Often, he only remembers what might have been.

He looks up, eyes blurry. He won't live long.

"Cathy, are you there? Are you waiting?" he whispers.

The woman beside the bed takes his hand,

"I'm here," she says.

Minutes pass. He suddenly says:

"Did I do right?"

The woman presses the hand tighter.

"Yes, you did right," she says.

He smiles as he dies.

Later, Alice disengages her hand, and goes to join the man in the wheelchair outside.

It is her way of remembering his father, John Caine.

†

Caine dragged himself into consciousness, found he had tears on his cheeks. Maudlin again. False futile tears of a stupid old man. Imagining how it could have been. A world of justice, a fantasy world that allowed reparation and redemption, a realm where albatrosses finally could fall off the necks of Ancient Mariners, and Lord Jims freely offer themselves to the grieving bullets of dead friends' fathers. Tragedy, cruel and unstoppable, but given meaning and resonance.

But in this real world, tragedy came without the trappings. It came naked and ugly and shivering, sharp bones jutting through the skin.

For Michael Stevens, a tooth for a tooth would mean just that.

He wouldn't go looking for John Caine. He'd go looking for his son.

He hurled the whisky bottle to the ground, and picked up the phone, this time weeping real tears.

REVERSE PINOCCHIO SYNDROME

†

Name: *rhinolalia illuminata* (Reverse Pinocchio Syndrome)

Country of Origin: Italy

First Known Case: Don Camillo Guareschi, La Spezia, 1978

Symptoms: This illness affects only people whose profession or happiness depends on sustained and conscious mendacity – priests, politicians, parents of unspeakably ugly babies, etc.*

Stage one: One nostril dilates and expands alarmingly, while the other decreases in size to such an extent that it soon disappears completely, being replaced first by a modest indentation, then a more ambitious tunnel, and finally a supremely arrogant black void, with an unpleasantly greenish glow around the edges, similar to the solar corona during a total eclipse. At this point, the other nostril becomes smaller again, while, at the same time, a constant stream of mucus passes from it into its companion, as if being sucked into it.

Simultaneously, the owners of these noses undergo an amazing transformation: they cease to tell lies! They become, in fact, quite unable to do so. Even under controlled torture, when they are told that they only have to say that two and two is five for the torture to stop, they will scream out, provided that they didn't go to schools in the inner cities, that two and two is four.

Stage two (the Ouroboros Gulp): After about thirty days, the nostril that has been losing mucus disappears into its companion, and almost immediately the upper lip curls up into oblivion, followed by the four upper incisors. An ominous sucking sound is also heard from inside the skull, presumably the frontal lobe making its exit. At this point, the victim is shot.

History/Causes: On 27 June, 1978, halfway through a sermon, Don Camillo Guareschi, a much-respected Protestant priest in La

Spezia, suddenly remarked that there was more truth and beauty in a choirgirl's budding breasts than in the whole of Holy Scripture. In hospital later (his wife was twice his size) he forcefully informed the nurse that he wished to 'insert his woefully underused member into her deliciously rotund rump'. In addition to this and other frank comments, unusual even for an Italian, it was observed that his nose had been undergoing a profound transformation, and that his left nostril in particular was shrinking at such a rate that from certain angles what was left came to resemble a filed-off eagle's beak.

The hospital's ear, nose, and throat specialist, called Geppetto, gimlet-eyed and chisel-featured, quickly related cause to effect. "Every time he tells the truth, his nose becomes shorter," he declared woodenly. It was, as it transpired, the other way round.

The first clue as to what was really happening, and why, was provided by the famed Welsh astronomer, Pulcheria Raskolnikov Dzhugashvili, who happened to be in hospital for a severe case of nystagmus caused by prolonged study of pulsars and Italian traffic accidents. She noticed that the void that had formerly been Don Camillo's left nostril was emitting vast quantities of x-rays. She asked about Don Camillo's personal hygiene, was sick, and then delivered her verdict.

"It is a well-known fact that lies only breed more lies. A time comes in the life even of professional liars when more lies are bred than can be actually uttered without fear of exposure or ridicule. Denied egress through the mouth, these lies accumulate in the nasal mucus. Unless the nose is forcefully and ever more frequently blown, in time the mucus in one or other of the nostrils becomes so impacted and dense with the weight of trapped falsehood that, just as in the process of star formation, that nostril develops its own gravity. As the two nostrils constitute a binary system, like Cygnus X-1, the emission of x-rays by one of the nostrils (which in our analogy is like the secondary body in a binary star system) is an indication that the gravity is so powerful that it is attracting and burning up the mucus from the other nostril. What we astronomers call the accretion disc, but might here be more accurately termed the *se*cretion disc, is clearly visible. Once the mass of mucus in the lie-packed nostril has passed the Chandrasekhar limit, it becomes a black hole. All the monstrous lies that the victim wishes to tell remain forever trapped behind the event horizon, redshifted out of existence by the Schwarzchild radius. Since no falsehood can now escape, the patient can only tell the truth."**

Subsequent studies have shown that although the black hole has a very limited range (for quantum reasons beyond the scope of this article) there inevitably comes a time when it has devoured its nasal companion, and sets about those parts of the body nearest to it. **IT IS IMPERATIVE, ONCE THE SKULL HAS GONE, TO LAUNCH THE REST OF THE BODY INTO SPACE!** Otherwise the world might be left with a homeless maverick black hole, with unforeseeable consequences.

No one is certain why this disease should only have appeared in the last few decades: people have, after all, always lied. The generally accepted explanation is that increasing pollution has resulted in the production of more nasal mucus, resistant to the occasional delicate dab with a silk handkerchief of the average professional liar, and that the vastly increased temptation to lie that has accompanied the rise of the media, especially television, has bred and generated more falsehood than ever before.***

Treatment/Cure: Despite the vast amounts of money being poured into research by priests, politicians, and the more well-off parents of unspeakably ugly babies, no cure is yet in sight. Many people, in fact, hope that a cure will never be found, believing that in the interests of overall world health it is better to allow this extraordinary disease to spread unchecked.

*Sarah Goodman, 'Increased Incidence of Nasal Collapse among the Clergy and in Parliament', *The Lancet*, June 1999
** Pulcheria Raskolnikov Dzhugashvili, quoted for some quite inexplicable reason in *The Guide to Psycho-tropic Balkan Diseases*, edited by Geraldine Carter, M.D.
*** For a dissident view, see Dr Yetan Other, *Aliens Bring Gift of Truth*, 1999

HOT CROSS SON
†

For most people, the name Ian Whiting simply recalls a somewhat gruesome Easter Day prank. For those of us who knew the full enormity of his crime, it was a little different. We were aware that we were facing the threat of the end of civilisation as we knew it.

Yes, it really was that bad.

Here's what I was able to piece together from the local newspaper reports. The Reverend Ian Whiting was celebrating Mass in the small church in the Devon village of Ashleycombe as he had done for years now. Everything went fine up to the saying of the Lord's prayer. But then, instead of offering consecrated wafers and wine, he produced a small plastic bag from behind the altar, and emptied its contents on the table. Splosh! Out poured what looked like chunks of stewing steak.

"Bread and wine, me hearties!" said he, departing somewhat from the liturgy.

Even the most devout found it odd that the bread was bleeding.

"It's the latest style," announced the priest, "you get to eat the body and drink the blood all in one go. Saves problems with the chalice if any of you lot have got any poxy diseases!"

It is not for nothing that a church congregation is called a flock. Despite wondering looks, five pillars of the community meekly accepted the 'host' until:

"But this is raw meat!" protested an old lady who had once shaken hands with Mrs Thatcher, and so wasn't afraid to speak her mind.

"Isn't that what I just said? Come on, tuck in!"

228

But she staggered back, spitting the offering out of her mouth.

Her decisive action at last broke the sacrosanct spell. The communicants who had been obediently chewing away finally came to their senses, and followed the lady's example.

The priest became furious. "You fools! All these years you've been quite willing to be fobbed off with bread and wine, and now I offer you the real thing, you don't want it! Bloody well eat it, you stupid cretins!"

And he leapt over the altar rail, picked up a bit of the 'host' that had been spat out, and tried to force it into the mouth of the lady who had defied him.

Churchgoers are usually a placid lot, and loyal to their priests. As old Neetzchy said, Christianity is pretty much a slave morality. But this *was* Easter Sunday, and they were all wearing their best clothes: clothes which were now getting spattered with wine/blood and assorted retchings. That is the only way I can explain the ferocity of their attack on their pastor. A well-wielded crutch put him into a coma, which lasted a week.

There's a fascinating letter in the State Archives in Florence, dated July 24, 1567, from one Piero Gianfigliazzi in Pisa to Prince Francesco dei Medici.

'On the 19th of the present month, while celebrating mass in the Cathedral of this city . . . the priest registered a most fetid taste and odour in the act of receiving the consecrated wine. However, he swallowed it down as best he could. Then, when he came to the purification, he wanted none of the wine that they wished to give him, saying that he didn't want any more of that piss (non voleva più piscio*). After expressing his displeasure to the choir master and the sacristan, he was brought another chalice and given good wine, which he was told he could purify. From all of this, I deduce that he*

was given urine to consecrate in place of wine. Though the Vicar has not been able to uncover the truth regarding who is responsible for such an obscenity, he has put a priest named Giobbo in solitary confinement . . . "

I never did find out whether they finally hung it on poor old Giobbo. I guess with a name like that suspicion was bound to fall on him.

I mention this little anecdote to show that this wasn't the first time the host and wine had been interfered with. The police were informed, but didn't find it important enough to investigate, or even to check just *what* meat it was. The deacon had already thrown it in the park for the local dogs, anyway

But a contact of mine was so amazed by what the priest told her when he came out of his coma that she gave me a call. I was passing my Easter vacation in Torquay for sentimental reasons, revisiting the spot which had witnessed one of the most satisfying moments in my long tumultuous relationship with my darling Katie – the place where I had thrown her first lover off the cliffs. Well, he should have known better than to mention my accident.

I asked to be alone with the Reverend (my Ministry of Defence ID secured acquiescence) and he at once burst into an amazing diatribe.

"The Central Mystery of the Church! Poppycock! The only mystery is why people have swallowed it for so long! It's just word games. Transubstantiation: the bread and wine no longer exist, though there it is, sitting right in front of you. Consubstantiation: the bread and wine do at least exist, but they are *also* the body and blood of Christ. Impanation, Eucharist, host, elementals, accidentals, sacring bell, fraction, epiclesis, oblation, credence table, chalice, paten – words, words, words! Verbal foliage to hide the greatest con trick the world has ever known! Our version of the Emperor with no clothes!"

Strange stuff, coming from such a meek-looking priest, but in my profession we deal with all sorts.

"You're preaching to the perverted," I said. "But I don't see that making the congregation sick with raw meat is any solution, do you?"

"Flesh."

"What?"

"*Flesh*, not meat. You, poor lost soul, indulge in the sins of the flesh, not the sins of the meat."

I was on holiday, so I didn't break his arm.

"You mean, that was *human* flesh you gave them?"

"Of course. A real Eucharist is the only way to save mankind! John 6:53-54, *'Then Jesus said unto them, Verily, Verily, I say unto you, Except ye eat the flesh of the Son of man, and drink His blood, ye have no life in you.'*"

Well, you couldn't put it much straighter than that!

"I've still got the rest of the body at home," he added, clearly concerned lest I doubt his word.

Well, I called in my contact, and we got him dressed and into his detached house faster than a premature orgasm. First, the fridge. Contents: week-old skimmed milk, a few shivering veg, and a plastic bag containing maybe ten kilos of what looked liked diced stewing steak. Then, the freezer. Contents: sundry innards, two arms, one leg, and a head attached to maybe half a torso.

I felt a new respect for this guy. Maybe we could recruit him later.

Only . . . that head. That head, I swear, was looking serenely up, with a warm forgiving smile on those frozen lips. Just looking at it, I felt that this guy would have immediately understood why I'd arranged for my darling Katie's second lover to come into a terminal headlock with a bulldozer.

But that wasn't all. There were nasty-looking holes in the hands and the foot.

You can't blame *everything* on junk food. I was starting to get a real bad feeling about this whole thing.

I kept my voice even.

"Who was this . . . gentleman?"

"Jesus, of course."

I'd expected that.

"No, I mean, who was he *really?*"

He looked at me, puzzled.

I went on: "Yes, of course, *you* knew it was really Jesus paying a secret Return Visit, but who did other less discerning people think he was? How did he disguise his Divine Effulgence? What did he do? Where did he live?"

"He lived here, down in the cellar, of course. No one else ever saw him. That's not what I cloned him for."

Well, that one threw even me, and I'm trained for the unexpected. Yes, cloning's the in-thing these days, but you still need something to clone *from.* That's why I still keep my darling Katie's little finger, just in case I go too far one day, though at the time I was cutting it off I admit I was doing it simply for pleasure: we were going through one of our little tiffs.

The good Reverend smiled indulgently.

"You're wondering where I got the DNA? Let me remind you, St John again, chapter 20, 6-7: '*Then cometh Simon Peter following him, and went into the sepulchre, and seeth the linen clothes lie, and the face-cloth, that was about his head, not lying with the linen clothes, but wrapped together in a place by itself.*'"

What did he think I was? Your average uncultured assassin?

"The Turin Shroud? That tatty old sheet that's supposed to

have been wrapped round Jesus' body in the tomb, and seems to have got a negative photographic image of a crucified man on it? Don't come that old chestnut with me. That was Carbon-14-dated ages ago, and proved to be medieval, not first century."

"Hardly *proved*," muttered Whiting, for the first time looking a bit nettled, "since they only took tiny samples from the edge of the cloth, which could well have been contaminated by later accretions. But, yes, its authenticity is in doubt, and besides it would have been impossible to break into Turin Cathedral and steal it. Too well protected. And anyway, what I needed was blood. And there was much more chance of finding that on the Oviedo Sudarium."

Damn, he'd got me there. Sudarium? But come on, my hobby is to break limbs, not read up on Fairy Tales For Religious Nutters.

He told me that the Cathedral of San Salvador in Oviedo in northern Spain is now really famous for one thing – it's the only cathedral in the world with just one tower. This wasn't minimalist design, it was poverty. But it used to have a lot of prestige. El Cid himself had a quaff or two in 1075. The reason was the silver chest in the Cámara Santa, which contained what was believed to be the Sudarium, or face-cloth, which had been wrapped round Jesus' head on the Cross to mop up the blood and serum coming out of his nose, and which was taken out of Jerusalem at the time of the Persian invasion, reached Seville, and then moved north in stages before the Moorish advances. But times change, and very few have even heard of the Oviedo Sudarium, all the glory being stolen by the Turin Shroud. The Italians just have more razzmatazz than the Spanish, and besides, the Pope lives there.

Whiting went on to explain how the Sudarium is only brought out to be viewed three times a year, twice on saints' days in September, and then again on Good Friday, and how he had broken in and stolen it at the end of September, knowing that it wouldn't then be missed again for six months.

He'd then cloned Jesus from the DNA he'd found there.

By now I was growing impatient. OK, so the guy was funny, and had a neat way of hacking off limbs, but was he trying to take me for a sucker? I know all about Dolly, Polly, Golly. And all the mice, cows, cats, cockroaches, and top models cloned since then. Cloning takes *time*. Not just six months.

"There speaks an abandoned soul!" Whiting said sadly. "You think a *god* isn't going to grow a bit quicker, you idiot?"

I saw that he had a point, but I gave him a backhander anyway. Guess in my job it's a kind of reflex. Besides, my darling Katie's third lover had been a vicar.

He turned the other cheek, bless him, so I gave him another backhander, and then we went down to the cellar, and, yes, there sure enough was a pretty impressive looking laboratory. (I learned later that Whiting wasn't the first priest to play around in labs. Apparently, Hoffman's mad scientist in *Der Sandmann* was modelled on the Roman Catholic priest Lazzaro Spallanzani who filled in his time blinding bats, decapitating snails, and resurrecting dried microscopic animals. It also turned out, would you believe it, that Whiting had once turned down a job in the Roslin Research Institute – you know, where they cloned Dolly – because Wilmut and the other researchers were 'amateurs and charlatans' and had 'a pathetically superficial knowledge of genetics'!)

In one corner of the lab, there was another freezer with the door hanging open and shelves full of what looked like a lot of Easter eggs for undernourished Hobbits. But I only noted that subliminally. Because next to the freezer was a cross.

A used cross. Unoccupied now. But used.

Don't ask me. In my profession, you just *know*.

"But why the hell did you have to *crucify* him?" I asked the

Reverend, who was tenderly releasing a fly trapped in a spider's web.

He looked at me pityingly. "Don't you know *anything*? A lot of good it would have done us if the Son of God had turned up the first time, taken a look round Palestine like Queen Elizabeth visiting Australia, and then just gone back to Heaven with unwanted gifts of Middle Eastern coffee pots and pictures of the Roman emperor! He had to die and be crucified to absolve us of our sins. The power lay in the *crucified* body, that was the whole point of it. The same with my new Jesus. Don't think I enjoyed it! Or that it was easy! Have you ever tried to lift a struggling man up on to a cross by yourself?"

Well, not entirely by myself. My darling Katie and myself were still close at that time. That was the guy who'd sliced off . . . but I don't want to think about that. But then *he'd* deserved it!

The Reverend was reminiscing. "And the names he called me! You could tell he had royal blood all right!" The gentle smile of the tolerant fanatic played about his lips.

I'd always thought the original Jesus must have done a bit of name-calling, too! 'Forgive them, for they know not what they do' my ass!' Sure, I can just see it!

Well, we had a pretty gruesome murder on our hands. A benign-looking parish priest somehow breaks into a Spanish cathedral, steals one of its relics guarded behind an iron grille, impossibly clones a man from *old* DNA in the cloth, accelerates the growth so that there's a full-grown man within a few months, crucifies him, chops him up into wafer-sized pieces, and offers the pieces to his congregation on Easter Day.

Pretty bad, eh?

Well, that wasn't the worst of it!

Those Easter eggs, you see.

The good Reverend suddenly noticed the open freezer, dashed across, and scrambled among the eggs – which I now saw were made of glass, not chocolate – with the ferocity of a tumescent, but unprepared, man searching for an unused condom. The eggs all had a spherical hole at one end.

"They've escaped!" he screamed.

The Reverend Ian Whiting was a true visionary, a man who cared deeply about the whole human race, who hadn't just wished to save the souls of his own small flock on this one Easter Day, but had planned to stamp out the Eucharistic fraud everywhere for a long time to come. A passing lamb had provided the uterus for his Jesus (no longer the Lamb of God, but the God of Lamb), but he had retained a hundred embryos which he had intended to later implant in other unwary passing lambs.

Now I admit I'm only guessing here. Very little research, it seems, has been done on divine chromosomes. A divine cell doesn't necessarily obey the same laws as a humble undivine one, as Whiting had found out with his accelerated Jesus. Certain faculties may be developed before the organs normally associated with them. The auditory sense, for instance, might precede the ear. Prayers not only have to reach as far as Heaven, which I'm told on *very* good authority is quite some distance away, but frequently aren't even uttered until one reaches one's death bed, by which time one's voice tends to be muted. Maybe straining to hear these deathbed prayers had preternaturally developed the Divine audition.

Now the good Reverend had crucified his Jesus just a few feet away from the embryos. What if they'd heard the nails going in, sensed what was in store for them, and during the week the Reverend had been in a coma, done a bit of accelerated growing up by themselves, and then scarpered? Can't say I'd blame them really.

Of course, I had to report all this to Section Thirteen. And the instructions went out just as I'd expected.

Search and destroy.

The world is ruled by economic imperialism. But judging from the antics of the original JC in the temple with the moneylenders, his clones wouldn't be likely to accept that. And some of those Commandments! No other gods: end of the pop music and film industry. No killing: end of the armaments industry. No bearing false witness: end of politics and international diplomacy. No coveting your neighbour's cow or wife: end of capitalism and good healthy competition.

In short, living by Christian precepts would rapidly bring the Christian world to its knees.

The next few days were tense. The Section's greatest stroke of luck was when the main body of jaycees got cornered in Portsmouth, remembered their old skills, and cockily walked across the Solent to the Isle of Wight, making rude signs as they went. Hubris. Next day the island was nuked. Pity about the local inhabitants, but Section Thirteen has to see the bigger picture.

After that, it was a case of mopping up. Three jaycees foolishly headed for the Vatican, and were brought down by the halberds of the Swiss Guard on the direct orders of the Pope himself twitching furiously, and still mumbling incoherently, on his Balcony. Well, he stood to lose most, I suppose. Bit like King Lear: once you hand over your power, people don't want to give it back.

The Simon Wiesenthal Centre used their expertise and accounted for half a dozen more jaycees. Quite a few were spotted because of their allergic reaction to the sight of a cross, and a fair number were nabbed in brothels: well, each generation does tend to rebel against the earlier one. One particularly cunning fugitive even set himself up as a pawnbroker, but gave himself away by offering fair prices for the articles pawned.

Oh yes, Whiting's jaycees got up to all the tricks in the book, but Section Thirteen has branches in every country in the world.

Soon we were pretty sure we'd bagged the lot.

Except one.

Like Woody Allen in *Zelig*, this one popped up everywhere. Tiananmen Square, the White House Lawn, Red Square in Moscow, Mecca, the banks of the River Ganges, Super Bowl stadiums – anywhere where there was a crowd he would appear, stick his tongue out, blow raspberries, make dire threats, and somehow melt away just before our agents could get there.

Me, I bided my time. I knew that he would become more and more human every passing day. I knew that in the end, he would fall victim to that most elemental of weaknesses – the desire for vengeance. I knew that some day he would come back to settle the score with the Reverend Ian Whiting.

And he did.

And I was waiting with my Kalashnikov.

†

He's got plans. Big plans. Big horrible plans.

Losing ninety-nine brothers. That's a lot. Kind of hardens your character. Seeing as he got resurrected on Easter Day, he declared last night as we placidly drank daiquiris, he's going to wait till All Hallows! Samhain. And it won't be the *spirits* of the dead he'll be raising, but what's left of their bodies. They'll start with the World Bank. Chuckling, he said to me: '*For as the Father raiseth up the dead, and quickeneth them; even so the Son quickeneth whom he will.*' Check in St John, chap 5, if you don't believe me, you heathen!" He slapped me on the shoulder. "It's not just the Devil who quotes scripture, you know!"

Oh, come on! The gun was just to show him I wasn't negotiating out of weakness. You think I was going to blow away a guy who could heal the sick? Raise Lazarus? For a guy like that, my embarrassing problem was nothing. I don't limp any more, and it sure does feel good having my balls back again.

My darling Katie's back with me now, of course, now that I'm complete again. I guess that was the root of our problem all along.

Of course, I had to give him the Reverend in exchange. And I did feel a bit sorry for the old guy, dying like that – upside down, too, and in such a public place as the Dome of St Paul's! – but then he *had* planned to crucify another five score jaycees.

Yep, I really do believe I'm going to enjoy working for my new boss.

A HELPING HAND

†

The beggar descended on my neighbourhood, a middle-class suburb of Madrid, in the middle of December, in time to feed on the carrion benevolence of Christmas. He was young, mid-twenties, unusually tall, and lean rather than thin. Despite the long lank hair, swarthy gypsy complexion, dirty uneven teeth, and filthy clothes, he didn't really give the impression of being one of life's victims — not with those insolent dark eyes seeking out his prey with ceaseless vigilance.

With the cunning of those of his kind, he positioned himself at an angle between two shops. One was the small local supermarket, the other a kind of butcher-cum-fishmonger which also sold bread — a fairly common arrangement in Spain. The construction of the shops was somewhat unusual. They formed two rectangles at right angles to each other, so that as you walked along the road on the left the corners of both shops jutted out — the supermarket more than the other — while their entrances were hidden in the 'V' between them — it reminded me of a giant axe, or meat cleaver, lying with the cutting edge facing the road, the shaft being the meat-fish shop and the axe head the supermarket.

It was this corner between the two shops that the beggar made his own, polluting it with his greed and odour like a cat spraying its territory. As the shops together provided for most everyday necessities, they were nearly always full, usually with the same customers, squat overweight mothers of families, many of whom went there every day. The beggar had clearly calculated that familiarity would breed, not contempt, but pity and pesetas, that even those who resisted at first would eventually succumb, through either attrition or contrition, or a mixture of both. And so it was, many of the weak-minded women deliberately keeping their loose change in their hands to pay their Danegeld as they came out of the shops. They really had little choice, because it was impossible to enter or leave either of the shops without passing beside his two-square-metre territory, within which he would lurk, ready to spring out and accost with outstretched hand. As for passing from one shop to the other, one had to venture right through his territory or make a very obvious and embarrassing detour around him.

These were merely the regular victims. What made his position even stronger was that the entrance to the Metro and the main bus-stop were just a few metres further on. Hence, there was a constant stream of people passing by, and from his lair, the beggar, in between fleecing middle-aged women with permed hair and silly smiles, would pounce out, almost (but not quite: the creature was too sharp for that) blocking the pavement, asking in a mockingly polite voice for *una pequeña ayuda, por favor*, 'a little help, please', and stepping back sardonically if refused or ignored.

Oh no, not for him the humility of others of his ilk who kept to the Gran Vía in the city centre, kneeling on the ground, eyes down, while a badly scrawled placard in front of them informed the world that, despite their revolting appearance, they not only had a wife but had even managed to engender a disgusting litter of hungry offspring. Our man despised such trumpery: placards, whining, and kneeling were not for him. He did not even bother with the ubiquitous begging bowl, which always contained just enough miserable coins to make you believe that others had contributed, and yet few enough to make it obvious that the holder was not going to be able to eat that day without your help. No, the only stage props he allowed himself were three tiny, emaciated, large-eyed puppies, which lay in a basket beside the supermarket wall. The message was obvious: if you don't give, these poor innocent creatures don't get fed, either. I could well imagine him breeding them, selecting for piteous eyes and pathetic yelp, and slashing the throats of the older ones once they no longer served his purpose.

In short, for him no glazed eyes, no monotonous whine, no sickening appeals to God. No *pordiosero,* he. Rather, he presumed to meet you as your equal, dark eyes challenging as he darted out to the pavement to scratch the conscience of a passer-by, or slithered back with unerring timing to trap a victim passing from one shop to the other.

Yes, you're right: I didn't like this beggar. I'm not a mean person, or selfish, whatever you may have heard from my ex-wife. I have frequently, maybe even too frequently, given money to cripples in the street. But those people had kept to the city centre, huddling abjectly on the pavement where they belonged, showing proper humility, not strutting outside my local supermarket, day after day, slowly turning my life into a nightmare.

It was, as I told you, near Christmas when I first saw him. As I approached that first time, I only noticed what I thought was a customer bending down to stroke some puppies, but suddenly the figure straightened up, darted forward, and asked point-blank for an *ayuda.*

I am fifty-seven years old, and suffer from a bad back. Ever since that ambush outside Pretoria. Ask Wendy: the bitch wouldn't lie about that, at least. It is rare for me to pass a full day without some pain. At that time, my back was particularly bad, despite a recent laminectomy, and I could only walk for short distances. But I had had to go out to buy food. And here was a strong, fit young man, capable of casually bending down and straightening up without pain, thrusting his slimy hand at me like a rapier point, demanding money! Yes, demanding! Oh yes, the voice was polite, but I knew from that first moment that he *expected* me to capitulate, that the mere fact of being a foreigner, and wearing a tailored suit, carried with it the obligation to be an easy touch.

If I'd been twenty years younger, like the old days when nobody would have *dared* . . . anyway, I gave him a puzzled look, as if I didn't understand his gesture, and went on into the shop. Yet when I came out, a carrier bag in both hands, he was waiting for me again, the hand insistently held out. I confess I was weak, I allowed him to catch my eye, and I nodded at the shopping bags, shrugging slightly to indicate that my hands weren't free. He said nothing, just stepped back, almost condescendingly, as if saying 'very well, but don't let this happen again'. Ashamed of my weakness, I decided there and then I would never surrender to this insolence.

I saw him only a couple of times more before Christmas, which I spent alone, as I always do – it's better to avoid people at Christmas, they only want things from you, and it gave me the chance to rest my back and reread a couple of my favourite books, and watch a few special videos – *very* expensive, but well worth it. And on those occasions there were so many people milling around the two shops that it was easy to avoid him.

It was after Christmas that things became more difficult. The beggar by now had realised that I wasn't just a visitor, but lived here, was part of his constituency, as it were. Each time I went to the shops, he increased the pressure just a little. The most dangerous stretch, of course, was between the two shops – you had to pass directly through his stronghold. At first, I simply tried to outface him, but there was something unnerving – worse, taunting – about his eyes, so soon I had no choice but to avoid that route. If I needed to go to both shops, I would go to one first, return home, and then come back to go to the second. That way, I could wait until he was facing one of the shop entrances, and then enter the other shop behind him. But, of course, the extra walking aggravated my back problems. After the second week, I limited my visits to the butcher by buying half a dozen chicken breasts at a time, and freezing them, but this meant foregoing daily fresh bread. Because of a damned beggar!

The real problem, moreover, was in coming out. Even if he didn't spot me going into the supermarket, from his vantage point he could see (and hear) the doors of the shops opening, and thus be standing directly in front of them as a victim emerged. At first, I dealt easily with this. After passing through check-out, I would wait and read the small ads stuck on the wall, until another person passed through, and then follow her out of the shop, using her as a human shield. Trapped stupidly with that hand outstretched as the silly woman looked up at him kindly and gave him her twenty-five pesetas, he could do nothing to prevent me turning and escaping unscathed from the zone of fire.

Had he accepted his defeat with dignity, he might still be there today. My days of violence were over, I only wanted peace and tranquillity now. But no, the arrogant fool chose to fight on. Aware that I would not enter his redoubt, he took the battle into no-man's-land, and would intercept me as I approached the supermarket. As I have already explained, due to the odd alignment of the shops, as I came up the road on the left he would have me in his sights for a good minute or two, and he took to toying with me, making a preliminary sortie, deliberately staring down the road to make me feel uncomfortable, disappearing back into his lair (either to feed on an old housewife, or, I suspect, to raise false hopes in me) and leaping out again just in time to assault me with his outstretched hand, causing me to take sudden, and frequently painful, evasive action.

My revenge was simple. By leaving his sheltered corner, he was exposing himself to the freezing winds and rain of a Madrid winter, so I started going shopping only on the most intemperate days, knowing I had some nice central heating waiting for me at home, while he would be stuck there till the shops closed. Yes, I did catch a bit of a cold, but, to my great delight, *he* was taken with a racking cough, and the eyes that gazed at me with hatred were now sunken deep in their sockets.

He survived the winter, however – that sort somehow always does – and by March, it was obvious that more concrete evasive measures were needed. One day I tried walking along the opposite side of the road, only crossing after I had passed the shops. By coming from the opposite direction, with the besieged shops now on my right, I prevented the beggar from seeing me until I actually passed the jutting-out corner of the supermarket, and then I moved rapidly to the entrance, gazing in through the window, thus leaving him no possibility of eye contact. This worked beautifully, and I can still remember the sheer joy I experienced when I came out of the shop (both arms full, of course) and saw the surprised and frustrated expression in his eyes.

I had a week or two of bliss until, one day, I crossed the road as usual, backtracked to the shop, sauntered round the corner – right into that outstretched hand! He had been lying in wait for me! I had to suddenly flick my fingers as if I had just remembered something, look at my watch, give a surprised exclamation, and turn on my heel, heading in the direction I had just come from. Heading? No, fleeing! I knew he was watching me, laughing to himself. In those few seconds of eye contact, I had seen his hate, his determination to conquer me.

It was clear that he had spotted me going down the opposite side of the road, and was therefore prepared for my arrival. I tried this route a couple of times more, but with the same result. I therefore had to go down another street behind the row of shops, and round a small park, before being able to approach on his blind side.

This added another ten minutes to my walk, just enough to start my back pains again. But now the only way for him to catch me was to stand well out on the pavement, and risk losing all the easy shop-to-shop victims. Even so, a few times, so furious was he with my stratagem, he did just that, stood right near the jutting corner of the supermarket – and I simply sauntered along, before turning into the chemist, or bar, or whatever shelter was near. Sometimes, to rub it in, I stopped a mere five feet away from him, staring into the window of the ironmongery next to the supermarket, admiring the thrilling beauty of the knives, axes, and hacksaws, while glancing across at him until he had to retreat to milk his old ladies. You can't imagine the satisfaction it gave me to know that I had made him lose a few hundred pesetas through his futile sallies.

I had more or less solved the problem of getting into the shops. The problem was still getting out of them. My initial ploy of using human shields, and making sure both hands were full, only worked for a short time, because such was his unreasoning hatred of me that he preferred to accept losses rather than allow me to foil him so easily. Now he wouldn't even waste time with whatever little old lady I was using as a decoy, but simply stared straight at me over her head; an easy thing to do since the generation of Spaniards born during the early Franco years – now *that* was a man who would have known what to do with my beggar! – are notoriously short and stocky. All I could do was avert my eyes, and shuffle away, but I could hear him whispering *viejo cobarde*, 'old coward'. It surprised me that no-one else seemed to hear him.

It did occur to me to retaliate by giving him, with a grandiose gesture, a deliberately insulting five pesetas (two pence), thus forcing him to thank me for nothing. But no, his would still be the moral victory. Besides, it would give him the right to *know* me, to *speak* to me, for God's sake!

By April, I was beginning to get deeply angry. I pride myself on being reasonable. Like the lion spider, the beggar had prepared his trap, and if other people chose to fall into it, that was their affair. But instead of being content with his easy victories, he had set out to persecute me. *Me!* Until his arrival, my life in Spain had been calm and uneventful, allowing me to forget the vindictiveness of my ex-wife and her conceited little lover, who had gloried in letting the whole world know about their affair, just to make me seem ridiculous. Not so ridiculous as he was, mind you, when he was attacked and robbed one night and had a knife stuck through his groin for good measure! You must have read about it. I believe his penis was rather badly slashed and that he lost a testicle. Poetic justice, when you think about it.

By all means, help yourself; there's another bottle in the kitchen. I can see by your expression what you're thinking: if he was poor, why not give him a few coins now and then, like everyone else? Poor? Him? One day I got a small boy to carry a chair for me into the street, and I watched for hours from behind a parked lorry on the other side of the road. I calculated that someone came out of one or other of the shops every six seconds, and that about one in five gave him a coin. That meant two coins a minute. Since nobody would be likely to give him anything less than a twenty-five-peseta coin (around ten pence) that's twenty pence a minute. Which comes to twelve pounds an hour, which is around a hundred pounds a day *at least*, for obviously many of the coins would be more than twenty-five pesetas. It wouldn't be unreasonable to double or even treble that figure. A hundred pounds a day or more for doing nothing apart from slouch around disturbing people by sticking that grasping grimy hand in front of their noses! Nearly two and a half thousand pounds a month. Tax-free. More than *I* was getting, even with the aid of the old mercenary network who always look after their own.

No, don't talk about poverty to me! Why, he hadn't even been bothering to put in a full 'working' day. I know this, because I spent a few days watching from a distance to see if there were any safe times for me to go shopping. The shops were open from ten to two, and then again from five to eight. He turned up punctually at ten with his puppies, but in the evening didn't arrive till six. He probably needed a long siesta after enjoying a slap-up meal with wine at the little old ladies' expense. Perhaps he even half fed the puppies.

I decided to give him one last chance. I began to go shopping between five and six, but one day, after having avoided him for a couple of weeks, I was caught in a queue, and walked right into him as I came out, with not even a single housewife as a buffer. It was a tense moment, enough time for us both to establish that this was going to be a fight to the death. You think I was imagining things? So how do you explain the fact that after that he was always there bang on five o'clock? He had repaired the breach in his defences, though I at least had the satisfaction of knowing that I had spoiled his siesta – even though this satisfaction in turn was vitiated by the knowledge that by forcing him to 'work' longer I was making him even richer.

You'll say I could have gone to different shops, and indeed I did consider this. But I immediately saw it was out of the question. Not only would I have to walk much further, with the consequent discomfort to my back; it was now a question of honour, of personal integrity. God almighty, I'd been going to that supermarket for years before the beggar arrived, what right had he to drive me away? That shop belonged to me, just as my wife had belonged to me: it was mine, not his. How did he dare to defy me by staying there, healthy and fit, mocking my age, my pain? Was he really so stupidly blind as to think that the old lion had lost all its teeth?

What would *you* have done?

By May, I found I was quite unable to sleep. I lay awake at night, trying to find a comfortable position for my back, recalling how not so long before, the black cousins of this damned beggar used to cringe if I so much as glanced at them; and now this . . . Dago had the insolence to be lying in a comfortable bed somewhere nearby, free of all pain, laughing to himself over my discomfiture.

I repeat, what would *you* have done?

Well, that's all over now. These days, I sometimes go shopping two or three times a day. Just for the pleasure of being able to walk in and out of the shops without anyone pestering me. I sometimes listen to the fat old housewives talking about the sudden disappearance of 'that nice polite young man, even though he was poor'. Occasionally, another beggar wanders into our neighbourhood, shoulders stooped, eyes lifeless, pleading for money in a dull, hopeless monotone, and I never fail to give something. Poor bastards, life's pretty tough for them.

Yes, it *is* an unusual ornament, isn't it? Very realistic, very lifelike. Actually gives some people the shudders. I suppose it could be used as an ashtray, though I just use it to keep loose change in. Comes in very handy for that.

Oh yes, very handy indeed. Almost as if that's what it was designed for.

SPLIT DECISION
†

"Next!" barked St. Peter. He was actually quite a gentle man, but bitter experience had taught him that any sign of weakness at this stage could lead to trouble from the ones who would have to go Elsewhere.

A quiet scholarly soul stepped forward.

"Name!"

"Henry, sir."

"And what makes you think you belong here?"

"I cured many people, sir. I gave my life for medicine." His voice had a gentle sadness.

"Very well, if you'd just stand on those scales a moment . . . "

The soul obediently did so. The needle fluctuated wildly.

"Oh dear, they seem to have broken," said Peter. "Never mind, I see no reason why I shouldn't let you in." His smile was just a little bit ingratiating. After all, he *was* a couple of millennia old, and the old crucifixion wounds were starting to play up a bit. A friendly doctor in the House wouldn't hurt. Then he thought he heard the muffled words:

"Just you try to stop me, you silly old sod!"

"What!"

The soul looked at him in surprise. "I didn't say anything."

Peter glared suspiciously, but the soul continued to look up at him meekly. (One nice thing about the job was that the souls always looked *up* at him. They had to, as they were never above three feet tall when they arrived. Something about travelling faster than the speed of light. They soon stretched out again, however.)

Peter assumed he'd been hearing things – over the centuries his ears had been seriously damaged by the unnecessarily hurtful

250

comments of those sent Elsewhere, as well as by the loud recordings of cock crows played, in the flat above him, by an unemployed angel who felt Peter shouldn't have come to Heaven in the first place – so he stood back to allow the soul to pass.

"I hope we'll be seeing more of each other," he said.

The soul gave him a grateful look, bowed slightly (Peter liked that: the angels never allowed him to forget his humble beginnings) and walked through the Turnstile. Once through it, however, he suddenly turned round and hissed, *"Up yours, you stupid old fart!"*

At this point, Peter decided he really ought to check the new soul's file, after all.

†

"Simple," said Solomon. "Cut him in two, keep one half here."

"Surprise, surprise!" muttered Peter. Subtlety had never been Solomon's strong point.

The Archangel Michael was busy force-feeding the baby Beast: it still weighed less than a hundred tons, and he only had a century or so to get it big enough for the Apocalypse. Peter had just begun to explain the problem, when the Beast lashed out with one of its tails, and Michael went flying into the distance.

The Archangel Gabriel jumped away guiltily from the Virgin Mary as Peter entered the Library. His wings were still twitching.

"Not my department," he panted, "better ask God. If you can find which Mansion he's in."

"And knock next time you come in!" snapped the Virgin. The Corporeal Assumption had gone to her head.

Peter glowered and left. In his cups one night, the Holy Ghost had confessed that he'd never even been near Nazareth. Why did they bother to keep up the pretence?

He went to see Jesus, but they told him he was away in the Andromedan Nebula. Probably being Crucified yet again, thought

251

Peter. Poor sod. Though in public everyone defended God – you couldn't just Save one little bit of the Universe and not the rest – behind his back not a few wondered whether he might not be a bit short on the paternal instinct. That, or it was an aggravated case of Münchausen Syndrome by proxy.

"Oh, don't bother me now, come back later," said God, with a look of irritation. He was playing chess with Satan, who sometimes popped over to have his tail groomed, to cool off, and to get a bit of peace and quiet. The game was going badly: God decided to sacrifice a bishop. You couldn't do that with dice.

Ah well, thought Peter, he'd tried. He was just the Doorman. It wasn't his job to make this impossible decision. Anyway, perhaps things would now liven up a bit in this dull place.

He slipped a bottle of confiscated whisky into his pocket – and a revolver, just in case – and wandered off to invite Dr Henry Jekyll to have a drink.

LATE DEVELOPER

†

'I just don't think they'll accept me,' Liza said, as we strolled along the winding pathway to the mansion.

'Don't be silly. They're very open-minded, you'll see.'

'All the same, I think this might be a bit too much for them. A conservative place like Devon. My colour . . . "

'My family are above all that,' I interrupted, 'they would never hold it against you.'

That wasn't just words; I really *was* sure. Yes, in some ways Father was a bit strait-laced, fixed in his ways, and Lorna my ten-year-old sister wasn't talking to me because of what she termed my perverted attitude towards her, but I knew that taking home a classy girl like Liza would impress them. And as for Mother and Grandfather, they would be absolutely delighted. I would no longer be considered the odd one out in the family.

True, Liza wasn't a virgin, which might be considered an obstacle in a traditional aristocratic family like ours, but she *had* been until four nights ago, when she had been cruelly assaulted in the middle of the night.

This time, I was sure, I had finally found the perfect partner.

†

My family, except my mother, had never hidden their disappointment in me. I frequently heard words like 'throwback' and 'sport' bandied around.

For a start, I'd never had any success with girls. Maybe I was too shy, or too sensitive. But the local girls expected you to whip it out, and then in, after half a pint of scrumpy. I found this coarse and off-putting.

But there were other more fundamental things.

Once Father had indulged in an uncharacteristic outburst:

'My God, Pete, what's wrong with you! Nearly fourteen years old, and you've never even killed anyone, let alone dismembered or eviscerated them. You've never raped anyone, you've never drunk anyone's blood, you've never burnt down anyone's home, or slaughtered their cattle, or castrated their cat, or buggered their sheep . . . You're just not *normal*, lad!'

I noticed that the axe hanging on the wall was shining brightly. When I was very young, he didn't use to clean it after a small nocturnal outing, but Mother had told him off for 'setting a bad example' to the children, and since then we only knew he'd used it when it was newly polished. Apparently, he felt that axe-murdering was an adult pastime, not suitable for children. I was often surprised how narrow-minded he could sometimes be.

'Watch what you're saying about my son,' interposed my mother with a voice deceptively like the sound of black orchids dancing to the slower bits of Handel's *Sarabande in D Minor*. Whenever she and Father had an argument over me, I became 'her' son. Despite her usual sweetness, it wasn't wise to forget why they'd repeatedly failed to burn her at the stake (her Cat hadn't fared so well). Once or twice, after a more serious disagreement than usual with Father, she had proved that a spell was considerably faster and more painful than an axe stroke.

But Father always showed more bravado after an axe-outing:

'What's more, you refuse to have sex with any of the rest of us. Lorna's already ten years old, and you haven't molested her even once! Why, last Sunday, after Mass, she was crying all night; she told me she'd climbed into your bed, and asked you – *begged* you – to at least put your fingers inside her, to show you weren't completely unnatural, and you wouldn't even do that! Have you no respect for her feelings? This family has had a respectable history of incest for

centuries. I wouldn't even have been born if your granddad had had the same perverted attitude to *his* sister!'

I wanted to explain that it wasn't my fault, that I was no more responsible for my desires than a werewolf or a Catholic priest or a bluebottle fly, but deep down I knew there *was* no defence. I was a vile unnatural animal.

†

I thought things would be better when I did at last find a girl who attracted me. I felt so happy. Not just because I was tired of being alone, but because it meant I might at last earn the respect of my family.

Her name was Isabel Valiño-Hijosa, a slim dark-eyed Spanish girl who'd come to work as a nurse in the UK, since not only was it difficult to find enough English girls to enter the profession, but those who did were so unattractive that patient morbidity and even mortality had increased alarmingly. Isabel, despite being weighed down with names, had been a corker! But Mum − luckily, as it turned out − had spotted me on the way out of the house. We've always been completely open with each other, so I told her what I was planning. She shook her head patiently as she took the shovel out of my hands.

'I'm glad you're starting to make up your mind at last where your preferences lie, I always did think you'd take after Grandad,' she said, 'but don't touch the Valiño-Hijosa girl.'

'But I want her!'

'She's not the one for you, dear.'

I was baffled. 'But why? She's only been buried two days.'

'Your first experience of necrophilia is very important. A bad initiation into sex could turn you off it for life. The Valiño-Hijosa girl might be all right when you have much more experience, more skill, more *manoeuvrability* . . . "

255

'But Mum, she's not going to complain. Beggars and corpses can't be choosers.'

'No, my darling, I don't mean that. I'm sure your youthful impaler erectus will do you credit. After all the training your father and I have given it, you're more than prepared in that department. No, the problem is, she's been embalmed.'

'But . . . I saw her in the coffin in the undertaker's! She looked so beautiful, so natural!'

'Just a touched-up "memory-picture" as they call it in the trade. All false. Cosmetics, moisturizing creams, baby powders, pink-coloured lighting to make up for the lack of blood.'

'I don't care. She can still be my true love.'

'You weren't listening. I said she's been *embalmed*.' She stroked my hand. 'Take my word for it, darling. You won't even get a kiss, as her lips will have been sealed with a needle ejector gun. And even if you tore them open, she'd stink of formaldehyde. And all her insides will be as hard as rock; you could permanently dent your impaler.'

I went back to reading my comics.

✝

Then the living dead appeared, and I realised what I'd been missing all along.

There are various theories about the outbreak of zombies in Devon, and the complete failure to eradicate them. The ones most commonly accepted are that the mass burnings of cattle following the latest outbreak of foot and mouth had warmed the earth so much that many bodies had been revived by the heat; and that Devonshire people moved so slowly and laboriously that the zombies were able to mix with them in broad daylight without drawing attention to themselves. They simply learnt the local lingo, went about mumbling 'Yer gurt gawk, yer vest be back-ze-fore! Get rid o' th' bissly ole thing, will 'ee? Baint right', and nobody noticed a thing.

I was now thankful that Mother had stopped me losing my virginity to the corpse of Isabel Valiño-Hijosa. She wouldn't have been able to respond at all, of course. With Ana Sánchez-Iglesias, a delightful freckled girl who had been working as an au-pair before being poisoned by the family's traditional British cooking, and who was just as beautiful to my thirteen-year-old eyes, things would be different. I met her as she was stumbling through the cemetery gates, and immediately took her home to meet the family.

But, after a few minutes' embarrassed silence, my parents called me quietly into the kitchen, and shut the door.

'You could have picked someone with more interesting conversation,' Mother said quietly.

'Well, I know she doesn't talk much,' I said defensively.

'Darling, she doesn't talk at all!'

'Oh come on, Mum, there's no need to exaggerate!'

She sighed. 'I know you always like to see the best in a corpse, and that's a commendable thing, of course. But has she ever said one word?'

'What a silly question! She . . . "

I trailed off. Now that it was pointed out to me . . . I'd foolishly assumed, on our way to the estate, that she was a bit shy.

'Let's face it, son,' said Father, 'she's a mindless zombie.'

There's Father for you. Tactful as a shark. I flushed angrily.

'That's an unkind thing to say. OK, I know she shambles a bit, and has a bit of a pong, what else do you expect, but to call her mindless . . . Just because she's a bit slow on the uptake doesn't mean . . . "

'It does!' stated Father flatly.

I stared at him.

'What he means, dear,' said Mother gently, 'is that she's had an autopsy. We can spot these things. Her brain was removed – and not put back. And even if she could think, she couldn't speak, because they always remove the larynx too. And they not only take out the organs and slice them up, but afterwards they shove them back – that's if they bother to replace them at all – inside the thoracic cavity all higgledy-piggledy, and sew them up again with about as much skill as a Boris Karloff Frankenstein head job. You might well find the . . . er . . . entrances blocked by a misplaced liver or something.'

I thanked her and impulsively kissed her for saving me from such a terrible error.

Her tongue slithered under mine like one of the *Shai-Hulud*, the sandworms in **Dune**, and she automatically clutched my scrotum before she remembered my peculiarity, and reluctantly drew away from me. I felt guilty, but what could I do?

'Sorry, Mum. It's just that . . . well, you still taste a bit . . . um . . . *charred*.'

That wasn't the real reason, of course, and she knew it, but was too finely bred to say so.

'It's OK,' she whispered, 'all in good time. I'll always love my little boy, however odd he is.'

Father just shook his head in despair.

'Why can't you be more like your sister?' he grumbled. 'Nice and normal. She seems to be taking most to fetishism – don't forget to wash the spoon and knife handles, by the way, before you use them – but she's also made great strides in exhibitionism and frotteurism, as well as scatophagy and coprophilia.'

Bloody little goody two shoes!

†

But now, with Liza, I had no qualms at all. She really was very special.

258

'Liza, this is Mum and Dad. Mum and Dad, this is Liza.'

'It is, for me, an honour and a pleasure to meet you,' said Liza. She curtsied.

Oh, did I enjoy their shock! Everyone knows your average zombie can't manage more than a mumbled 'baint' or 'innum'.

'It's a joke. Just paint and makeup . . . ' Father tried to sound confident.

'Oh no,' I said, 'that's real pallor mortis you're seeing. Liza died six or seven days ago.'

Mother gazed at Liza, her eyes shining, and touched her face impulsively.

'I knew, I just knew, Petey was keeping himself for someone special! I knew it would happen one day. The next step in the evolution of the dead! The intelligent zombie!'

'Come on, she only said, "Pleased to meet you"', muttered Dad. I suspected that he feared this new development would make mere serial axe-murderers a bit dull and passé. Which, frankly, they were. In Devon, at least.

'You're right,' said Liza with exquisitely fetid tact. 'I hardly think I could be classed as intelligent compared with you. But I hope to learn from you, and from your son. That is, if you have no objection to my seeing him now and then.'

'Objection? We're delighted!' said Mum. 'Oh, you can't imagine how worried we were about our Petey! Come in, come in, sit down, sit down! Don't worry about the mud. Oh, I do love your perfume, perfect putrescence! Promise me you won't decompose too quickly, try and hold yourself together, give us time to really get to know you.'

'You are really very kind,' murmured Liza. 'I didn't expect to find so much sensitivity among the living.'

'Liza is only half a zombie,' I explained proudly. 'She's really a

zompire. Half zombie, half vampire. They're special, there are only a
hundred or so in the whole world. Vampires can't bear to bite dead
flesh, but just occasionally the victim dies, usually of fright, a split
second before the vampire bites, and it doesn't realise. The victim
doesn't become a vampire, of course, but the brain cells are still alive
enough to receive the vampire virus, which prevents mental decay
and slows down physical decay too. The victim is conscious almost
immediately, but unable to rise until the third day.'

Just then, Grandfather hobbled into the room, followed by
Lorna still adjusting her panties, and the Hound. Liza looked up at
the sound, stared, then leapt to her feet and hurled herself upon him.
We were all too shocked to react for a moment, but when we realised
what was happening – she was ripping his neck open – we pulled her
off him. And then we pulled the Hound and Lorna off her.

'Liza,' I said, 'I don't want to criticise you, my love, but in our
circles it's a bit rude to try to murder someone's grandfather on a
first visit.'

'It's him!' she screamed, 'he's the one who took my virginity
my first night in the grave! The filthy old fucker never even asked
me if I minded!'

Father was shocked. His hand strayed towards the axe.

'We don't allow that kind of language in this house, young
lady, zompire or not!'

I stared at Grandfather.

'Grandad, you didn't!'

Grandfather fell heavily into a chair, out of breath, pushing
his carotid artery back into place.

'I don't understand. How can she talk? What's she doing
here?'

Mother explained Liza's zompire nature, and how I had
brought her home. I was still too angry to speak.

'Petey, how was I to know she'd even rise as a zombie, let alone that you'd take up with her? She was just another corpse to me, although a damn fine one!'

'There's no need to get so upset,' said Father, frowning at me. 'Dead bodies usually have a miserable life, no fun, no love. Bored stiff. They should be thankful there are people like your grandfather around, willing to show an interest in them, offer them a bit of human warmth.'

'Your father's right, darling,' said Mother, unexpectedly taking his side. 'And it gives your Grandad an interest, a hobby, in life. You of all people should appreciate that.'

'And don't think Granddad screws just any old corpse, willy-nilly,' added Father. 'He's always been a finicky one. He goes to as many funeral parlour open-coffin viewings as he can, and only visits the corpses who have really attracted him in some way. And that's not many, let me tell you. And it's hard work desecrating a grave at his age, buggers the back, gets him covered in filth, so any corpse who has so much trouble spent over them should feel honoured.'

'Oh, I didn't think of it like that,' said Liza, looking a bit contrite. 'I'm being so selfish, putting myself ahead of everyone else.'

'It's all right, dear,' said Mother, 'we're not going to hold it against you. Are we, Father?' she added significantly.

Grandfather glowered, unwilling to be so forgiving.

'What are things coming to?' he whined. 'You do someone a favour, and they throw it in your face.'

'I'm sorry, I really am,' said Liza, 'I've only been dead a few days, and . . . "

'We understand, dear,' said Mother kindly, 'let's say no more about it.'

†

At last we were alone together, lying beside a grave which

Dad had thoughtfully opened up for Liza near the gazebo. I think it was of some aunt or other: the bones smelt spinsterish and familiar. He had even slung in a bucketful of fresh worms. Clean ones, that wriggled alluringly in the moonlight.

As I lay smoking a cigarette and sipping absinthe, trying to pluck up the courage to finally lose my virginity, Liza lay on her side, looking at me. A big tear fell from one eye socket, a small maggot grub clinging desperately to it.

'What's the matter?' I asked tenderly.

'Pete, you must tell me.'

'Tell you what . . . ?'

'Will you still love me when . . . ?'

'When . . . ?'

'When . . . When all my flesh is gone! Oh, my love, I'm so frightened! Will you wish to have osseous knowledge of me when I've got no flesh left at all?'

I ran my fingers down her cheek, fascinated by the sensuously sickly tints of her pallor mortis, and kissed her glabella where a frown was forming. Our time would be all the more precious because it would be limited. At that moment, I felt so much in love that I really didn't rule out the possibility of a platonic if rickety relationship with her skeleton when the time came. I suppose all adolescents feel the same.

How can I put into words what happened then? And why should I even try? Most people have experienced that incredible joy sometime or other in their lives. But in my case, the real happiness, finally, didn't come from my groin. It was something deeper, much more profound. Unexpected, not asked for, never dreamed of, as if the heart of Heaven itself had opened and poured all its eternal joy over me in a scalding rush of bliss!

And yet I almost let the numinous moment pass me by!

262

Liza was stretching up towards me, gasping with the effort. The smell of decay was delicious. Mephitic bliss. I breathed it in deeply. A tiny fragment of her shoulder broke loose, and I licked it lovingly while trying to push it back into the gap with my mouth and teeth. It wouldn't stick. I gave up. Liza sighed. She removed her fingers from my impaler's accoutrements, and used them to push the piece of shoulder between my lips, her supraorbial foramen glinting in the moonlight.

'Eat it,' she said.

'But . . . "

'Oh, you're such an unselfish lover, so thoughtful of me all the time! And I know you want to. And I can't keep it any more, I'm losing nothing that isn't already lost.'

'Are you sure?' I was surprised by the excitement in my own voice.

'Of course. Go on.'

I opened my teeth, allowing the putrefying flesh to slip between them. I rolled it round my mouth, feeling it disintegrate like a biscuit dunked in tea, then swallowed it with reverence as a true believer does the communion wafer. My throat burned with a blissful heat. The praying mantis, brown bush cricket, and certain spiders knew a thing or two, I realised. In touch with nature, as I now was.

I couldn't stop myself. I took another nip at Liza's shoulder. Then another . . .

'Pete!' There was panic in her voice, as she tried to pull away.

'Just a bit more,' I gasped. 'You can't feel pain anyway, can you?'

'Not much. But how can we be lovers if you eat me? There'll be nothing for you to love!'

It was the hardest thing in the world, but I just managed to stop my teeth closing again. I forced myself to roll away, but the need was agonizing, I clutched my stomach with the pain. In a few seconds I had become totally addicted.

But I loved Liza.

But I had to eat her.

I found myself moving towards her again, my will destroyed by my need, but still able to shout at her to run away from me . . .

†

Of course, my family (except Mother) are disgusted with me.

'A *platonic* relationship?!' My sister almost spat the words at me.

I don't care. Liza's zompire nature hasn't completely stopped her physical decay, but we have a few more months. We lie beside each other in the grave in the garden, and talk of more things in Heaven and Earth, and, of course, under it, than Horatio ever dreamed of. And sometimes Liza unwraps a tiny handkerchief where she has guarded a piece of herself that even vampire blood could not save.

That is the Sacrament itself.

And as for my daily bread . . . well, the zombies I catch are too stupid to realise what's happening to them even when they're half eaten.

And the Hound is never short of a bone or two.

CYBERSOUL

†

His name, I learned later, was Gilbert.

I knew as soon as he sidled furtively into the office that he would be ideal. A sort of cross between a Tenniel illustration for a Lewis Carroll character and one of Goya's unfortunates, he was also so squint-eyed I wondered for a moment whether I'd moved; and he obviously couldn't cut his way out of a paper bag even with a Stanley knife. Perfect.

"And what can I do for you?" I asked, as if I didn't know.

He found the strength somewhere to shuffle his feet, looked round nervously, and, his lower lip trembling, muttered: "I've been told you have the most realistic Virtual Reality simulations in town."

"That is quite true: we allow people to enact the Hero that is already in them, but which, due to congenital circumstances beyond their control, and a society blind to inner worth, has little scope in the normal world." Well, it would have been bad for business to have answered bluntly, "Yes, and we specialise in wimps".

Since he was still struggling to recover from the effort of shuffling his feet, I went on: "We've got the very popular Van Damme model, for example: within a few seconds of having three bullets removed from your chest, *and* a beating by five thugs, you'll be able to run, jump, and hang from an iron girder by one hand, and . . . "

I paused. It was clear he wanted to interrupt me, but didn't dare.

"I'd rather not be Van Damme, if you don't mind, please." He seemed proud of his forcefulness.

"I'm pleased to hear it. I could tell as soon as you came in that you were a man who could see beyond passing fads. Perhaps you'd

265

like to look through our catalogue, which goes from fairy-tale to avant-garde cross-genre fiction. We aim eventually to provide for *everyone*. We've had so many requests from pederasts, for example, that we even designed a Pied Piper of Hamelin simulation – first deal with the rats, and then the blissful reward in the mountain! Others wanted to be Little Red Riding Hood's Wolf – I dread to imagine why. But I'm quite sure, just from the look of you, your interests do not lie in that direction." In fact, I really *was* quite sure, having just been in touch with the new agent. "In the less . . . *specialised* lines, our Aragorns are fairly popular, as are our Lancelots, our Napoleons and Tamburlaines, our James Bonds . . . "

I paused again, to encourage another interruption. He licked his lower lip – nervously, of course; I wasn't sure if he even *had* an upper lip. The tongue, I noticed, was a sick turmeric yellow. A shifty look came into his right eye: the other gazed behind him. Then he blurted:

"I heard that you have this new system where . . . where we don't just re-enact pre-programmed roles, but we can really be ourselves."

"Ah, you mean the TI System – Total Immersion. Yes, that's quite right. We provide the environment, the *decor*, as it were, and you enter it as yourself – or, to be more exact, as a copy of yourself, right down to the last atom – with absolute freedom of movement. You become your own Hero, not somebody else's idea of a Hero. A far better choice, if I may say so, far better. But also much more expensive."

"Oh," he said. It would have taken a much stronger man to say "How much?" at this stage.

"The most usual," I continued, "and so the cheapest, is a Quest."

"A Quest?"

"Yes, you know, like the Knights of the Round Table, you travel the land looking for an old wine glass or something, having lots of Adventures on the way."

"But I don't like travelling. Why can't I stay in Torquay?"

"I don't think it's quite the place for an Adventure. Hasn't got the, um, same *resonance* as Camelot, or Avalon, or Minas Tirith, or even Ankh-Morpork, come to that. All of which, let me say, we can provide. Still, if you're not interested in a Quest, I'm not going to push you. Perhaps, instead, you'd be interested in Saving the World, or at least the important white Anglo-Saxon part of it. Some customers try to jump right in with Saving whole Galaxies, but my advice would be to start with the World first, just for practice."

He still had that slightly belligerent look of the very weak, so I stopped to allow him to be a daredevil and interrupt me again.

"Erm, I wasn't thinking about Saving the World. I'd be quite content to Save . . . well, a village, or, um, maybe a Damsel in Distress."

I had to give him credit: he'd come to the point quickly.

"Also a worthy and respectable aim. And you're in luck. Princesses are very cheap these days."

"Princesses are *cheap*?"

"Yes. At one time, everybody wanted them, so we ran off a few thousand, but since certain unfortunate revelations in Monaco and here in England, Heroes are now scared – no, that's clearly not the right word for a Hero, Heroes are *wary* – that they might catch something rather nasty. Apart from which, Princesses aren't what they used to be; I mean, do you really think the Duchess of York would notice a pumpkin under the mattress, let alone a pea? So the market has plummeted."

His eyes now became so shifty, I couldn't tell whether he was looking at the ground, or the dark side of the Moon. He leaned forward, though whether conspiratorially or simply because his own weight was now too much for him, I couldn't tell.

"I heard something about a new so-called Solaris Effect," he muttered.

"Ah, *now* I understand! I should have seen you were too discerning to be interested in being limited by the imagination of our programmers. Tell me, what do you know about the Solaris Effect?"

"Only that it's something to do with having real people in the Simulation."

"Other than yourself, you mean. Well, look, I can see you're a serious customer, so I think the best way to explain what we can offer is for you to *experience* it first. I would like you to go into this booth here behind me, put on the wraparound visor you'll find there, and then concentrate on someone – anyone – you know, and after a moment a shutter will rise, and you will see . . . But I say no more. The booth is, of course, completely private."

He nervously entered what had once been a Peep Show booth – with the Millennium fever, Soho had been razed to the ground to appease the Avenging Angels, who hadn't bothered to turn up, anyway – and closed the door behind him. I heard him lock it from the inside: old habits die hard. After a few minutes, from the monitor I had hidden on my wrist, I saw the new agent materialise for the third time that month: she certainly had her admirers! This Gilbert at least had the decency (or the lack of imagination: it was pretty clear to me he'd spent all his life keeping a vow of chastity he'd never made) to visualise her with *some* clothes on. I gave him twenty seconds, then clicked off. I had to wait another minute or two before he stumbled out. Again, nothing unusual. His eyes, when he finally emerged, were even more strabismal than before.

"Now," I lied, "I've no idea who or what you've just seen, but I do know that you now realise that this is much more than your common or garden Virtual Reality nonsense. The *decor* of that scene, the *ambience*, is pre-programmed – the default setting is Quest Four, Interlude Seven – but it was *your mind* that added whoever you saw in that scene. That's why we call it the Solaris Effect, if you've ever read Lem's novel. It's much more than cutting edge technology, it makes all other technology seem primitive and blunt, as I'm sure you'll agree. It is, of course, a *very* expensive process, and unless you particularly wish to take a certain person into the Simulation with you, I feel I should tell you, in all fairness, a pre-programmed Princess, despite what I said earlier, is maybe a better bargain."

"Well, actually, I did have someone in mind. I know someone – well, not exactly *know*, but there is a check-out girl, in Woolworth's . . . "

That was odd: I thought we'd agreed on Marks & Spencer's. "Say no more! Now I understand! What a kind thought on your part! Tell me, do you want to Rescue her from a keep?"

"I suffer from vertigo."

"A dungeon then. And that way, we can throw in a few rats free, to make her all the more pleased when you Rescue her."

His eyes had now achieved a veritable Crick and Watson. "Erm, do I actually have to *rescue* her? I mean, can't I just *be* with her?"

"But you can be with her in the real world . . . ah ha, I see! She doesn't appreciate your true worth, is that the problem?"

He nodded abjectly. Somehow, I couldn't imagine him nodding in any other way.

I put on my Suitably Sympathetic expression.

"Oh dear, this is difficult. We shouldn't really have people just idling around doing nothing. Company regulations . . . I mean, we've already dispensed with the Heroes, the Princesses, the Quest and Saving the World. I suppose we might get away with it provided

269

there's a Villain or two . . . Look, we've got a couple of top-quality Orcs which don't cost very . . . "

"Aren't Orcs a bit old-fashioned?" He must have realised that this time he really *had* interrupted me, for he bit his tongue – I know, because I could hear the taste buds popping.

"*Old-fashioned!*" I know I'm not supposed to get involved in my work – at least outside the Booth – but how dare this etiolated sebaceous bone-bag refer to an O*rc* like that? OK, what we had on offer weren't really Orcs at all, they were job lot Gremlins, but the principle still remained. However, I had a job to do, so I controlled myself.

"Well, what would you like, then? Though I have to warn you we don't provide Dragons because of the fire hazards."

"Well, I'd prefer not to have any Villains at all."

"But you can't just Rescue the Damsel from nothing in the first minute and then live happily ever after!"

"Why not?"

My job usually involved finding a client's weak spot, and then playing on it. In this case, it was obvious we were dealing with Achilles' Willy rather than his Heel – all this creature really wanted was to shaft the checkout girl. Well, it made my job that much easier. So I pretended to ponder a while, and then nodded. "Indeed, why not? The customer is always right, after all. If you're content with the check-out girl from Marks & Sparks . . . "

"Woolworth's."

"Sorry, Woolworth's. Very well. Now, before we go into any more detail, perhaps we should discuss the financial aspect . . . "

†

I lay back, my hands behind my head, listening to the unearthly humming coming from the Booth, and wondering how much longer he could keep at it. What they say about skinny men was obviously true. I didn't begrudge him, considering the price he had to pay.

I recalled how, a few months before, The Venerable Nicholas, as he styled himself, had calmly strolled into my garage, where I was halfway through dissecting my wife and her lover – I hadn't decided whether to kill them both afterwards or not – and said, "It's quite obvious you're a very very sick person – I trust you don't mind me expressing my admiration so openly – but if you go on like this you'll soon be behind bars. But I have a proposition for you."

The Venerable Nicholas was scrupulously straight in his crooked dealings. The client always got what he was paying for, even though he might be unaware who was really providing the service. And if the client turned out to be a heavyweight boxing champion, or a kung fu expert, that was my lookout. I was only allowed to reject two out of every three potential clients. "You'll soon get to appreciate the thrill of potential danger," said The Venerable Nicholas, with one of those smiles that looked like a freeze-dried flame. Maybe so, but my arm still hadn't healed properly from the last time. Thank the devil today's client was more interested in removing the Woolies' girl's knickers than in really being a hero!

As usual, it all boiled down to filthy lucre. The Venerable Nicholas had been quite honest with me – at least, I *think* so! "The cost of living never stops going up," he said, "and people are becoming more and more materialistic. True spiritualism, alas, is a thing of the past. Quite frankly, I'm running out of cash. But I have to be able to fulfil my side of the bargain for those people who *do* still want to sell their soul. That lazy sod God can get away with answering maybe one prayer in a million, and everyone says 'Hallelujah!' but if *I* failed just once to come up with the goods, it'd be in all the tabloids the very next day, 'Satan Screws Up!' So a little sideline like this is a way of bringing in a bit of cash to finance the

271

soul-deals. Moreover," he added thoughtfully, while he helpfully put a hand over my wife's mouth to stifle her screams as I was tearing her liver into strips, "it's about time some people paid *me* for the pleasure of my eternal company, instead of me always paying *them*." At that point, my wife expired for some reason, and he rummaged around inside her a bit, then popped her soul — at first, I thought she'd swallowed a rabbit dropping — into his pocket. He never did pay me.

So, that is the main purpose of our Solaris Booth — to collect funds: I suppose you could say we're a bit like a charity stall, offering bric-a-brac in aid of a higher cause.

But while we're at it, we collect something else as well. When a client enters that Booth, he really is entering Virtual Reality: but he's also entering the Other Reality.

The new agent communed with me, saying she thought Gilbert had finally run out of steam (not, I might add, a figure of speech when you do it with a she-devil!) and telling me to get ready. "And tell the Master," she added, "I want a change: I don't like the types who shop in Marks & Spencer's."

So the little bastard *had* lied to me!

†

There was absolutely no visible difference between the man who entered the Booth, and the man who walked out, tottering from sexual exhaustion, an hour later. Except that the man who walked out was, without realising it of course, the copy, not the original. Maybe he felt a strange unease, an emptiness, a sense of loss, which would never leave him.

Because, of course, it's quite impossible to copy a soul.

Now you may ask what there was in all this for me. That's easy.

Someone has to whip the trapped souls into obedience, before they go to meet their new Master.

There's no doubt about it: having a steady job gives a man real self-respect.

THE LAST QUESTION
†

A roadside anti-tank mine exploded in Afghanistan as a UN reconnaissance convoy was passing. This time, only one soldier was killed. He was twenty-one. Years. His child was also twenty-one. Weeks.

God summoned the Devil.

"Was that your doing?" he asked.

The Devil had lately grown used to such questions, and now only felt resignation rather than anger. He simply shook his head wearily.

"I didn't think so," said God.

An infinite sadness was emanating from him, stronger than any the Devil had ever noticed before.

"You don't look well," said the Devil. There was no irony in his voice. "If there's anything I can do..."

"You can," said God. "I tried to prevent that soldier from dying, as I have tried to prevent so many millions of similar tragedies. And I failed, as I have always failed. Find out once and for all why that soldier died."

God had never made a joke in his life, so the Devil answered:

"You do realise the impossibility of what you have just asked me, don't you?"

"I realise the difficulty. Not the impossibility. At least, not for you."

"You mean, you already know the answer?"

"I think so. But I need you to confirm it. There is no other way to stop it."

The Devil was far from sure whether he was up to the task, but God was his oldest friend, and had never asked for help before.

"I'll try to find the answer for you," said the Devil, "but I'll need some time."

"Take as much time as you want. Only..."

The Devil looked at him expectantly.

"Only?"

"Only not *too* long. Please? The weight, the weight..."

Aeons later, the Devil appeared in God's ruined palace. God was slumped against the base of his throne. The Devil had half expected this. He filled a chalice from a nearby fountain, knelt down, and supported God's head with one hand as he helped him sip at the liquid.

"I knew you would come," said God.

"Of course you did," said the Devil.

"Have you got my answer?"

The Devil leaned forward and kissed God gently on the lips.

"That man died for no reason at all," he said, and now there were tears in his eyes, "and because you don't exist. Perhaps you have never existed."

"Thank you, " said God. "You have always been free. And you've used that freedom to free me. At last. Not all my choices have been wrong." He clutched at the Devil's hand. "Will you look after them for me?"

The Devil closed his eyes for a few seconds, wondering how God could be so blind, then nodded his last and noblest lie, and gently stroked God's hair as the life force poured out of his crumpled body. The force flowed over and through the Devil, recognised him, bathed him in a glow beyond golden, until his last tears and he himself dissipated into a suddenly meaningless universe.

Acknowledgements

Some of the stories in this collection originally appeared in the following publications:

Book anthologies: Bare Bone, Darkness Rising, Mammoth Book of New Comic Fantasy, Minotaur in Pamplona, New Writings in the Fantastic, Thackery T Lambshead Pocket Guide to Eccentric & Discredited Diseases

Magazines: Cimmplicity, Dreamzone, Enigmatic Tales, Eureka Literary Magazine, Here & Now, Literary Bone, Midnight Street, Polluto, Quality Women's Fiction, Roadworks, Serendipity, Whispers of Wickedness

Other Works by Steve Redwood

Fisher of Devils, novel (Prime Books USA/UK 2003)
(Spanish edition: **El pescador de demonios** (El Tercer Nombre, Spain 2007)

Who Needs Cleopatra? novel (Reverb UK 2005)
(Spanish edition: **¿Quién necesita a Cleopatra?** (AJEC Editorial, Spain 2009)

The Heisenberg Mutation and Other Transfigurations, chapbook (D-press UK 2005)

Dog Horn Publishing presents...

Queer AND LOATHING on the YELLOW BRICK ROAD

a preview of Deb Hoag's upcoming novel

Chapter One
Dorothy: The Meeting

I don't know much, but I know this: magic is all around us, every day. It's in the air we breath, the water we drink. Sometimes it's wonderful, and sometimes it's absolutely horrid. Magical things are happening to all of us, all the time, without rhyme or reason, without a care in the world about who deserves it or who doesn't.

Magical things have happened to me. My name is Dorothy, and this is my story.

*

I met Frannie in the spring of 1890, the night I got thrown into the hoosegow for getting overly friendly with a couple of guys at the local saloon. I stomped into the cell and threw myself dramatically on the bunk, except it wasn't the bunk I landed on – it was another woman. I hadn't seen her there in the dim light leaking in from the booking room.

She made an 'oofing' noise and I jumped off the bed faster than I had jumped on, and the guard laughed. A small horde of adolescent jitterbugs that were prancing around on the ceiling giggled shrilly, but my mundane companions didn't notice.

"Well, excuse me," the woman said with a sniff, sitting up and putting a hand to a hairdo that had seen better days.

"Sorry, sister," I replied, scooting over to the wall, where I slid down into a sitting position.

The jitterbugs went back to their endless, intricate mating dance, having approximately the same attention span as the gnats they so closely resembled.

The tiny flashing disco light was annoying, but I did my best to ignore it. I'd learned early that people who see things no one else does get a one-way ticket to the nearest loony bin.

Even jail was better than that, which reminded me of exactly where I was. Jail. Fuck!

I thunked the back of my head against the concrete. It hurt like hell, so I did it a couple more times. Stupid, stupid, stupid getting caught like that! A few more dollars and I would have been on my way back to Kansas, chasing cyclones till I could find one that would take me back to Oz.

"Hey, honey, it can't be that bad," said the woman, eying me with alarm.

I stopped banging my head and sighed. "I was this close to going home, and I got picked up by some needle-dick copper for soliciting. Now I'm stuck here until I can see the judge, pay a fine, maybe a bribe, and then earn the money I'd saved all over again. And I'm on a deadline. I need to get back to Kansas before cyclone season hits."

She laughed. "If you can make enough money out of these hayseeds to bribe a judge, you're even better than you look. Most of these hicks would rather boink a sheep than pay money for a tumble with an actual woman."

I sighed again. Completely true. I should have known two guys with cash money in a frontier town like Aberdeen, South Dakota were too much of a good thing.

"Look," I said, "I didn't mean to sit on you. I really didn't know you were there. I'm Dorothy. I just blew into town a couple of weeks ago. Who are you?"

She shook her head sadly. "I'm Frannie, from right here. For the last few years, at least. I hale from back east, originally."

"God, you actually live in this podunk town? You poor thing."

We sat in companionable silence. Eventually, my thoughts brought me back around to what I'd been doing that landed me in jail, and from that to what my cellie had been doing that landed her in jail.

"So, what exactly got you thrown in here?"

Her face grew sulky. "I committed a lewd act in public."

"Wow. What constitutes a lewd act around here?"

She shrugged and looked annoyed. "Looking cross-eyed on a Tuesday, if the constable is in a bad mood. It wasn't really even in public. We were in a perfectly respectable alley. It just happened that the alley was behind the police chief's house, and his wife picked that very moment to look out the bedroom window."

"Gee, that sucks."

"Yes, and so did I. That's why I got arrested."

I laughed out loud. Frannie started laughing too. Just like that, I knew we were going to be good friends.

When we stopped laughing, Frannie stretched on the narrow cot and stood up. "I've got an extra blanket," she said. "It gets quite cold in here at night. You want it?"

"Sure," I said, and she walked over to drape it around my shoulders.

When she stood up, the jitterbugs' disco ball illuminated her face and figure. She had a square, short jaw, and lush, full lips. Her nose was a little large for her small face, but it lent humor to an otherwise serious visage and her eyes were beautiful and large, thickly lashed. In the dim light she was altogether pretty, and she had a grace of movement that gave her lithe frame an inviting wiggle when she moved, top-heavy the way men liked. The farmers probably ate her up. She looked closer to thirty than twenty, but I prefer older women, myself. She wore boots she must have sent all the way to New York for, and had the goodies wrapped up in a scarlet silk dress that suggested all kinds of mischief.

If I wasn't heartbroken over Glinda, that wicked bitch, I might have eaten her right up myself.

I must have been staring, because she blushed, and reached up a hand to check her hair again. Her hands were large but well-shaped, with long, sensitive fingers. When she tucked the blanket around me, I smiled up at her, and noticed an unfortunate Adam's apple, nearly as large as a ma--

Was that a wisp of mustache on her upper lip?

"Are you . . . ah, you wouldn't happen to be . . . I know this sounds crazy, but are you a man?" I blurted out, watching as her painted cheek turned even rosier than it already was.

Frannie raised one of those large hands to tidy hair I realized now was a wig, askew on her head. I reached up and gave it a tug to set it straight.

She slid down to the floor and leaned against the wall a scant distance from me.

"You've found me out. Our guard doesn't know that I sat next to him on a pew just last Sunday in a suit coat and tie. Are you going to tell him?"

"Your secret is safe with me. It's no skin off my nose."

Frannie blinked. "Really? That's a refreshing attitude. You didn't grow up around here, did you?"

"Well, I'm from Kansas, originally, but . . . "

"I've been to Kansas. I didn't realize they grew 'em so liberal there."

"Oh, Kansas isn't really my home."

"Then why do you want to get back there?"

"It's a long story."

She laughed. "Sister, time is one thing we both have plenty of, given the present circumstances."

I had to agree.

I didn't suppose for a second that she would believe a word I said, but I didn't think she'd call the local loony bin about me, either.

I nestled in more comfortably to begin my tale.

"It all started in New Orleans . . . "